THE DEATH OF A POPE

PIERS PAUL READ

THE DEATH OF A POPE

A Novel

IGNATIUS PRESS   SAN FRANCISCO

Cover design by John Herreid

© 2009 by Piers Paul Read
Published in 2009 by Ignatius Press, San Francisco
All rights reserved
ISBN 978-1-58617-295-4
Library of Congress Control Number 2008936283
Printed in the United States of America ∞

Christianity did not bring a message of social revolution like that of the ill-fated Spartacus, whose struggle led to so much bloodshed. Jesus was not Spartacus, he was not engaged in a fight for political liberation ...

—Pope Benedict XVI, *Spe Salvi*

No one dares to talk ... about the completely obsolete medieval rules for electing the Pope. Here in particular the Roman system goes on and on. The Pope chooses those who will elect his successor solely according to his taste; with good reason he addresses the bishops not as 'brothers' but as 'sons', since they have been created simply and solely by him. They are therefore officially named 'creatures of the Pope', who will choose the next Pope—of course from their own ranks ...

—Hans Küng, *Disputed Truth*

The Pope kills millions through his reckless spreading of AIDS.

—Polly Toynbee, *The Guardian*,
September 6, 2002

Contents

Author's Note

This story takes place against the background of actual events and inserts fictional characters into real institutions such as London's Central Criminal Court (the Old Bailey), the British Security Service (MI5) and Secret Intelligence Service (MI6), and the Italian Security Service, Servizio per le Informazioni e la Sicurezza Militare (SISMI), which in 2007 was reorganised as the Agenzia Informazioni e Sicurezza Esterna (AISE). However, the Catholic relief agency Misericordia International and the Vatican Congregation for Catholic Culture are both fictional, as is the description of how to make an explosive device that would disseminate poison gas.

The Trial

In the dock behind a screen of thick glass sit the three accused men. The two Basques have sun-tanned complexions while the Irishman has pale white skin as if he had spent little of his life in the open air. The Irishman and one of the Basques wear dark suits, shirts and ties; the second Basque, Uriarte, is dressed more informally in a blue herringbone jacket and open-necked shirt. O'Brien looks straight ahead, or down at his hands, avoiding the eyes of either the judge or the jurors—on his face a look of patient resignation: How can an Irishman expect justice from a British court? The Basque wearing a suit also looks at some notional point in the middle distance with vacant staring eyes. His companion, Uriarte—the one with the open-necked shirt—studies the judge and the advocates in their wigs and gowns with an air of amused curiosity, as if they are figures from Madame Tussauds or the London Dungeon.

The charges are read out by the Clerk of the Court. Fergal O'Brien, Juan Uriarte and Asier Etchevarren are charged with conspiring to cause an explosion with the intent to take human life.

The chief prosecution counsel stands to open the case. 'It will be established', he tells the jury, 'that two of the three defendants had links with terrorist organisations. Fergal O'Brien was a member of the Provisional IRA and now associates with members of the Real IRA, while Asier Etchevarren—he stumbles over the name—was a member of the Basque separatist organisation, ETA. A senior officer from the Irish Garda and another from the Spanish Gardia Civil will confirm the defendants' terrorist credentials, but the conclusive evidence of a conspiracy to commit the offence will come from a British police officer from Scotland Yard's Special Branch.

'This officer will describe how the Security Service, MI5, had informed Special Branch that O'Brien, a resident of Dublin, was coming to London looking for toxic gas. The officer had posed as a chemist who was able to supply it. An intelligence source in the Irish community had introduced him to O'Brien, and O'Brien in turn had arranged a meeting with the two Basques at the Elgin public house on Ladbroke Grove in West London. A microphone and transmitter had been concealed in the lapel of the officer's jacket. The questions the two Basques put to him were recorded by a second police officer in a van parked nearby. The jury will hear how the Basques enquired about the relative merits of Sarin and VX, the mechanism required to vaporise the gasses, and what quantities would be required to ensure that several hundred people would be killed within an enclosed space such as the House of Commons or the Spanish Cortes.

'You may have become bored, members of the jury,' the prosecutor continues, 'with talk about weapons of mass destruction and begun to doubt whether they exist—in the Middle East or anywhere at all. But let us be quite clear: whether or not Sarin is to be found now in the Middle East, it was most certainly used in conjunction with mustard gas, and possibly VX gas, by the government of Iraq against Kurdish insurgents in 1988, and Sarin was the agent used only ten years ago in a terrorist attack on the Tokyo subway by Aum Shinrikyo, a cult intent on hastening the end of the world.

'Now you may have read that this atrocity, though it affected five thousand people, killed only twelve. The relatively small loss of life was not thanks to the ineffectiveness of Sarin; it was due to the incompetence of the Japanese terrorists who simply left punctured packages of liquid Sarin on the seats of the underground train. If they had disseminated it with aerosols, the results would have been quite different; and it is our contention, members of the jury, that the two Basques among the accused knew this because they specifically asked the police officer whom they believed to be a chemist how the gas could be vaporised and what would be the effect of that vaporisation in a confined space.

'And what *would* be the effect, members of the jury? Sarin is a substance that disrupts the nervous system, over-stimulating muscles and vital organs. Given a sufficient dose, Sarin will paralyse the muscles around the lungs. One hundred milligrams—one drop of Sarin—will lead, within a few minutes, to death by suffocation. Sarin is five hundred times as toxic as cyanide. A fraction of a drop is enough to cause almost instantaneous death.'

The police officer is called to the witness box: he has a solid London-Irish face, not unlike that of the accused O'Brien. The prosecuting counsel takes him through the events of that Saturday night six months earlier. Later O'Brien's barrister cross-examines. 'Was *any* evidence presented to Special Branch or the Security Service that O'Brien had been engaged in any terrorist activity after the Good Friday Agreement and the IRA ceasefire?'

'No.'

'And is it not the case that Mr. O'Brien told you that he was engaged in a confidence trick and, not realising that you were a police officer, offered you a share of the proceeds?'

'It is not.'

A third barrister now gets to his feet. 'It is correct, is it not, that my client, Juan Uriarte, asked what amount of gas would be required to cause the death of all the members of a national assembly?'

'It is.'

'Did he not *also* ask about the effect of poison gas if released in the open air?'

'He did.'

'And is it not true that *at no time in the course of his questioning* had Uriarte said that he intended to use the gas to take human life?'

'Implicit in the whole line of enquiry . . .'

The police officer is interrupted by the barrister. 'Please answer with a yes or a no. Did Juan Uriarte *say anything at all* about the intended use of the nerve gas?'

'No.'

The Press

The case of *The Crown v. O'Brien* and his associates has aroused the curiosity of the general public. On the opening day of the trial, vans with satellite dishes were parked outside the Old Bailey and reporters addressed hand-held cameras. Inside Court No. 4, a dozen or so journalists sat on the press benches scribbling in their notebooks. However, as the days have passed the interest has waned. It seems that terrorism is newsworthy only where Islamic fanatics are involved. The British public has grown bored by the IRA and has never been interested in ETA. The vans and cameras disappear from outside the Old Bailey and the number of journalists on the press benches diminishes day by day. By the end of the first week, only four journalists remain in Court No. 4: three are from the more serious national broadsheets—two middle-aged men and a woman in her early thirties. The fourth is a young man who tells his colleagues that he is covering the trial for *The Law Review.*

At first, during the lunch break, the four journalists had gone their separate ways—to buy a wrap from Pret a Manger, a sandwich from Eat or, in the case of the two older men, a pint of beer and sausage roll at the Almoner's Arms. On day four of the trial the two younger journalists coincidentally find themselves at the same sandwich bar in Carter Lane and, since they now know each other so well by sight, sit down at the same table to eat their lunch. The young man is a few years older than the girl but seems less assured. He has neatly cut soft hair, high cheekbones and blue eyes. He wears a chain-store grey suit, a white shirt and a diagonally striped blue and red tie. The girl is dressed in a green skirt, a mustard-coloured top, a beige cashmere cardigan and, over tights, brown suede boots.

'Why is *The Law Review* interested in this case?' the girl asks as she squints down at her wrap.

'There are some legal issues involving jurisdictions and the application of new terrorist legislation', the young man replies. 'And why', he asks in turn, 'is your paper staying with the story?'

She shrugs. 'I don't know. Perhaps just to give me something to do.' Her mouth is filled with wrap: she mangles her words. 'There'd be more interest', she adds, when she has swallowed what was in her mouth, 'if the accused weren't all foreigners.'

'The offence was committed in our jurisdiction.'

'And so the British taxpayer has to foot the bill.'

The young man nods. 'Yes.'

'Legal Aid for the defence?'

'Almost certainly.'

'I might write something about that. Why should we pay for solicitors and barristers to defend foreigners planning to commit crimes in other countries.'

The young man frowns. 'Presumably other countries would prosecute terrorists planning atrocities in the UK.'

They walk back to the Old Bailey. 'I'm Kate Ramsey', says the girl.

'David Kotovski.'

They pass through the security checks and return to Court No. 4.

Day Four

O'Brien's barrister stands to defend his client. He is a plump, amiable man with a florid face. He sets out at once to defuse the forbidding atmosphere that has until now existed in the court. '*Of course* nerve gas is a very terrible thing, and it would be a very serious matter indeed if anyone were responsible for it falling into the hands of a party intending to use it to kill innocent people. But what O'Brien will tell the court is that he had *no intention whatsoever* of supplying nerve gas to ETA terrorists. What he meant to do was to relieve two gullible Basques of their money.'

O'Brien is called to the witness stand. Speaking quietly and with a thick Irish accent—the judge often asks him to repeat his answers for the benefit of the jury—O'Brien admits to his counsel that he was a member of the Provisional IRA in the 1990s and had been 'tangentially' (the word is the barrister's) involved in the sale of arms and explosives to the Basque separatist organization, ETA. After the Good Friday Agreement, however, he ceased his involvement in terrorist activities. He is, he agrees with his counsel, 'out of the loop'. He earns his living as a jobbing builder in Dublin. When visiting London he stays with his sister in Queens Park.

Why, then, had he come to London ostensibly looking for nerve gas? Six months before he had received a telephone call at his home in Dublin from the first accused, Asier Etchevarren, with whom he had had dealings prior to the Good Friday Agreement. Etchevarren had said he had a business proposition. O'Brien had agreed to meet him in London. Why? It seemed 'only polite'. But why in London? Because it would be safer than meeting in Dublin. Safer? 'More private-like.'

They had met at the Elgin on Ladbroke Grove. Etchevarren had said that he was on the same kind of mission as before. He asked

15

O'Brien if the IRA had a source for nerve gas. O'Brien had said that he would enquire.

'Why was that?' asks his counsel.

'I was playing for time.'

'And what did you discover after making enquiries?'

'That the gentleman's shopping trip had not been aut'orised by our Spanish friends. He was acting on his own.'

'Did you tell him that you were aware of this?'

'I did not.'

'Why was that?'

'Well, I thought it would be harmless to relieve him of some of his money.'

'You saw, in other words, the possibility of mounting what is commonly called, I believe, "a sting"?'

'I did, m'lud.' O'Brien turns towards the judge. 'I'm afraid that was what I had in mind—a sting.'

The judge writes the word down in his notebook, a slight frown on his brow.

The light is artificial; the conditioned air is blown in from rectangular vents in the ceiling. There is a faint aroma of paper, plastic and cloth. Another barrister is on his feet telling the jury, with apparent conviction, that his client Juan Uriarte is not a terrorist. Quite to the contrary, he is a man who has devoted his life to helping others, latterly as a senior aid worker for the Catholic refugee service Misericordia International. The director of Misericordia has come from Rome to London to give evidence to this effect. Though born in Spain, and retaining Spanish nationality, Uriarte has not lived in that country for twenty-five years. He is a man with strong convictions, but those convictions have nothing whatsoever to do with Basque separatism. Mr. Uriarte's only interest has ever been to improve the condition of the most oppressed, impoverished and neglected members of mankind.

'How, then', the barrister asks rhetorically, 'did Mr. Uriarte find himself in London with a former member of ETA shopping for nerve gas? Mr. Uriarte does not deny the facts. He does not pretend that the tape-recording that has been played in court—the transcripts of which, members of the jury, you hold in your hands—are anything but an undoctored if partial record of the conversation he had with the two other defendants. He was in London to buy nerve gas. What he *does* deny, members of the jury, is that he had any intention whatsoever to use this nerve gas for the taking of human life.

'To understand what he was about, members of the jury, we have to travel in our minds to the western part of the Sudan known as Darfur, where Mr. Uriarte has been working for the past four years. It is a region, as you will know, where a cruel civil war has been conducted for quite some time between the local inhabitants and the central government. You will have read accounts in the newspapers, and no doubt seen images on television, of the pitiful condition of the civilians, mostly women and children, who are innocent victims of this civil war. You will have read of the massacre of unarmed civilians by the Arab militias, and you will have read how little, how very little, has been done by the international community to protect them. You will hear evidence, members of the jury, from experts in this field as to the reasons for this remarkable reluctance of the international community to intervene—the interest of the Peoples Republic of China in the oil provided by the Sudanese government and the interest of the United States of America in the cooperation of the Sudanese government in the war against terrorism. And, after hearing this evidence, you will begin to understand the feelings of the defendant who had seen the atrocities perpetrated on the people under his care. Mr. Uriarte will tell you how he and his superiors had made countless appeals for better protection—to the local observers from the African Union and, through the headquarters of Misericordia in Rome, to the United Nations and individual Western nations. All to no avail. And you will then understand how, *in desperation*, he came to the conclusion that the refugees must defend themselves. But how? Their menfolk were either dead or hiding out in the hills. Most of the refugees were either women or children, quite incapable of shouldering a Kalashnikov or firing a mortar, even if such weapons had been at hand. No, there was no question of the refugees defending themselves by conventional means. The best—*the only effective method*—would be *deterrence*. If it became known that the refugees had at their disposal not guns or explosives but something simpler yet more lethal such as nerve gas, then the attacks on the camps would cease.

'How could nerve gas be obtained? Clearly, the defendant, Juan Uriarte, could not acquire it through Misericordia International: his superiors would never countenance such a radical plan. He would have to obtain it unofficially: But how? One can learn a great deal about nerve gas through browsing the Internet, members of the jury, but it is not as yet possible to *buy* it on the Web. If Mr. Uriarte were to obtain it, it would have to be through irregular channels.

'Now, as you will hear in due course, Mr. Uriarte has led a varied and unusual life: he was once a Roman Catholic priest but left the priesthood to fight with the liberationist rebels in El Salvador. He was a man who was prepared to take risks for a cause he believed right. He realized that to achieve his objective he might have to sup with the devil—the devil in this case being a member of a terrorist network who could provide him with what he required. It was now many years since he had fought in the jungles of Central America and his former *compañeros* had long since dispersed. He had heard, however, that a friend from his childhood in Spain, Asier Etchevarren, was deeply committed to the cause of Basque independence and had contacts with ETA.

'Mr. Uriarte flew to Bilbao, telephoned Etchevarren and visited him in his home. He told his friend what he wanted and why. Etchevarren agreed to make enquiries and, a week later, told Mr. Uriarte that there was someone in Dublin who might know how to obtain Sarin. They flew to London. They met the first defendant, Mr. O'Brien, at the Elgin public house on Ladbroke Grove. O'Brien told them that he knew a man who could supply the nerve gas but warned that it would be expensive. Uriarte said he could raise the sum demanded, and a second meeting was arranged at which Uriarte and Etchevarren were introduced to a man whom we now know was an undercover police officer. There was a further meeting where the conversations took place, which were recorded and played in court. Mr. Uriarte does not deny that these conversations took place, and in due course he will explain that the references to the British House of Commons and the Spanish Cortes were simply to illustrate the amount of gas that would be required. *At no point did he ever intend to use the Sarin or VX gas to take the lives of civilians or even members of the Arab militias, the Janjaweed.* At worst it would be used on their livestock or camels to demonstrate the potential of the deterrent and to bring their cruel raids on the refugees to an end.'

Colleagues

The trial moves at a snail's pace. Kate Ramsey and David Kotovski now frequently eat lunch together. Kate tells David that she thinks the law is a racket. 'Think of it. The barristers are paid by the day. The longer they can string it out, the more money they make.' They are sitting side by side in a Sushi bar picking dishes off a moving belt.

Kotovski smiles. 'Apparently', he says, 'the world's earliest decipherable writing, on a tablet in Mesopotamia, is a complaint about lawyers.'

Kate likes his smile. She is at present without a boyfriend and sizes him up for the role. She finds him attractive but hard to place. His accent—tell-tale in most cases—does not reveal whether or not he comes from her side of the tracks. Kate's father is the senior partner in a firm of corporate lawyers. Her mother is 'well connected'. Kate was educated privately at Wycombe Abbey and has a degree from Oxford University. She moves in a circle of interesting, amusing, high-achieving friends—architects, writers, actors, barristers, fund managers. Her only problem: she lacks a lover. She has been out with all the possibilities among her friends. She needs to break new ground.

'What did you study at college?' she asks.

'History.'

'Where?'

'Leeds. And you?'

'Theology. At Oxford.'

'Theology? Are you religious?'

'No. But it was an easy way in.'

'And was it worth it?'

'What?'

'Studying a subject that didn't interest you for the sake of . . .' He waves his hand as if he might catch the word he is looking for in the air. 'For the sake of "the life"?'

She shrugs. 'It is interesting, once you get into it.'

'The life?'

'No, theology.'

Kate is annoyed. He is finding out more about her than she is finding out about him. She decides upon outright interrogation. 'Your name, Kotovski, . . . is it Polish?'

'Yes. It was Kotkovski but my father dropped the second *k*. It made it easier to pronounce.'

'He is Polish?'

'Second generation. Part of the Polish diaspora living in Acton. But not a plumber.'

She is being teased—gently, without rancour. 'I didn't think he was a plumber', she says firmly.

'My grandfather, on the other hand, *was* a sort of plumber.'

'What do you mean? A sort of plumber?'

'He worked for a builders' merchant. He sold taps and sinks to plumbers.'

Misericordia

The next morning the defence calls its first witness who gives his name as Cesare Bianco and his profession as an aid worker. He is director of Misericordia International and works from its headquarters on the via Chieti in Rome. In good English he confirms that Juan Uriarte has worked for Misericordia for the past twelve years; that he is one of the most esteemed members of the organisation with an extraordinary capacity for administration but, more importantly, an ability to empathise with the refugees. If he has any weakness, it is 'too great a sensitivity to the suffering of others. In our line of work, one must have a soft heart but a thick skin.'

The prosecutor rises to cross-examine this witness for the defence. 'Father Bianco . . .'

The witness waits.

'You are, I think, a Catholic priest?'

'I am.'

'Did you know that Juan Uriarte had also been a Catholic priest?'

'Of course.'

'Is it the policy of the Misericordia to employ de-frocked priests?'

'We do not use that expression. Juan Uriarte was laicised following canonical procedures.'

'Did you know, when you employed him, that he had fought for the Frente Farabundo Martí para la Liberación Nacional in El Salvador?'

'I did.'

'Had your organisation no objection to employing a man who had used violence in pursuit of a political objective?'

'We judge that God's calling may be understood in different ways at different times.'

'By which you mean ...?'

'The situations in El Salvador in 1990 and in Darfur today cannot be compared.'

'You did not think that Mr. Uriarte might join the insurgents in Sudan?'

'No. Quite to the contrary. Mr. Uriarte was trusted with the most difficult negotiations with the Janjaweed.'

'Negotiations?'

'He worked to reconcile the two sides of the conflict at great risk to himself.'

'He was in contact with the Janjaweed?'

'Yes, with their leaders in Khartoum.'

'Didn't it therefore come as a surprise when you learned that he had been caught shopping for nerve gas?'

'At first, yes.'

'And subsequently?'

'Subsequently, when I understood why, I was not surprised.'

'You accepted his explanation?'

'One hundred percent.'

After Cesare Bianco, a tall, sallow man enters the court and crosses to the witness stand. He gives his name as Jacques Belfon and his profession as a doctor working for *Médecins Sans Frontières* in Darfur. He tells the court that he has worked closely with Juan Uriarte for the past two years. He has never come across a more effective aid worker, or a man with a greater rapport with the people he had been sent to help. Belfon speaks good English with a French accent. 'You find, in our profession, many aid workers with high ideals and great compassion but often these are, how can one put it—*de haut en bas*.'

'Patronising or condescending?' the counsel suggests.

'Yes ...' Belfon hesitates. Neither is quite the right word. 'It is commonly "I am here to help you." But with Uriarte it is more "I am one of you. We are in this together." The difference may be small but it is important.'

'Were you surprised when you heard that Uriarte had been arrested for trying to buy Sarin?'

Belfon laughed. 'Nothing would surprise me about Uriarte. He was always one for *l'audace*.'

'"*L'audace*"?' says the judge. 'I believe I know what that means, but members of the jury may not.'

'Audacity. The unusual solution to a problem', says the barrister. 'I believe that is what the witness means to convey. One also hears the term "lateral thinking" or "thinking outside the box". I believe, My Lord, they mean the same sort of thing.'

The judge nods and makes a note.

The barrister turns back to Belfon. 'In the course of your acquaintanceship with Mr. Uriarte, have you ever heard him express any opinion about his people, the Basques?'

'No.'

'About whether or not the Basques should have an autonomous state?'

'No.'

'Has he ever expressed any sympathy with the Basque separatist organisation, ETA?'

'Sympathy, no. The only occasion that I can recollect when he mentioned ETA was when he expressed surprise that prosperous people should use violence in pursuit of political autonomy, which, because of the European Union, has become irrelevant.'

Uriarte

Juan Uriarte is called to the witness stand. He wears the same sports coat but a fresh blue shirt, open at the neck. In answer to the opening questions, he agrees with his counsel that he is Juan Uriarte, born on 12 November 1956, in Bilbao, with a permanent address at 12 via Manzoni in Rome and a temporary address at Camp No. 16, Darfur, Sudan. Slowly, with an eye to the judge's note-taking, the barrister elicits from Uriarte the information he gave to the jury the day before. Uriarte trained in Spain as a Jesuit priest; he was sent to El Salvador, where, after witnessing the brutal treatment of the poor by the military government, he left the priesthood and joined the rebels—the FMLN. When the civil war ended, he returned to Europe and was employed by the Catholic relief organisation Misericordia International. He has worked for Misericordia for the past twelve years, mostly in the field. He has been in the Darfur region of Sudan for the past four years. He is unmarried.

Uriarte speaks in a soft but perfectly audible voice. His English is fluent but he has a Spanish accent: when he uses the word 'poor', the sound of the vowel is protracted and the *r* is enunciated with a slight rattle of his tongue. He has a strong physiognomy with sallow skin, dark brows, taut cheeks and a sharp, aquiline nose. He is not tall but seems lean and fit. His manner is relaxed. He does not look or sound like a man facing grave charges under the Terrorism Act. His tone of voice is matter-of-fact, as if he does not particularly mind whether the court accepts what he is saying or not. *Qui s'excuse s'accuse.* He does not make excuses. He does not protest his innocence. He tells the court why he wanted to obtain nerve gas as if, under the circumstances, it was a perfectly reasonable thing to do.

The manner in which his counsel takes him through his story suggests that he, too, thinks it was a reasonable thing to do. He returns, time and again, to the purpose to which the nerve gas was to be put. 'Have you ever, *at any time*, had the intention of using the Sarin or VX or whatever gas you might have obtained to take, or to endanger, human life?'

'I never had that intention, no. My life is dedicated to saving human life, not taking it.'

'Were you persuaded that possessing nerve gas, and at worst using it on animals to demonstrate its dreadful efficacy, would do just that— would save human lives?'

'I was.'

'Thank you, Mr. Uriarte. I have no more questions at present.'

Uriarte's counsel sits down. The judge turns to the accused. 'Mr. Uriarte, it is now the duty of the Crown to cross-examine. Would you like a brief recess before this begins?'

'No, My Lord. I am ready to proceed.'

'Very well.'

The atmosphere in the court changes. All the bored-looking barristers and solicitors look up from their briefs (or concealed copies of *The Spectator*) to watch the spectacle of one of the best minds at the bar demolish the evidence of one of the accused. The prosecutor stands and for a moment says nothing, his hands clasping the sides of his gown. He glances at the few notes he has scribbled on a single sheet of paper and then, after an intake of breath, he begins. 'Mr. Uriarte, you will understand, I trust, how the jury may be somewhat confused by what it has heard in evidence so far. On the one hand they have heard a tape-recorded conversation between you, your friend Mr. Etchevarren and the third defendant, Mr. O'Brien, in which you seek to obtain nerve gas, ask how it can be most effectively dispersed in an enclosed space such as the debating chamber of the House of Commons or the Spanish Cortes; and on the other, they have heard one Italian, Father Bianco, and a Frenchman, Doctor Belfon, tell them that they know you well, that you are an experienced and dedicated aid worker and wouldn't hurt a fly. No, I have got that wrong. You might hurt a fly, or a horse, or a camel, but you wouldn't hurt a human being.'

Uriarte says nothing.

'You will understand why they might be confused?'

'No longer, I think.'

'No longer because you and your counsel have made it all crystal clear? Though you were in the company of a member of a terrorist organisation, ETA—which continues to place explosive devices in public places and assassinate government servants—a man you admit is a childhood friend, you have asked the jury to believe that neither you nor your friend were seeking to promote the objectives of the terrorist organisation to which your friend belonged, but that he was acting on your behalf and your objectives had nothing whatsoever to do with ETA?'

'That is correct.'

'You are a Basque, are you not, Mr. Uriarte?'

'I am.'

'Not only was Mr. Etchevarren your childhood friend but no doubt you also had many other childhood friends who shared his views on the desirability of political autonomy for the Basque region of Spain?'

'One or two. But only Asier, so far as I know, joined ETA.'

'You yourself would never use violence in pursuit of political autonomy for your people?'

Uriarte shakes his head. 'No, I would not.'

'You do not feel that the end would justify the means?'

'I think the end—political autonomy—is an irrelevance.'

'An irrelevance?'

'Yes.'

'Which makes the use of force in this context morally wrong?'

'That is correct.'

'But am I not right in saying that this has not always been your view?'

'It has always been my view in relation to ETA.'

'But not, perhaps, in relation to other political objectives?'

'Not necessarily, no.'

'Because if we go back fifteen years or so, Mr. Uriarte, we find you wielding a Kalashnikov in a guerrilla army—the Frente Farabundo Martí para la Liberación Nacional?'

'That is correct.'

'You had been a priest—a Jesuit, I believe?'

'That is correct.'

'But then left the priesthood to fight the government?'

'That is correct.'

'You did not feel that the use of violence in this context was morally wrong?'

'No. I thought it was clearly the will of God.'

'The will of God ...' The barrister repeats the phrase in the tone of dry scepticism for which he is renowned.

'The will of God ... for me', says Uriarte.

'You heard voices, perhaps?'

'The voice of conscience', replies Uriarte. 'You will remember that five Jesuit priests had been murdered by the Salvadorian Army.'

'And this is what provoked you to change the course of your life?'

'Yes.'

'And so you joined the FMLN?'

'Yes.'

'And fought the government forces?'

'Yes.'

'And took human life?'

Uriarte hesitates. 'It is possible, yes.'

'Only possible? Surely, Mr. Uriarte, if you were engaged in a guerrilla war, there were times when you pointed a firearm—I have said it was a Kalashnikov, but it may have been some other kind of firearm; you pointed it at another human being and pulled the trigger?'

'Yes.'

'So, in all likelihood you took a human life?'

'Yes. But it was in self-defence, which is allowed.'

'Allowed? By your conscience?'

'By the Catholic Church.'

'Did the Catholic Church allow you to leave the priesthood?'

'Initially, no.'

'So when you made the decision to stop ministering to the spiritual needs of the people of El Salvador and start killing Salvadorian soldiers, it was not with the permission of your religious superiors but rather in obedience to this voice of your conscience that outranked them because—am I not right—you considered it to be the voice of God?'

'That is correct.'

'So if this voice of conscience had told you to detonate a bomb, or some other deadly device, not to defend the oppressed of El Salvador but your fellow Basques, you would obey it?'

'If it did, but it did not.'

'That is what you say. But the evidence, Mr. Uriarte, suggests otherwise.'

'I am not a member of ETA.'

'So you say. And there has been no evidence presented to prove that you are. But the jury may well decide that even the Spanish security forces, in all their wisdom, may not know the identities of *all* the members of ETA, in particular someone who took up the cudgels of Basque separatism later in his life, having seen the other cause for which he had fought—a Marxist revolution in El Salvador—come to naught.'

'That is absurd.'

'Is it, Mr. Uriarte? Or is it absurd to suggest that you wanted these deadly nerve gasses to kill horses and camels and cattle?'

'That is the truth.' ·

The barrister sighs—an ironic sigh. 'I am not an expert on the military situation in the Darfur region of the Sudan, Mr. Uriarte, and I do not think that the court would expect that of me, but I do know something of human nature, and it beggars belief—yes, Mr. Uriarte, *it beggars belief*—to accept that mechanised units of the Arab militias would be deterred from doing what they had otherwise intended to do by the killing of their livestock. Their women and children, perhaps, but not their livestock.'

'You are correct', says Uriarte, now with a glint in his eye and an edge of contempt in his voice. 'You are *not* an expert on the military situation in the Darfur region of the Sudan, and even less are you an expert on the psychology of the Arab militias because if you were you would know that they value their horses and camels more than their women and children. They are hard men, as hard as the rock in the desert from which they come. Their horses and camels and cattle mean mobility and the means of survival. How did this civil war start? Competition for scarce resources. The desert is encroaching on the fertile land in the west of Sudan. The Arabs moved into Darfur. The inhabitants resisted. The government in Khartoum supported the Arabs; the inhabitants proclaimed their independence. The men went to the hills. The civilians—women and children and the old—took refuge in our camps. But we cannot protect them. Many of them die because they are—isn't it an English expression?—"sitting ducks". The militias cannot find the men so they rape and kill their wives and children. We feed them and clothe them and draw up reports for the different agencies, but we do not protect them. The officials of the United Nations sit in their comfortable offices in Geneva and New York and draw their tax-free salaries. President Bush condemns the genocide. But they do nothing. *Nothing.* And after a time the voice of conscience cries out within you. *Basta!* Enough! Something must be done.'

A Drink

Kotovski and Kate go for a drink. The pub is crowded. Kotovski is masterful. He places Kate like a marker on a plush banquette behind a glass-topped table, then returns with two glasses of vodka and tonic. A moment later the bartender brings olives and potato chips. How did he manage to fix that when they were so busy?

Kotovski asks her about the trial. How does she think it is going? What impression does she think Uriarte made on the jury?

'I think they'll get off.'

Kotovski frowns. 'It's a preposterous story.'

'Maybe. But this afternoon . . . you could see it on their faces . . . the jury was spellbound. And not just the jury. Uriarte made us all feel that we are part of the inert establishment which does nothing to prevent genocide. I felt it. The lawyers felt it. Even the judge. We felt ashamed.'

Kotovski looks annoyed. 'He made a good witness', he says grudgingly.

'He made a *very* good witness', Kate says. 'He sounded as if he really cared. And the way he spoke . . . his sincerity. It was so refreshing after the pomposity and falsity of the Queen's Counsel—the mild sarcasm, the feigned astonishment, all the tricks of his trade. They didn't work. However far-fetched Uriarte's plan might have been, it has not been proved beyond a reasonable doubt that Uriarte is an evil man.'

'*Mens rea*', Kotovski mutters.

'Exactly. *Actus non facit reum nisi mens sit rea.* The act does not make a person guilty unless the mind is also guilty.'

'But the *actus reus* is beyond dispute.'

'Of course. And, if the charge was simply handling dangerous substances, then I am sure the jury would convict. But the charge is conspiracy to cause an explosion *with intent to take human life*. And that has *not* been proved. And so what we have is a monumental cock-up that has cost the taxpayer hundreds of thousands of pounds.'

Kotovski's brow remains creased in a frown. He finishes his drink. 'We'll see.'

'Do you want another?' Kate asks.

'No, thanks. I'd better get back.'

If Kotovski had planned to ask Kate out on a date, he has changed his mind.

The Verdict

The next day the second Basque, Asier Etchevarren, is called by his counsel to give evidence in his own defence. This is linked to that of his childhood friend Uriarte, as a trailer is to a truck. He knew in advance, he insists, that his friend *never intended to use the nerve gas to kill human beings.* Kate is proved right. This becomes the crucial question that the jury must decide. For, as the judge explains in his summing-up, even if it is clear that there *was* a conspiracy to obtain toxic substances, it would be a crime only in the terms of the charges that had been brought by the Crown if it was proved beyond a reasonable doubt that the substances were intended to be used to take human life. 'Explosives', he says, 'may be bought in the same quantity by the same man. But whether he intends to use the explosives to kill and maim innocent people on a train in the rush hour, or to dislodge quantities of rock in a limestone quarry, wholly alters the nature of the transaction according to the law. Certainly, Mr. Uriarte's stated purpose for the purchase of phials of nerve gas was not as innocent as that of the hypothetical gentleman, or lady, who purchases explosives for use in a quarry. But the charge here, members of the jury, is that the three defendants conspired to cause an explosion *to take human life.* If you are satisfied that Mr. Uriarte did indeed intend to take human life, then you will find him guilty. But if you believe Mr. Uriarte's contention that he did not, then you must find him not guilty.'

The jury withdraws. It is three in the afternoon on the twelfth day of the trial. By five there is no verdict and the judge instructs the jury to spend the night in an hotel. At eleven-thirty the next day the judge is informed that a verdict has been reached. The court reconvenes. The foreman stands and is asked by the Clerk of the Court: 'Do you find the defendant Fergal O'Brien guilty or not guilty of the charge that he did conspire to cause an explosion to take human life?'

'Not guilty.'

'And Asier Etchevarren?'

'Not guilty.'

'And Juan Uriarte?'

'Not guilty.'

'And is that the verdict of you all?'

'It is.'

The judge turns to the defendants: 'You are free to go.' O'Brien looks astonished; Etchevarren, relieved. Uriarte shows no reaction until, as he leaves the dock, he looks towards the jury and smiles.

29

Post-Mortem

A committee room at the Home Office: a long table with a pine veneer top, chairs with tubular frames and cloth-covered seats, a view over Saint James's Park. At the head of the table sits a middle-aged man in a pin-striped suit, white shirt and bright mauve tie. Strands of his remaining hair are brushed back from the shining dome of his forehead. Next to him, a young woman waits with an open notebook and ballpoint pen. He introduces himself to those present as James Miller from the Home Office, and then he asks those sitting around the table to do the same: Anne Grayson from the Crown Prosecution Service (CPS); Bernard Ashton from Scotland Yard's Special Branch; Brian Butler from the Security Service, MI5, and at his side a younger colleague, David Kotovski.

'There can be no doubt', Miller begins, leaning forward, his elbows resting on the table, 'that the acquittal of the Basques is an embarrassment: there has been comment in the Press and there may be more.'

None of those sitting at the table disputes what he says.

'It seems clear to me . . .'—he glances across the table towards the police officer, Ashton, and the lawyer from the CPS—'that there may have been an undue readiness to take the conspiracy at face value.'

'How else was one to take it?' asks the CPS solicitor, Anne Grayson— a middle-aged woman with thin blonde hair. 'The evidence presented by our colleagues here . . .'—she nods towards the officer from Special Branch and the two men from MI5—'was *prima facie* . . .'

'But wasn't it established', Miller interrupts, 'that O'Brien was *not* acting for any known terrorist organisation?'

'That is correct', Ashton, the police officer, replies in a drawling *faux* Cockney accent. 'But it does not change the nature of the offence.'

'It was our sources in Dublin', says Brian Butler, the older of the two men from the Security Service, 'who in fact alerted us to what O'Brien was up to. He led us to the Basques, one of whom had been a member of ETA . . .'

'But inactive?' Miller suggests.

'So we were told by our friends in Madrid', says Ashton.

'One can never be certain', says Butler, 'that former members of a terrorist organisation are not going to branch out on their own like the Real IRA.'

'But wasn't it apparent', asks Miller, glancing down at his notes, 'that the key figure here was not O'Brien or even Etchevarren but the man for whom Etchevarren was acting, Juan Uriarte?'

Again, no one dissents from this judgement.

'The mistake, it seems to me,' Miller continues, 'was the failure to analyse Uriarte's character and motivation before prosecuting the case.'

'With hindsight, I agree', says Anne Grayson. 'But analysis is the job of analysts, not lawyers.'

Miller looks across at the two men from MI5, Brian Butler and David Kotovski.

'The Security Service may alert Special Branch to a criminal conspiracy,' says Butler, 'but it is not our job to collect evidence or make arrests. Nor is it our job to decide whether the evidence merits prosecution.'

Miller turns back to Anne Grayson. 'If you had framed lesser charges which made no mention of the intent to take human life, do you think that the verdict might have been different?'

'Certainly', says Grayson. 'We might have secured a conviction for the unauthorised handling of toxic substances resulting in a fine or eighteen months imprisonment.'

'The connections with ETA and the IRA', says Butler, 'led us all to assume that the gas would be used to take human life.'

'But you were surely appraised of this man Uriarte's line of defence?'

'Yes,' says Grayson, 'but we all thought it inconceivable that a jury would accept that Uriarte wanted the gas to kill camels.'

'It still seems daft', mutters the police officer.

Miller fixes his languid gaze on Brian Butler and David Kotovski. 'Did either of you feel, when you first learned of this conspiracy, that it represented a terrorist threat?'

Butler shakes his head. 'No. But whenever a toxic gas like Sarin comes into the equation, we have to assume the worst.'

'Of course.'

'Even if we were confident that the British public was not at risk, we could see that something dangerous and unlawful was intended and that it was therefore a matter that had to be referred to the police.'

Miller sits back in his chair. 'It seems to me', he says in a worldly-wise tone of voice, 'that everyone acted in good faith and nothing is to be gained from any recriminations. As you say'—he looks across at the solicitor from the CPS and the Special Branch detective, Ashton—'juries are unpredictable and in this case it was sufficiently impressed by the chief defendant to find him and therefore the others not guilty. What we have to decide now'—he turns to Butler and Kotovski—'is what we here in the UK should do in terms of further investigations.'

'All three of the accused have returned to their countries of residence', says Brian Butler.

'Yes', says Ashton. 'O'Brien to Dublin, Etchevarren to Bilbao and Uriarte to Rome.'

'So presumably we can leave any further investigation or surveillance to the agencies in those countries?'

Butler nods. 'I think that would be appropriate unless, of course, any of the three were to return to the UK.'

'Are we agreed on this?' asks Miller.

'We do not intend to bring any further charges', says Anne Grayson. 'Bernard?'

'With no further evidence,' says the Special Branch officer, 'I can see no reason to keep the case open.'

'Brian?'

'I concur.'

Kotovski raises his hand.

Miller looks down at his list of those present. 'Yes, Mr. . . . Kotovski?'

'There is surely a slight inconsistency in our position. If, as was believed at the time of the prosecution, Uriarte was trying to get hold of toxic gas for some purpose *other* than the killing of camels, then surely the jury's conclusion should not necessarily lead *us* to change our mind. He may have been acquitted. He may have left the country. But if he still has that purpose in mind, shouldn't he be kept under surveillance?'

There is silence. Miller looks down at his blotting pad as if the younger man's intervention will pass like a shower of rain.

'How can we keep him under surveillance if he is abroad?' asks Ashton.

'We could alert the national agencies', says Brian Butler, his tone reluctant, his brow furrowed as if annoyed that his subordinate was taking a view different from his own.

'But will the Spanish keep an eye on Uriarte while he is living in Rome?' asks Kotovski. 'And what interest will the Italians show in a

Spaniard who is not even a member of ETA? Should they not, at the very least, be informed of our concerns?'

There is a further half minute's silence as those around the table consider what has been said.

Miller, at the head of the table, breaks the silence. 'It is true that if Uriarte were to go on to perpetrate some atrocity abroad, questions might be raised. So perhaps Kotovski here is right.' He looks across at Butler. 'Keep the file open until you are quite satisfied that Uriarte presents no threat to us or anyone else.'

The Analyst

David Kotovski walks back to Thames House. He is angry. He is angry with his superiors for their obtuseness and angry with himself for his lack of *sang froid*. Out of sight, out of mind. What kind of solution is that to the acquittal of a man trying to buy poison gas? Juan Uriarte. He had watched him throughout the trial. What lay behind his insouciance? How could he have been so sure that he would be acquitted? Kotovski had not interrogated him before the trial—that had been a matter for the police—but the trial had been his baby. It was Kotovski who had received the intelligence that an old link between ETA and the IRA had been reactivated, who had put O'Brien under surveillance, who had invented the corruptible chemist who could obtain Sarin, who had tracked the two Basques after their arrival at Heathrow. The operation had been overseen by his chief, BB, Brian Butler, but because there had been no connection to Islamic extremists, BB's interest had been slight. He had left the whole thing to Kotovski, and yet he had had to take the flak from Miller—rebuked for his department's failure 'to analyse Uriarte's character and motivation'. And the riposte from the CPS: 'analysis is the job of analysts, not lawyers.'

To the world outside the Security Service, Kotovski is a civil servant who does something dull at the Ministry of Defence. He lives *incognito*. The strong feelings for Queen and Country are hidden under a shroud of affected ordinariness. But Kotovski is ambitious and now wonders if the acquittal will affect his career. Would the 'adverse press comment' be blamed on him? No doubt Miller had been thinking of the piece Kate Ramsey had written after the acquittal. 'An outrageous waste of public funds! Misjudgement amounting to incompetence!'

The thought of Kate Ramsey confuses Kotovski. From the start of the trial, when he had not been watching Uriarte—trying to judge what lay behind his sly nonchalance—he had been taking sidelong glances at the pretty dark-haired girl in front of him on the press benches. Occasionally, going in and out of the courtroom, they had exchanged a smile. Then, finding themselves in the same sandwich bar, they had had lunch together. She had seemed intelligent, friendly, funny and prepared to put herself down. When the trial ended, they had exchanged cell phone numbers and promised to keep in touch. Kotovski had meant to wait for a week or so before asking her out. But now, after her article, he is not so sure.

Kotovski has had a number of girlfriends. Some have been his colleagues in the service, some not. It is easier to date colleagues because there is no need to invent cock-and-bull stories about his job. Kotovski's first girlfriend had been a fellow student at Manchester. Judy. They had started to sleep together after getting drunk at a party. She came from York and had a soft Yorkshire accent. She was quiet, gentle, affectionate, sharp and pretty. On graduating, she had come to London, gotten a job in magazine publishing and shared a flat with friends. Though they never lived together, they were a couple: Dave and Jude. They took holidays together, went to movies together, had dinner together with their friends.

At Christmas each went home—Kotovski to Ealing, Judy to York. One Bank Holiday weekend, Judy had taken Kotovski to stay with her parents. They lived in a Persimmon Home in Huntingdon, a dormitory suburb to the north of the city. Judy's mother was house-proud: everything was tidy and clean with little frilly mats under the cups of tea to protect the polished table. She fussed over Kotovski, constantly glancing nervously at her daughter. The father, a middle manager at Rowntrees, asked Kotovski about his job at the Ministry of Defence. Kotovski was well practised in disinformation. 'Nothing interesting. Personnel. A good pension.'

Had Kotovski gone off Judy because of her parents? Would it have been different if they had lived in one of those beautiful country houses that Kotovski saw on the property pages of *Country Life*? No. It was because he had not been in love. Their relationship had been no more than a habit based on companionship and sex. At first there seemed no reason to break up. Then a couple they knew got married; soon after, another; and suddenly it seemed that they were going to a wedding every weekend. Things became pointed. The brides threw their bouquets at Judy. Kotovski knew that he was expected to whisk her off to Venice or Rome and propose on the Rialto Bridge or at the Trevi Fountain. A ring. A hen night. A stag night. A white wedding in Huntingdon Parish Church and a reception afterwards at the Horse and Hounds. A honeymoon in Bali, then back to a Persimmon Home.

Kotovski had dumped her on their seventh anniversary amid the clatter of her favourite restaurant, Kensington Place. While tears ran down her cheeks, he tore into himself and his parents, blaming his aversion to the idea of marriage on their divorce. He told Judy that he liked her better than anyone else in the world: she was warm and attractive and a wonderful friend, but he did not want to get married now or in the foreseeable future. She must find someone else. Both agreed to remain friends. To him this meant letting her down lightly: to her it meant giving him a chance to change his mind. They went to a movie or had dinner every couple of weeks. Then once a month. Then every six weeks. Then Judy gave up on London and moved back to York.

Kotovski had gone out with other girls, but the relationships rarely lasted as long as a year. The *coup de foudre* never came. He now wonders whether he is capable of falling in love, or whether the kind of passion he envisages is not a chimera. Perhaps he should resign himself to the fact that one girl is always going to be much like another. They look different, of course; some are better looking than others and there are other qualities to be measured—intelligence, sense of humour. There are also the negative qualities—neurosis, self-obsession. Why do his affairs always end? Because of their neediness, their baggage. Baggage from ex-boyfriends; above all, baggage from their families—oafish fathers, nervy mothers, envious siblings. They seem to expect him to provide a psychic panacea: solve their past problems and assure a flawless future.

Are their demands unreasonable? What is love if not a psychological quid pro quo, an *egoisme à deux*? I will think you wonderful if you think me wonderful and fancy you if you fancy me. But how long does it last? The space of time between that first kiss and the emergence of plaintive, nagging neediness. 'Most men fall in love with a pretty face but find themselves bound for life to a hateful stranger.' That is Schopenhauer quoted by Germaine Greer in *The Female Eunuch*, which Kotovski read while at Manchester. Greer thought that the traditional family was a nightmare and Kotovski is disposed to agree. His parents divorced when he was twelve. He grew up in Acton with his mother, his sister and, two years after the divorce, a step-father, Trevor Oxley, an apparatchik in the Ealing Education Authority. Oxley was silent and dull: like boron rods in a nuclear reactor, he absorbed his wife's radioactive neurosis. For that, Kotovski was grateful: living alone with his mother and his sister had been hell.

His father, Michael Kotovski, had also remarried—a woman who was dull and undemanding. Kotovski now understands why his step-mother's passivity appealed to his father. She never nagged; she had no social ambitions; she was not ashamed, as his mother had been, of her husband's Polish name. But their marriage was not an enticing model: it was a compact for mutual aid at a low level. He earned money as a solicitor in Ealing; she cooked supper and washed his clothes. To Kotovski they are like a male and female baboon he had once watched lugubriously picking nits off one another's bodies at the London Zoo.

Perhaps in the end, Kotovski decides, that is as good a basis for a marriage as any. Why, then, is he still unable to proceed from a date to a relationship, and from a relationship to a proposal by the Trevi Fountain or on the Rialto Bridge? Is it just that he has yet to find the right girl? Or is it something more profound, more existential? Is it because Kotovski does not really know who *he* is? Or what sort of person he wants to be?

Throughout his childhood and adolescence, the only man Kotovski admired without reservation was his grandfather, Jan Kotkowski. He had called him Zazu, short for *Dziadziu*—grandpa in Polish. As Kotovski had told Kate, Zazu had worked as a stock-taker at a builders merchant in Acton but had been born on his parents' small estate south of Cracow and his mind, his demeanour, his *soul*, had remained that of a Polish nobleman. Zazu had joined the army. As a young cavalry officer at the outbreak of World War II, he and his squadron of mounted

Uhlans had charged German tanks. His horse was killed beneath him, but Zazu survived. He escaped from Poland through Romania, enlisted in Sikorski's Polish division in France, later joined the Polish Legion in Italy and was decorated for valour at the Battle of Monte Cassino.

The freedom of Poland had been the *casus belli* of World War II, but at Yalta Roosevelt and Churchill had thrown Poland to the Stalinist wolves. Zazu's parents were dead; their estate was expropriated by the Communist government. Zazu remained in England. He was demobbed from the Polish Legion with a puny pension. Speaking little English and with no professional qualifications, the best job he could find was as a stock-taker at a builders merchant in Hammersmith. He fell for a typist in the front office, Mary O'Connor. They were married in 1950. Her family members were London Irish. 'Peasants', Kotkowski would call them: but at least they were Catholic and drank whisky and danced jigs.

It was their son, Michael, Kotovski's father, who in his twenties dropped the second *k* from the name Kotkowski and changed the *w* to a *v*: it made it easier for the English to pronounce. Michael had done his best to shed both his Polish and Irish heritage and become British. He had married someone emphatically English—Kotovski's mother. She had infected her son with a measure of disdain for his Irish cousins—Kotovski loathes the jigs and the Blarney—but not for her Polish father-in-law: Kotovski had adored him until his death at the age of eighty-four.

Zazu had been tall with an unmistakably Slav physiognomy—high cheekbones, Asiatic eyes. As a child Kotovski had looked with awe at his medals and sabre. Zazu was stylish and grand and curious and well read. He never changed his job but lived as if the external circumstances of his life were of no significance. Destiny was destiny, and if it left you in a semi-detached house in Acton rather than a country house in Poland, then so be it. Aristocracy was a thing of the spirit, not the body. The Polish Club in Queens Gate might not be the Club of the Nobility in Warsaw—but then in Warsaw the Club of the Nobility was no more. 'In England', Zazu told his grandson, 'you can be who you like. If I had gone back to Poland, I would either have had to change, or to pretend.' That perhaps was why Kotovski had wanted to work for the Security Service—to protect the liberties that had meant that his grandfather had no need to change or to pretend.

As Zazu had grown older, he had tested the tolerance of his adopted country. He liked to argue, and to be told that he was a fascist or a bigot only brightened the gleam in his eyes. Going out with Zazu became hazardous: he refused to lower his voice and, as he grew deaf in old age, would shout out his views on the Irish, blacks, homosexuals, asylum seekers, unmarried mothers, Americans, feminists, Muslims, Jews ... 'Poles are anti-Semitic? What do you expect, when they are despised by the Jews? If a Jew eats with a gentile, he is *defiled*. Read Tacitus; you'll see that there was anti-Semitism long before Christ.'

'Am I not eating with you now?' Zazu's friend Ackerman would ask, and Zazu would answer: 'There you are. A typical Jew. Always the subjective point of view. You are eating with me because you are not observant. You think you are liberal because you give money to Amnesty International and say we should let blacks into the country, but if your daughter had married one of those blacks, or a Catholic or anyone but another Jew, you wouldn't like it and you wouldn't like it if your grandsons weren't circumcised; and when it comes to Israel, you're like all the others—you say you have the right to a Jewish state because of the Holocaust! As if two wrongs make a right!'

Ackerman would shrug his shoulders in a gesture of mock despair. He owned the dry-cleaning store to which Zazu took his clothes and let out the waistbands of Zazu's trousers when he put on weight in old age. Next to the dry cleaners was the barber's shop where Zazu had his hair cut: the barber, a Greek Cypriot, was another of Zazu's friends. Next to the barber's shop there was a newsstand run by Kurds. The Kurdish husband was less friendly towards Zazu, misunderstanding the gallant manner in which Zazu kissed the hand of his wife.

Next to the newsstand there was an Indian restaurant where every two weeks, on a Wednesday, Zazu had supper with Ackerman. The Indians were in fact Bengalis and, as Muslims, shared many of Zazu's views—though not his views on Islam. 'The Koran—a patchwork quilt made up of snippets from the Old and the New Testament. Some of it good, of course. The One True God. Charity. Care of widows and orphans. And not just for the Chosen People as it is with the Jews but for anyone who converts. But for those who don't convert?' Zazu would slit his throat with his finger. 'Death or enslavement and, for the pretty girls, the life of a concubine. Why? Because Muhammad was a bandit. He led his raids against other tribes and then against the Byzantine Empire. So Islam was spread with the sword, and we would all be Muslims now if they had not been stopped at the Loire by Charles Martel and at the gates of Vienna by Jan III Sobieski. Yes, a Pole, my dear Ackerman. Christendom saved by a Pole!'

The Journalist

It is hot. Kate Ramsey makes her way through the crowds that have spilled out of the pubs onto the pavement in Soho and enters a restaurant on Greek Street. She breathes in the refrigerated air. Her eyes adjust to the dimmer light. Her face loses some of the lines of tension.

'Ramsey', she says to the waiter who greets her.

The waiter finds her name on the list of reservations, then he leads her to a table set for two at the back of the room. Kate sits down. A second waiter brings two menus to the table. She orders a Campari and a bottle of still mineral water. They are brought to her table with a small dish of olives. The minutes pass: her brow puckers into a look of irritation. She takes out her cell phone. 'Where on earth are you?' She listens. Whatever she hears does not mollify her: the look of irritation remains on her face.

Kate Ramsey is ambivalent about her own good looks. She finds it tiresome that men glance at her as they pass in the street and worrisome if they do not. She is brisk and can be abrupt. On the top of her right ear are three small circular scars left by the studs she had worn in her rebellious teenage years. She wears black designer jeans and a blue cotton shirt. She seems confident—and controlled. In the twenty minutes or so she is kept waiting, she drinks only half her Campari and eats three olives.

The man who finally joins Kate at her table also wears jeans, adding to them an olive green shirt and one of those loose multi-pocketed waistcoats favoured by plumbers, photographers and architects. Like Kate, he is in his mid-thirties.

'I'm sorry', he says as he stoops to kiss her on the cheek.

'You don't change.'

'Punctuality is a Western fad', he replies as he sits down at the table. 'No one in Phnom Penh or Moscow or Montevideo would expect one to be on time.'

'You don't think that when in Rome you should do as the Romans do?'

'No one keeps appointments in Rome.'

'In London, then.'

'As I said, I'm sorry.' He gives another disarming smile which does not in itself lead the lines of irritation to fade from Kate's face but rather seems to trigger some kind of resignation: if he had not changed during the five years they had gone out together, why would he change now? She beckons to the waiter: they order and ask for more mineral water. Neither wants to drink wine.

'Where have you been?' she asks.

'Canary Wharf.'

'No, I mean . . .' She waves her hand to signify the world beyond London.

'Honduras.'

'What's the story?'

'The last great disaster. Hurricane Mitch. What happened to the money? What has been done?'

'Your idea?'

'No, theirs.'

'Are you safe?'

'In Honduras?'

'On the paper. Aren't people being laid off?'

'My name never comes up because I'm never there.'

'No,' said Kate, her face turned down, 'you were never there.'

He shrugs as if to say 'That's the way I am.'

They talk about this and that. Whenever they meet, Kate wonders whether it had been a mistake to dump him. She had no longer loved him; she had seen through him; he was passive and self-obsessed. But he had been a bird in the hand and now there seemed to be none in the bush. It is a truth universally acknowledged that there are more thirty-something women in London wanting a husband than thirty-something men wanting a wife. Was true love a chimera? Should a woman settle for whomever she happens to be sleeping with when she hits thirty?

40

Kate tells Barney about the trial and Uriarte. Barney looks bored. It is her story, not his. He tells her about Honduras and Hurricane Mitch. Then, over their double espressos, Kate looks up at Barney: 'I want some advice.'

'About your love life?' He smirks.

'No. My career.'

'Go ahead.'

'They want to lose people on our paper too.'

'So I hear.'

'From where you stand, on the outside, would you say I was safe?'

Barney hesitates, then says: 'You've got a good reputation. I would say you were as safe as anyone.'

'But no safer?'

'Circulation is dropping. Advertising is drying up. People are getting their news off TV, the Internet, even their cell phones.'

'I used to write a column. Now I'm a crime reporter.'

'Did Digby give a reason for dropping the column?'

'My scope was too narrow.'

'He thinks you're posh.'

'And a woman. He thinks we're only good for one thing . . .'

'Has he come on to you?'

'He chatted me up over a drink one evening after work but quickly got the message.'

'That you didn't fancy him?'

'That I'd no more consider dating him than a skunk, even without the wife waiting for him in the suburbs.'

'A yob and a snob. Not a good mix.'

She frowns. 'The thing is this. Do you think I should resign?'

'Why resign?'

'More dignified than being sacked.'

'You'd get some sort of pay off if you were sacked.'

'It wouldn't amount to much and . . .'

'You've got a rich dad.'

Kate blushes. 'It might look better if I resigned. I could say I was head-hunted.'

'If you get another job.'

'Don't you think I would?'

Barney shrugs. 'When it comes to journalists, there's more supply than demand.'

Kate frowns. 'Time for a career change?'

'Go into the City. You've got the contacts.'

'Too dull.' She thinks to herself for a moment. 'The law, perhaps?'

Barney smiles. 'You studied theology and are good at preaching. Become a woman priest.'

Kate scowls. 'We don't have women priests in the Catholic Church.'

'You're no longer a Catholic.'

'I'm certainly not an Anglican.'

'You can always convert.'

'Uncle Lolo would never forgive me.'

'He would have to forgive you. He *is* a priest.'

The Priest

Kate Ramsey's uncle, Father Luke Scott, lives alone in Marylebone in a mansion flat. He remains a priest of his diocese, but when he had reached the age of sixty, his bishop had agreed to let him withdraw from parish work and decide for himself the scope of his vocation. Given the shortage of priests in the diocese, this showed how estranged Father Luke had become from the bishop and the bishop from Father Luke. He is still kept busy. He says Mass every morning at Saint James's, Spanish Place, marries the children of old friends, goes to Rome where he is held in greater esteem than he is in England, acts as a locum tenens in certain parishes which welcome a 'traditionalist' priest, gives occasional missions or retreats to dwindling communities of nuns, and is a shoulder to cry on for those like his niece Kate who find they can talk to him in a way that they cannot talk to their parents.

Luke Scott is not a monk: he has not taken vows of poverty and chastity but only of obedience to his bishop, who, like all bishops in the Roman Catholic Church, enjoins commitment to a celibate life. But he was not asked to renounce all worldly goods. Luke has private means. He does not depend on the diocese for his livelihood because his brother-in-law, Kate's father, has, over the years, turned Luke's modest inheritance into a substantial portfolio. As a result he can afford the flat in Marylebone, subscriptions to the London Library and the Travellers Club and occasional visits to elegant restaurants with his friends.

This comfortable life strikes a number of Luke's fellow priests as unseemly: they do not know of the sums of money he gives to the needy. He is described as 'pre-Conciliar', which means a throw-back to the days before the Second Vatican Council and the Church's 'preferential option for the poor'. If any were to accuse him to his face of misdirecting his vocation, he would reply that someone has to minister to the rich—to guide them, as it were, through the needle's eye. Had not Jesus taught that they were at greatest risk of eternal damnation? 'It is the man who is sick, after all, who has most need of the doctor.' However, Luke never has to defend himself: the slurs are only made behind his back.

Luke does recognise that in some ways he is a 'spoiled' priest. He does not drink or download pornography, but he watches too much television—particularly *films noirs* or Westerns where there are clear heroes and villains and good always triumphs over evil. He accepts that if he were to spend as much time in prayer as he does watching television he would be a better priest, but he knows his own limits and assumes that God knew them too.

A more serious vice is the fourth of the seven deadly sins—*acedia*—a state of cynicism, disillusion and spiritual sloth. How straightforward a priestly vocation had seemed when he was a young seminarian among other young seminarians, all certain that their calling came from God. How many of those vocations, he now wonders, were the product of disorders and distortions in the development of a child? Was not a commitment to celibacy often the result of a devout adolescent deciding that his indifference to women was a sign that God called him to the priesthood—'eunuchs for the sake of the Kingdom'—only to find that he was powerfully drawn to teenage boys? How many priests had weak fathers and domineering mothers? Had Luke become a priest simply to please his mother? Or was it to anaesthetise himself from human emotions after being jilted by his fiancée at Cambridge? Was loving God merely a front for his failure to love human beings? He thought back to his reading of Thomas à Kempis' *The Imitation of Christ*. 'Nothing defiles and ensnares the heart more than a selfish love of creatures.' How heady it had been in his youth to believe that he had been chosen by God to rise above the humdrum turmoil of the human condition.

Luke had not sustained it—this holy detachment from human affection. Two months after Kate's birth, he had baptised his niece Kate in the font of Saint Laurence's Church in Petersfield, and in the years which followed had seen the bald baby grow into a child with dark hair and large blue eyes. He had felt flattered that she had crawled happily towards him when she saw him and later toddled around the garden holding on to an extended finger and calling him Lolo. All the priest's immunity to emotional attachment was lost in the delight he took in the company of this child.

Ripe plums drop off the tree. During adolescence, Kate had lost her faith. Was it because of sex? The Church taught that outside marriage it was a mortal sin and those who died unrepentant in a state of mortal sin went to Hell. No one believed that any more—neither in the sinfulness of consensual sex, nor the existence of Hell. From Kate and Charlie, her brother, Luke had learned to interpret the jargon used by her generation: 'Going out with' meant 'sleeping with' and a 'relationship' was an affair. When Kate told him about her love life, Luke found he could not bring himself to talk of damnation. He dropped the role of the strict priest for that of the worldly-wise uncle. The power of sexual attraction, he had warned her, could sometimes conceal a temperament incompatibility. He had not told Kate that he found Barney immature and narcissistic; he had done his best to like him and had watched in anguish as Kate slowly came to realise that her heroic war correspondent was in reality a posturing Peter Pan.

A penitent in the confessional had once asked Luke whether it was a sin to fail to forgive someone who had harmed someone he loved. Luke had counselled, without reflection, that it was, that we are commanded to forgive those who trespass against us collectively—severally and singularly, as a solicitor might say. But he acknowledged it was hard. And while he now feels confident that he has forgiven those, such as the vicar general of his diocese, who have conspired against him and even the girl who jilted him at Cambridge, he finds it less easy to forgive those who have harmed Kate—Barney, with his sins of omission, and now a man called Digby, who, Kate tells him, has given her the sack.

44

They are dining together in a small restaurant where, because Luke is a regular customer, the waiters are not fazed to see an older man wearing a clerical collar dining with an attractive young woman half his age.

'I can probably get another job of some sort', she says. 'But it isn't good to be let go. You look like a loser.'

'Of course you'll get another job', says Luke—confident not just in his niece's talent but also in the efficacy of prayer.

'Sure', says Kate. 'But in fact I wouldn't mind going freelance for a while and writing some features—perhaps from abroad.'

Luke frowns. Is this an unacknowledged ambition to be more like Barney? Has she seen through him or not?

'Did you read what I wrote about the trial at the Old Bailey?' asks Kate.

'Of course. I read everything you write.'

'Do you remember the man who was acquitted?'

'Weren't there three?'

'Yes. I mean the main man, Uriarte—the one who was once a priest. His story would be interesting. Perhaps I should write about him?'

Luke says nothing.

'He's not your kind of Catholic, I know,' says Kate, 'but nowadays people are fascinated by Africa and what's being done or not done to help solve the problems there.'

'Or what has been done', says Luke, 'but hasn't worked.'

'Exactly. It hasn't worked. Why hasn't it worked? What would work? Those are just the kind of questions I'd like to put to Uriarte.'

'Sarin would work. Isn't that what he'd say?'

'In that context, yes. But overall. Consider the poverty that exists even when there isn't a war. Should we just dole out more money or improve their terms of trade?'

'Tesco sells *mangetout* from Kenya', says Luke, 'but I can't believe that that solves the country's problems.'

'And AIDS', said Kate. 'All those people dying of AIDS and . . .' She stops.

Luke knows why she has stopped. 'And the Church's ban on the use of condoms?'

She hesitates, as if she had wanted to avoid the subject but, now that it has been raised, must go on. 'It really is difficult for someone of my generation to understand it. Even Catholics.'

'You read theology at Oxford', Luke reminds her. 'You know the arguments.'

'Natural law . . .'

'Which is not the law of nature, but the law *of* our natures, or the nature of anything created by God—the law inherent in its design.'

'God as a Bauhaus architect . . .'

'More or less.'

'But what use is it, Uncle Lolo, to tell the wife of a migrant worker that she can't have sex with her infected husband when he comes home because Saint Thomas Aquinas, following Aristotle, judged that our bodies were made for having children, not having fun?'

'Fun is not altogether excluded', says Luke, 'but it is a secondary end.'

'Secondary ends. Primary ends. These theological niceties don't mean much when it comes to love.'

'I dare say.'

'When you were engaged to that girl at Cambridge', says Kate, 'did you think about primary and secondary ends?'

'I did, which was almost certainly why she went for the man who didn't.'

'You didn't sleep with her?'

'No.' Seeing the shade of a smile come onto Kate's face, Luke adds: 'It wasn't just Catholics who held back at the time. Girls didn't want to get pregnant.'

'I can see that before the pill it was difficult to disentangle sex from procreation, though I guess there were condoms, weren't there?'

'Difficult to come by. They were sold in seedy barber shops.'

'Do you think if you *had* slept with her you might have kept her?'

'Perhaps. But it would have been a mistake.'

'How can you be sure?'

'The pleasure of sex can blind one to certain incompatibilities.'

A pensive expression crosses Kate's face. 'Did she marry the other guy?' she asks.

'Yes.'

'And?'

'So far as I know, they lived happily ever after.'

'You didn't keep in touch?'

'No.'

'And you never fell for anyone else?'

'No. I thought ... well, I decided that I'd been going down the wrong road. That God didn't want me to marry. That he wanted me to be a priest.'

'Did you ever find *men* attractive?' asks Kate.

Luke smiles. 'No.'

'Because now it turns out ...'

'I know. Priests are all repressed, or not so-repressed, homosexuals.'

'Not all, but some.'

'Some, certainly.'

'Didn't you realise it at the time?'

'Of course. There were rumours about some of the monks who taught us, and we now know that there were cases where they molested the boys.'

'Did they ever molest you?'

'Not at school.'

'In the seminary?'

'When I was in Rome, a Dutch student at the Gregorian made a pass at me.'

'Is he still a priest?'

Luke laughs. 'He's a cardinal in the Curia!'

'But isn't that wrong?'

'I dare say he repented of what he had done and learned self-control. You must remember that at the time in all male institutions—in monasteries, seminaries, theological colleges, the army, the navy, public schools, prep schools—this sort of thing went on. People didn't make as much of it as they do now.'

'But to make him a cardinal!'

'I am sure that by the time he was made a cardinal, he had led an exemplary life for many years.'

The Cardinal

Cardinal Doornik, the Prefect for the Congregation for Catholic Culture, looks out from his office in the Vatican towards the windows of

47

the papal apartments. He is a man in his late sixties with an austere face that might have been drawn by Cranach or Dürer. Behind him stands a plumper, younger man—his secretary, Monsignor Perez. Perez is Spanish, Doornik is Dutch, and, since neither is fluent in the other's language, they speak to one another either in Latin or, more commonly, English.

'What was decided?' Cardinal Doornik asks Monsignor Perez without turning to face him.

'That it was a matter for the Holy Father.'

'But is the Holy Father able to decide?'

'His mind, they say, is clear and his spirit is ... sublime.'

'"They say"?'

'Those who have been admitted to the Holy Father by Bishop Dziwisz.'

'He alone decides?'

'Cardinal Soldano or Cardinal Ratzinger would not be turned away, but our matter is not deemed important.'

Now the Cardinal turns to face his secretary and, in an exasperated tone of voice, asks him: 'How long can this go on?'

'It is for God to decide.'

'Of course.'

'We have to accept, Eminence, that the matters that are considered urgent by our Congregation are not thought urgent by those close to the Holy Father. There will be no resolution until there is a new pope.'

For a while, the two men stand in silence, each with his own thoughts.

'Is it thought possible that the Holy Father might abdicate?'

'Cardinal Sodano has said it is a possibility, but many are against it.'

'I am sure. Bishop Dziwisz for one ...'

Monsignor Perez says nothing.

'What are the precedents?' asks Cardinal Doornik.

'Celestine V abdicated in 1294 and Gregory XII in 1417.'

'In what circumstances?'

'Celestine V had been a hermit. The cardinals thought that the choice of a patently holy man would lead to a reform of the Church, but he couldn't cope.'

'And Gregory XII?'

'There were three claimants to the papacy at the time. Two were deposed by the Council of Constance and the third abdicated. It was to end the Great Schism.'

'Which it did?'

'More or less. But when there is more than one man with a claim on the papacy it can confuse the faithful. It can lead to a schism.'

Cardinal Doornik sighs. 'So we have to wait for the Lord to call Karol Wojtyła in his own good time.'

'And hope that the Holy Spirit will guide us to choose a worthy successor.'

'And what would your advice be to the Holy Spirit, Monsignor?'

'Perhaps not the same as yours, your Eminence.'

The Cardinal laughs. 'I come from a rich country while you have spent much of your life working in one of the poorest, yet I would like to see a progressive pope while you want a reactionary.'

'"Man does not live on bread alone", your Eminence.'

'Tell that to the people living in the *favelas*.'

'I did.'

'You are incorrigible, Monsignor.'

'It was you who chose me as your secretary ...'

'I did. There's no point in working with a parrot.'

Monsignor Perez inclines his head to acknowledge the compliment. Cardinal Doornik goes to his desk. 'I think that will be all for now.'

Monsignor Perez nods again and turns to leave.

'Before you go ...', says the Cardinal.

Perez waits.

'I was talking this morning to Bishop Crowe, who has just been made the spiritual director of Misericordia, and he said he thought you might once of have known this man Uriarte.'

'Juan Uriarte? Yes. We were together in El Salvador.'

'Did you hear about his troubles in London?'

'Yes.'

'And?'

'It did not surprise me. He was always ...' Perez hesitates. 'He was always impatient.'

'As you may well imagine, he is now *persona non grata* in Sudan. Misericordia itself may be asked to withdraw from the region.'

49

'And Uriarte?'

'He will be reassigned.'

'They won't dismiss him?'

'He is a good man, I understand, and he has his admirers.'

'I dare say.'

'But you are not among them?'

'He remains a friend, your Eminence. We meet from time to time and grumble about the state of the Church but from diametrically opposed points of view.'

'It is good that ideological adversaries can remain friends like Pole and Bellarmine at the Council of Trent. But all the same, to associate with terrorists, to buy toxic gas ...' The Cardinal shakes his head.

'Pope Pius V called for the assassination of Queen Elizabeth of England', counters Perez.

'But he was pope! Your friend Uriarte is not even a priest.'

At the Questura

The interpreter provided for Kotovski by the British Embassy in Rome is an Italian woman in her early forties—the wife of a Welsh language teacher working for the British Council. On the evening of Kotovski's arrival, Signora Gwynn comes to the two-star hotel, near the Termini Station, where Kotovski is staying. They go over the arrangements for the following morning. She is not unfriendly but not friendly either: she declines the offer of a drink and, when Kotovski asks if she could recommend somewhere to eat, says, almost abruptly, 'No. We never eat out.'

Signora Gwynn returns to Kotovski's hotel at nine-thirty the next morning, and together they take a cab to the Central Directorate for the Anti-Terrorism Police at the Questura. An appointment has been made with a Comandante Paulo Franchetti for ten o'clock, but he is not in his office and a uniformed officer—a young woman—asks them to wait. At a quarter to eleven, Franchetti appears and, without apologising for being late, leads Kotovski and his interpreter into his office. Franchetti sits down at his desk; Kotovski and Signora Gwynn sit in two chairs facing the desk. Franchetti, a heavy man with wiry, receding hair, quietly drums his fingers on his desk while Kotovski, through Signora Gwynn, tells him about the trial at the Old Bailey. Halfway through the exposition, Franchetti's fingers suddenly stop: he picks up some sheets of paper laid out on the blotter on his desk—the surface upon which he had been playing an imaginary toccata—glances at them and says, in heavily accented English: 'Of course, yes. Juan Uriarte. The terrorist. But he was acquitted, yes?'

'He was acquitted', says Kotovski, 'but there are grounds for thinking that the verdict was unsound.'

'Unsound?' Franchetti does not understand the word. Signora Gwynn explains in Italian. Franchetti replies with a stream of Italian words, which Signora Gwynn condenses into one short sentence. 'Until we received your communiqué, we knew nothing of this man Uriarte and now, after our investigations, there is no record of any criminal activities or even grounds for suspicion.'

'The ground for suspicion', says Kotovski, 'is that he was trying to get hold of phials of toxic gas.'

'Of course, of course, that is a puzzle', says Franchetti through Signora Gwynn. 'But perhaps it was, as he says, to kill camels.'

'Of course', says Kotovski. 'But if it was *not* to kill camels ...'

Franchetti understands enough to shrug and raise his eyes. 'Of course. If it was not to kill camels, then to kill whom? The King of Spain, perhaps ...'

'We do not think he was acting for ETA.'

'*Un mistero*', says Franchetti.

'One it might be wise to solve', says Kotovski.

Another torrent of Italian words. 'You must understand that our resources are limited', translates Signora Gwynn when Franchetti pauses to catch his breath. 'We can put Uriarte on our list of terrorist suspects, but to keep him under surveillance takes many man hours. Teams would have to be diverted from the surveillance of Islamic extremists who, it has to be said, pose a more direct threat.'

Kotovski does not dispute this. 'I understand.'

'We are willing to act upon any concrete information that comes from you or from Madrid—particularly Madrid. In our view, it is the Spanish who should be concerned with Uriarte because Uriarte is Spanish, no?'

'Yes, but he resides in Rome.'

Franchetti shrugs. 'We will do what we can.'

The meeting ends at noon. Kotovski would like to have his interpreter's impression of what has been discussed, but Signora Gwynn declines his invitation to lunch and hurries away. Kotovski eats alone in a small restaurant off the Piazza Navona, reading a copy of the *Economist* that he has bought at Heathrow. Every now and then he pauses in his reading as his mind returns to the morning's meeting. Clearly, there will be no close surveillance of Uriarte by the Italians. Why should they spend time on a man who presents no threat to them? Why, then, should Kotovski still feel involved? Does he simply feel thwarted by Uriarte's acquittal? Frustrated that so many hours spent on the case had led to nothing? Or is he genuinely afraid that Uriarte planned some atrocity with poison gas?

Kotovski's flight back to Heathrow leaves Fiumicino at six. To fill the afternoon, he first considers doing some sight-seeing but then, because the case still presses on his mind, he decides instead to take the Metro out to Nomentano and look at the block of flats where Uriarte lives. What does Kotovski expect to learn from such an excursion? Anything or nothing. He feels as if he is doing a jigsaw puzzle depicting a landscape, and he is now trying to place a piece with nothing on it but a fragment of blue sky.

There is a map of the locality at the Bologna Metro station where he alights that guides Kotovski to the via Manzoni. It is a five-minute walk. There are some shops on the corner and newly planted trees line the street. The neighbourhood seems quiet and decent—neither smart nor squalid. Kotovski can imagine that the flats are lived in by doctors or lawyers or middle-ranking civil servants.

He comes to Uriarte's building. It is four storeys high and there is a balcony for each flat. Kotovski goes into the foyer. There is no porter or concierge: a line of post-boxes is affixed to the wall. Kotovski goes to the box for flat 8—Uriarte's flat—and sees that it is empty. A woman with a child comes into the foyer, and Kotovski, not wanting to arouse suspicion, leaves the building. He turns and looks up. Should he have gone up to the second floor to look at the door to Uriarte's apartment? What would be the point? He looks down again as a second woman passes him; after checking the number on the wall beside the entrance to the building, she goes in. She has not seen Kotovski. Kotovski has recognised her. It is Kate Ramsey.

12 Via Manzoni

The door to Uriarte's apartment is opened by a dark-skinned middle-aged woman with the wide cheeks and the straight black hair of a Latin American Indian.

'Signore Uriarte?' Kate asks.

The woman looks her up and down with expressionless eyes, then steps back to let her in. After closing the door, she leads Kate from the hallway into a large, light living room with modern furniture and a marble floor. Silently, she gestures towards a sofa. Kate accepts her direction and sits down.

'*Caffé?*' asks the woman.

'Yes. *Sì, per piacere.*'

The woman leaves. Kate waits, her briefcase on the floor next to her legs. It contains the pamphlets and press releases that she has been given at the offices of Misericordia International, a map of Rome, three notebooks, three ballpoint pens and a Sony tape-recorder. She likes to record her interviews as well as to take notes and, as backup, she uses one of the two concealed recorders she bought in a 'Spyware' store in New York—an MP3 recorder that looks like a watch with a 256 MB flash memory card, and another that looks like a fat Montblanc pen. She finds that even the interviewees who agree to speak into the Sony sometimes become inhibited when they see the tape turning in front of them. She once asked her Uncle Lolo whether it was a sin to record someone without their knowing. He had considered the question for quite a time and then replied that it would be if she lied about it or if she continued to record an interview after being told not to, but otherwise it could be considered the equivalent of a CCTV camera that records people's movements without their consent.

Kate looks around. The flat is spacious and comfortable but impersonal. There are etchings showing views of Rome on the walls, and there are books in a glass-fronted bookcase, but there are no personal belongings on the sideboard—no clutter. It looks like a flat used by a consular official or a first secretary at an embassy. It is not at all the book-lined shambles that she had envisaged after hearing Uriarte at the Old Bailey.

Uriarte appears from the rounded archway through which the dark-haired woman had left the room.

'Miss Ramsey?'

Kate stands. 'Yes.'

Uriarte wears beige chinos with a brown belt and a check shirt. 'I hope you don't mind coming out here', he says. They shake hands: it seems strange to Kate finally to touch someone she had observed from a distance for so long. 'The office ... did you go there?'

'Yes.'

'And they gave you the information pack?'

'Yes.'

'Well, you could see that we would have had no peace and quiet there, whereas here we can talk undisturbed.' He gestures to her to sit down again, and he himself moves to an armchair to face her.

'It always adds something,' Kate says, 'talking to people in their homes.'

Uriarte laughs. 'This isn't exactly my home. It is a flat that Misericordia puts at the disposal of field workers when they are in Rome.'

'It is very nice', says Kate, looking about her.

'They take the view', says Uriarte, 'that after the months of rough living we deserve comfortable rest and recreation. In fact, it takes a week to get used to the soft mattress and regular meals.'

'And you have staff!'

'Staff?'

'I was offered some coffee.'

Uriarte laughs. 'Lucia is not staff. She is part of the team.'

'I'm sorry.'

'"From each according to his abilities. To each according to his needs."'

'Marx, surely?'

'Marx, yes, but also the gospel message.'

'Marx, the "anonymous Christian"?'

'You have read Rahner?'

'I studied theology at the university.'

'You are interested in religion?'

'It was easier to get into Oxford if one applied to study theology.'

'You were at Oxford?'

'Yes.' Kate reaches into her briefcase. 'Would you mind if I used a tape-recorder?' she asks.

Uriarte hesitates. 'Will I see what you write before it is published?'

'You can see it, certainly.'

He smiles. 'And if I have said something I would rather not have said?'

Kate frowns. 'You want a right of approval?'

Uriarte laughs. 'You make it sound like censorship. No, I don't insist on the right of approval, but if I have it then I am more likely to speak freely. If I don't, then I shall have to watch what I say.'

'If you say something off the record ...'

'But that is inhibiting, too, because I shall always be asking myself "Should this be off the record on the record?" '

'Very well', says Kate. 'You can read what I write, and if you object *strongly* to anything I have written, I will take it out.'

'*Gracias.*' Uriarte sits back, looking more relaxed.

'Of course', says Kate, 'there are facts which are a matter of public record.'

'What facts?'

'Facts that emerged during your trial.'

'Ah, the trial. Yes. You were at my trial?'

'Yes. I covered it for my paper.'

'And this article is for the same paper?'

'No. I'm working freelance, but various papers have expressed an interest.'

If Uriarte wants more time to reflect on what he has learned, it is bought for him by the entry of the *mestiza* woman with a *cafetière*, two cups and a plate of biscuits.

'You have met Lucia?' asks Uriarte.

'Yes, indeed', says Kate.

Uriarte turns towards Lucia. '*Piensa, Lucia! Esta señora estaba un peri-odista que cubrio mi processo en Londres!*' [1]

The woman glances at Kate but says nothing. She places the tray on the table in front of Uriarte and leaves the room.

'Does Lucia ...?' Kate begins.

'She takes care of the flat.'

Kate opens her notebook. 'And cooks?'

Uriarte frowns. 'Yes, she cooks. But before you write about how Misericordia pampers those who work for it, you should understand that she too is part of Misericordia and accepts its philosophy.'

---

[1] Just think of it, Lucia. This lady was the journalist who covered my trial in London!

55

'Which is?'

'That God gives different talents to different people and all are equally worthwhile.'

Kate leans forward and switches on the tape-recorder. 'And is it the philosophy of your organisation that cooking and cleaning are talents God is more likely to give to women?'

Uriarte pours coffee from the *cafetière* into the two cups. 'Not at all. We have many women working in the field.'

'And men who cook and clean?'

'There are some. But you must remember that much of our work is in countries where not only the economies are underdeveloped but also people's assumptions about the roles of the sexes.'

'And you do not see it as your mission to change those assumptions?'

'Very much so. Empowering women is fundamental to development, particularly in Muslim countries, but we have to proceed carefully and not appear to be imposing Western concepts of political correctness.'

Kate notes what Uriarte says in her notebook.

'And what about imposing Christian concepts of right and wrong?'

'We impose nothing', says Uriarte, sliding one of the cups of coffee across the table towards Kate.

'Yet you are a Catholic charity.'

'Yes. Our inspiration comes from the Church—in particular the Second Vatican Council and the decree *Gaudium et Spes*.'

Kate pours cream into her coffee, adds a lump of sugar and stirs it with a spoon. 'Readers will clearly be interested in the work of Misericordia, and I know that you have agreed to be interviewed to make that work better known. But there are also deeper questions that I would like to address about the *people* who work in such charities and NGOs.'

'Clearly, we like to stress the work rather than the personalities.'

'I understand that. But are you and your colleagues doing this work—for little pay, in great discomfort and sometimes at some risk to your life and liberty—because you are misfits or adventurers or Don Quixotes, or simply as a way to save your souls?'

Uriarte laughs. 'You will find charity workers who fit any one or all of those categories.'

'Which fits you?'

Uriarte reflects before answering the question. 'In my case', he says eventually, 'I think there has been an element of all those things. As you know, I was a priest and a priest is, in a sense, a misfit and an adventurer and someone who tilts at windmills, and, of course, he hopes to save his soul.'

'But your plan', says Kate, 'to use poison gas against the Janjaweed—'

'Against their livestock.'

'Yes. Against their livestock. That was not tilting at windmills.'

'There comes a point', says Uriarte, 'when you want to tilt at the real thing.'

'But it was dangerous', says Kate, 'because your plan involved the use of poison gas.'

'*Ciertamente.*'

'And it was fortunate for you that the charges were framed in such a way that the prosecution had to prove an intent to take human life. If you had just been accused of handling dangerous substances or something like that . . .'

'They would have condemned me?'

Kate blushes. 'It's possible. There is something particularly dreadful about Sarin.'

Uriarte frowns. 'More dreadful than hydrogen bombs?'

'No. They're dreadful too.'

'Yet nuclear deterrence has saved the world from a major war.'

'I know, but all the same, for an individual . . .'

'To take the law into his own hands?' He speaks kindly but with a touch of sarcasm. 'You're right, of course. Matters of this kind should be left to the politicians and civil servants and men like those lawyers who, when they see what is going on in Darfur on television, send a cheque to Oxfam or Amnesty International.'

'No, I know, that isn't enough . . .'

'Oh, it is enough to satisfy their consciences, but it was not enough to satisfy mine. I was there. I saw the suffering, and I felt that God expected something more of me. Who was it who said, "I am the King's good servant but God's first"?'

'Thomas More.'

'Precisely. You would have said to him, I suppose, that it was not for an *individual* to defy the king?'

'No, because he did not use violence.'

'And Saint Joan of Arc? If God told her to kill Englishmen, might he not ask me to kill a few camels?'

'Yes, perhaps.'

Uriarte drains his cup of coffee. 'I was foolish', he says. 'I should have known that what I tried to do would be misinterpreted— particularly at a time when there is a fear of terrorism of one kind or another. The state—all states—hate terror because it is the only weapon that the weak can use against the strong. And I do not condone it. It is always wrong to take innocent life. But nor do I condone the complacency with which those who live in comfort and security in the First World lament the abject condition of the poor in the Third World yet permit it to continue from generation to generation. For a Christian or anyone with a sense of common humanity, the words of Christ ring out as a constant rebuke: "I was hungry and you did not feed me; I was thirsty and you gave me nothing to drink." Like Dives, the rich man in Saint Luke's Gospel, we sit feasting while the poor beggar starves at our door.'

The time passes quickly, and Kate becomes so absorbed in her interview that she hardly notices Lucia, the housekeeper, laying a cloth over the table by the window and setting out cutlery, glasses and mats. The smell of cooking wafts through the archway, and, glancing at her watch, Kate sees that it is past one o'clock. She switches off her tape-recorder, closes her notebook and prepares to take her leave.

'Won't you stay for lunch?' asks Uriarte.

Kate glances at the table and sees that it has been set for two. 'I wouldn't dream of imposing.'

'Have you another appointment?'

'No, but ...'

'Then you must stay. It would dishonour us if you were to leave.'

'Well, if there's really enough ...'

'There's always too much.'

Uriarte calls to the Indian woman, who comes in from the kitchen. There follows a conversation in rapid Spanish that Kate can hardly follow. It sounds as if Uriarte is telling Lucia that she should join them at lunch. The housekeeper is reluctant. Does she normally eat with Uriarte? Kate wonders. Or does Uriarte want her to join them now to make a point? For whom has she set the second place? Whatever the nature of the dispute between them, Lucia gets her way. She leaves the food on the sideboard and returns to the kitchen.

It is a good lunch—angel hair pasta with a Napolitana sauce, veal escallops, salad, *panna cotta* with raspberry *coulis*, a bottle of San Pellegrino, a carafe of chilled white wine. Kate quickly empties her wine glass and allows Uriarte to fill it again. The anxiety she felt before the interview is now dissipating; she already has enough material for a piece and anything more that Uriarte says over lunch is a plus. The tape-recorder is switched off, but her Spyware watch is still running and she keeps her notebook open on the table beside her, occasionally making a note—more to give Uriarte the impression that she is listening to what he says than actually gathering more material. She does listen, or half-listens; he is describing Misericordia's aid strategies in the different countries where they work, which is certainly important but somehow dull. There is something hypnotising about Uriarte—the emphatic, even relentless flow of words in his singsong Spanish accent—which, after eating the hot food and drinking a third glass of wine, makes it hard for Kate to concentrate. She feels sleepy and in that somnambulant state finds her mind wandering from the words to the man who speaks them. Is he always so earnest? Does he ever relax? Is he still celibate? Is his body pallid or bronzed like his face?

She thinks back to Barney's bony body and how much less attractive it is than Uriarte's stockier but more muscular form. The different physiques somehow reflect their personalities—Barney the bogus hero against Uriarte the real thing. Dreamily, she wonders whether she can somehow arrange to see Uriarte again and, as if this were a prayer immediately answered, she hears him say: 'You should see what we do rather than just hear me speak about it.'

Kate blinks. 'See it? Yes, well, clearly it would be more interesting for our readers ...'

'It can be arranged', says Uriarte.

'To go to Darfur?'

He laughs. 'Well, clearly *I* couldn't show you around our camps in Darfur. I am now persona non grata so far as the Sudanese government is concerned. But I am going to Uganda next week. I was there before I worked in Sudan. It would be a good opportunity for you to see our work firsthand.'

'It would be wonderful, yes ...' The wine has somehow lessened her tight control, and she is afraid that she must sound to Uriarte like a gushing Sloane. She is also trying to calculate whether she could get a paper to pay her expenses and at the same time realizing that it makes no difference whether it would nor not. She would pawn her car to pay for such a trip with such a man.

Lucia appears through the archway and begins to clear the dishes from the sideboard. Kate and Uriarte get up from the table and go back to the sofa. Lucia lays a tray on the table in front of them—this time with coffee in an aluminium espresso machine and demitasse cups.

'Would I have trouble getting a visa?' asks Kate.

'As a UK citizen, no,' says Uriarte, 'but better not say that you're a journalist. Museveni has things he likes to keep from the outside world. Go as a tourist; say you're going to look at the game reserves.'

'And how would I find you? Is there a Misericordia office in Kampala?'

'If you e-mail the details of your flight, I'll meet you at the airport.'

Spirito Divino

Father Luke Scott is in Rome at the same time as his niece. They meet for supper at the Spirito Divino, a restaurant on the via dei Genovesi in Trastevere. Luke can tell at once, from the tepidness of Kate's smile, that she is not particularly pleased to see him out of his Marylebone context and, from the blotches on her face and slightly bloodshot eyes, that she has drunk wine at lunch. He is not upset by this appraisal: he is familiar with Kate's grumpy moods—and anyway, priests take people as they come.

'What are you doing in Rome?' Kate asks once they are seated—in a tone that suggests that she would rather he were somewhere else.

'I come every three months to advise a committee.'

'What committee?'

'A committee which decides on the English translation of certain liturgical texts.'

She yawns. 'That sounds dry.'

'On the contrary', replies Luke. 'It's a minefield.'

'Why?' She asks without showing much curiosity.

'There are doctrinal implications in the choice of words.'

'Such as?'

'Well, the most obvious and most controversial is what is called "gender laundering". Christian feminists do not like the use of words such as "mankind" or "man" as a generic term for humanity. They would prefer "humankind".'

'Haven't they got a point?'

'Some of the more insistent', says Luke, avoiding an immediate answer to her question, 'don't like referring to God as "Our Father". They say that this suggests that God is male when in fact God has no gender, and that this therefore reinforces a presumption of male ascendancy. So the Lord's Prayer would begin: "Our parent, who art in Heaven ...".'

'Ugly but perhaps more accurate?'

'It is not what Jesus said.'

'I bet you're on the side of the male chauvinists', says Kate, a mischievous smile lighting up her face.

'I like to think that I'm on the side of truth.'

'So God remains our Father?'

'Yes.'

'And so, in a sense, a man.'

'God is not like a man but man is like God—made "in his image and likeness", as it says in Genesis.'

'And woman?'

Luke smiles. 'Made from Adam's rib as a helpmate for man.'

'Really, Uncle Lolo, you really do belong in the dustbin of history.'

'A wise man once said that one of the attractions of Catholicism is that it saves one from being a child of one's time.'

'Making you a child of what?'

Luke shrugs. 'Of eternity, I would hope.'

Kate professes not to be hungry and orders only a *primo piatto* of *bresaola*. Luke, in contrast, orders three courses—not because he is hungry or greedy but because charity towards the restaurant demands that he should counterbalance Kate's frugality and bump up the bill. Also, in the event—this has happened before—that Kate's appetite comes with the eating, she can pick a number of her uncle's *rognoni* and fried potatoes off his plate. Recovering from her hangover, she drinks some wine and becomes more cheerful. 'And are there feminists on the committee?' she asks.

'No feminists, no, but their proxies—mostly Americans.'

'Do you have showdowns?'

'No showdowns, no. In fact, they've more or less thrown in the sponge because they know that the man appointed by the Pope to oversee our deliberations, Cardinal Ratzinger, is on our side.'

'The reactionary Rottweiler Ratzinger.'

'So say the tabloids.'

'I'm not the only person who thinks he's a reactionary.'

Luke nods. 'That's true. Your camel killer, I am sure ... What was he like?'

'Impressive.'

Luke listens as Kate describes her lunch with Juan Uriarte and feels an increasing unease. 'You must be careful', he says when he hears that she plans to visit him in Uganda.

'Why?'

Luke cannot answer. He does not know why. He feels like a father whose daughter tells him that she is dating a well-known roué.

'Is he married?'

'No. He's celibate.'

'Did he tell you that?'

'No, but I could tell that his mind is on higher things.'

'They're the worst.'

She laughs. 'You priests have such dirty minds.'

'We're well acquainted with human nature.'

'He's ten or fifteen years older than I am, Uncle Lolo. And I'm not his type.'

Clearly, Kate has been pondering the possibilities, as women do. Luke does not want to encourage the speculation. 'Will you find a paper that wants yet another article on African refugees?'

'It'll be on Uriarte rather than the refugees. I know you don't like the sound of him, but he really is kind of charismatic ...'

From *charisma*, thinks Luke, the Greek word meaning 'a gift from the gods'. In Christian theology, a special God-given talent for healing, preaching, prophesying, celibacy. And now? Sex appeal, forcefulness, an ability to manipulate others—to make them see things as you see them. Still a gift from God perhaps, but, as so often is the case with gifts from God, purloined and misused by the devil.

'Your work on the translation of the liturgy', says Kate. 'Won't all that change when there's a new pope?'

'Change? Why?'

'Well, isn't a new pope likely to have more liberal ideas on questions like the role of women than a pope from Poland?'

'Not necessarily. Bishops in Africa and South America tend to be conservative on matters like that. Cardinal Arinze, for example . . .'

Kate looks perplexed. In her generation, Luke knows, progressive attitudes have been bundled together. A black bishop should have liberal views. She shakes her head. 'No wonder the Church is withering.'

'Only in Europe and the United States.'

'The developed world, Uncle Lolo, and as soon as the underdeveloped world catches up economically, they'll catch up in their social attitudes too.'

Luke shrugs. 'We shall see.'

This is the best he can do. He wishes he could argue more vigorously against Kate, but an inner voice whispers that perhaps she is right. The Church flourished where people were poor. How many girls had become nuns for want of a dowry? How many men had retreated into monasteries to avoid the vissitudes of war or misfortune? How many had become priests when Holy Orders were the source of a good living and a path to power?

They come out of the restaurant into the street. It is warm and there is the fragrance of blossom and pine needles in the air. 'Do you remember Saint Augustine?' Luke asks Kate. '"What do I love when I love my God? The sound that never dies away; the fragrance that is not born away on the wind; food that is never consumed by eating and an embrace that is not severed by fulfilment of desire. That is what I love when I love my God."'

He stops. Kate sighs. 'I wish I could believe that, Uncle Lolo, because it would mean, well—it would mean that one wouldn't have a worry in the world.'

Monsignor Perez

When in Rome, Father Luke sometimes stays at the English College, sometimes at the Benedictine monastery of San Anselmo, and occasionally at the newly built hostel within the Vatican itself, the Domus Sanctae Marthae—built on the orders of Pope John Paul II after the conclave that had elected him to the papacy. He had wanted to prevent a repetition of the ignoble spectacle of venerable cardinals sleeping on camp beds in corridors and queuing to use the lavatories and washrooms. When there is no gathering of bishops, rooms are made available to priests visiting the Vatican on official business.

Luke has a number of friends in Rome: an old school friend who is a member of the British legation, an American Vatican correspondent and an Italian *contessa* with a *palazzo* whom Luke first met when acting as the chaplain to the Knights and Dames of Malta on a pilgrimage to Lourdes. There are also priests and *monsignori* working in the Curia whom he has come to know over the years. He likes to see these friends not just to reminisce, but also to reassure himself that he is not alone in the dustbin of history; indeed, that he is not in the dustbin at all. Many of his friends in the Curia not only share his orthodox beliefs but are also as unhappy as he is about the present condition of the Church in England.

One of these is Monsignor Perez, the Spanish secretary to the Dutch Cardinal Doornik. He too is a friend of the *Contessa*, and on the day following his dinner with Kate, Luke is taken by Perez to dine at the Palazzo Freschi. There are eight others at the long marble table; Luke joins in as best he can the chat about Freemasons, Berlusconi and the failing health of the Pope. He speaks some Italian and understands most of what is said, but conversing in a foreign language becomes more onerous as the evening progresses.

When dinner is over and the guests move from the dining room into the ornate salon, Luke and Monsignor Perez, who had been separated at table, sit down side by side on a sofa. They speak in English. 'How are things progressing on your committee?' Perez asks. 'Have you saved God from ... how do you call it? A sex change?'

'Our progressive brethren are fighting a rearguard action,' says Luke, 'but we shall prevail.'

'Fortunately Spanish is closer to Latin so it is more difficult to alter the meaning of words. And we do not have powerful North American bishops lobbying for the feminists.'

Like Luke, Perez is a traditionalist Catholic, but in Luke's opinion Perez has a better claim to the tag than he does. While Luke believes that it is the duty of priests and bishops to pass on the beliefs that have been handed down from the original apostles and their successors, he is not wedded to Catholic customs and accretions that are not matters of doctrine. He always wears a black suit and clerical collar but never a cassock or a biretta. Perez, on the other hand, seems comfortable only in his Roman cassock with its thirty-three buttons and wears a biretta whenever he can. He values the sartorial privileges that go with the title of 'monsignor' as much as the title itself and is inordinately proud that, as a Monsignor of Honour, he is entitled to a cassock with piping that is amaranth red and therefore almost indistinguishable from the scarlet piping of a cardinal's cassock. He knows better than anyone else in the Vatican what kind of shoes with what kind of buckles and tassels are required of different bishops and cardinals, or what colour the ribbons should be that suspend a bishop's gold cross.

'I fear that if any criticism will be levelled by historians at our dear suffering Pope John Pope II,' Perez says to Luke, 'it will be that he temporised on the question of women—*Mulieris Dignitatem* is really quite confused. Christianity, like Judaism, is a patriarchal religion.'

'Is that what you tell Cardinal Doornik?' asks Luke.

'It is precisely because I cannot say such things to his Eminence that I say it to you. How do you put it? To "let off steam". Cardinal Doornik would ordain women.'

'Should he become pope, which is surely unlikely.'

'But not impossible,' says Perez. 'Doornik is *astuto, muy astuto*. I have just worked with him over the past nine months, but I have come to understand the way his mind works. Saint Paul said, after all, that we must be as innocent as doves and as cunning as serpents. Doornik seems simple but he is not. "Blessed are the peacemakers", he says, as he mediates between the quarrelling cardinals in the Curia or disputes between the Holy Office and certain bishops such as your late Cardinal Hume. It is a wonderful formula for making friends in both camps while sitting on the fence.'

'But at heart?'

'At heart he is a child of the 1960s—loyal to that radical vision of Vatican II.'

'I knew him in the 1960s. We were at the Gregorian together.'

'And wasn't he a radical?'

'He became radical, yes.'

'Now he is discreet. He never says anything that anyone might object to. He is, in his own eyes, eminently *papabile*.'

Luke shakes his head. 'I cannot see Doornik as Supreme Pontiff.'

'You may not see it,' says Perez, 'but there are others who do. He is third in line for the liberals. If Martini fails to get a majority among the cardinals, and after him Daniels, then their votes in the conclave would move to Doornik.'

'Why did he ask you to be his secretary?'

'To know the thinking of the traditionalists, perhaps.'

'And why did you accept?'

Perez smiles. 'Don't you say "better to know the devil"?'

'"Better the devil you know".'

A Man of Prayer

Cardinal Doornik is a man of prayer. He spends many hours in the private chapel of his apartment near the Vatican, a chapel he himself has 're-ordered' by removing the nineteenth-century accretions, covering with white paint what could be covered with white paint and placing a modern crucifix over the altar fashioned by the Belgian sculptor Anton van Trees—a twisted pewter cross with the figure of Christ, equally twisted but in a contrary spiral, lashed to the cross-beam with strands of miniature barbed wire. On one wall there is a contemporary Ethiopian depiction of the Virgin and Child and on the other, a framed photograph of Oscar Romero, the martyred Archbishop of San Salvador.

Prayer, Doornik knows, is the raising of the heart and the mind to God. When he was a young man, he had found this easier than he does now: or, to put it more precisely, he had prayed in a different way. He remembers kneeling transfixed before the fiery golden monstrance containing the consecrated host, whispering over and over again, 'My Lord and my God'. Now he wonders whether this had not been a kind of auto-hypnosis.

Cardinal Doornik had been brought up in the small Dutch town of Weldhoven. His father ran his own business supplying and servicing refrigerated storage for slaughterhouses. His mother was the daughter of two schoolteachers who, Doornik now realises, were disappointed that she had married an uncultured man.

Doornik now realises. . . . how many of the influences to which a man is subjected in his youth go unnoticed at the time? Had his mother, too, come to regret her choice of husband? She never spoke against him. She was devout and dutiful. 'A woman must give to her husband what he has a right to expect', Saint Paul had said in his first letter to the Corinthians. Doornik and his sister, his only sibling, were aware of those occasions when his father returned tipsy to exercise his conjugal rights. His mother would have liked more children. His father thought two were enough.

Doornik was sent to a school run by the friars of Saint Augustine. He had preferred school to home. He liked the company of other boys his age and the solicitude of the priests who taught him. He was never top of his class, nor did he excel at sports, but he applied himself to both and was commended. He preferred the priests to his father. Over a lifetime, a man is moulded by his day-to-day work: the refrigeration business, the company of other businessmen, reading the *Eindhovens Dagblad* and watching soccer on television had made Doornik's father a dull man. Had he ever been interesting? Amusing, perhaps. And attractive. 'He was handsome', his mother had said, 'and he made me laugh.' Doornik could not imagine his father handsome or his mother laughing: drink and gross eating had coarsened his father's features, while marriage to a dullard had wiped the smile off his mother's face.

By the age of sixteen, Doornik had come to realise, with a leap of joy in his heart, that God was calling him to become a priest. When he watched a priest say Mass or at Benediction raise the golden monstrance in the air, he was transfixed. For some months, he kept this knowledge to himself: it seemed almost impudent to suggest that God, who with a flick of his fingers had created Heaven and earth, should deign to notice the son of a Dutch businessman and say, as Jesus had said to Saint Peter, 'Follow me.'

Looking back ... looking back now, as he kneels before the twisted crucifix in his private chapel, Doornik wonders to what extent he had been moulded, manipulated and imperceptibly guided towards the priesthood by his teachers—to what extent they had sniffed out some vulnerability that made him susceptible to their influence. Had the inherent zeal for its own aggrandisement that is found in every institution—regiments and religious orders—led the friars of Saint Augustine to sign him up before he had a chance to consider the Jesuits or the Benedictines or to discern whether he had a religious vocation at all?

Certainly, from the moment he confided in his confessor, he was told to put all *arrière pensées* aside. He was to remember that, just as there would be rejoicing among the angels that God had chosen him to act *in persona Christi*, so there would be fury among the demons in Hell. He was never to underestimate the ingenuity of Satan, who would seek to undermine his resolution. The Evil One would whisper in his ear that he was unworthy or conjure up visions of worldly success—power, riches and beautiful girls with sparkling, impudent eyes and soft embraces.

As it happens, Doornik was spared most of the temptations that his confessor had predicted. Life in the world was hardly enticing if it meant selling refrigeration units to slaughterhouses. The young Doornik had liked cars and sometimes imagined the joy of driving a Mercedes along an open road, but there were few open roads in the Netherlands. A bicycle was enough. And—what seemed at the time the most emphatic proof that his vocation was genuine—he did not feel tempted by girls. His sister was moody and dull; her friends were trivial—preoccupied with pop songs and makeup and boys. When Doornik had told his sister that he was going to be a priest, she had simply said: 'Idiot'.

His father had been aghast: for the first time in his life, Doornik had seen the man look baffled, anguished, even ashamed. Then out came contradictory expostulations. 'We'll see how you feel about it in a year or two'; 'I don't blame you. It's an easy life.' And finally, in a bitter tone: 'Well, your mother will be pleased.' And his mother was pleased: her face had opened up into a look of serene delight. She had embraced him and then wept, and it was quite clear to Doornik that his calling was an answer to her prayer.

How many holy women, like Saint Monica, the mother of Saint Augustine of Hippo, or the mother of Saint Bernard of Clairvaux, had dedicated their sons to the service of the Lord? Looking back, almost fifty years later, Doornik wonders if, even before the friars had gone to work on him, his mother had not directed him in the way she wanted him to go. At his ordination in the Abbey Church of Traden, she had sat like a queen with a look of holy contentment on her face—or was it some kind of unholy psychic satisfaction? Doornik remembers the look but still cannot be sure what it meant. If Freud, after studying women for forty years, still did not know what they wanted, how should Doornik be expected to analyse how his mother had felt?

Doornik had started his studies at the Gregorian University in Rome in the autumn of 1965, when the Second Vatican Council was in session. Its decrees were causing mayhem among the teachers and pupils alike. 'Ours is a new age of history', wrote the Council Fathers in the decree *Gaudium et Spes*, 'with critical and swift upheavals spreading gradually to all corners of the earth.' Suddenly the professors who had been teaching Saint Augustine's *De Civitate Dei* and Saint Thomas Aquinas' *Summa Theologiae* were recklessly analysing the new ideas of Cougar, Rahner and Schillebeeckx. The world was changing; the Church was changing. No longer were Catholic priests to be the guardians of narrow dogmas, hurling anathemas at Protestants, Orthodox Christians, Muslims, atheists and Jews; nor were they the mere purveyors of sacramental grace to those who kept the rules for the sake of a payoff in the world to come. No, they were to be the yeast of social change in *this* world or, as *Gaudium et Spes* put it, 'a generation of new men, the moulders of a new humanity'.

'Bliss was it in that dawn to be alive, / But to be young was very heaven!' One of Doornik's closest friends at the Gregorian was an English seminarian who might have been expected to share the sentiments the English poet Wordsworth penned at the time of the French Revolution. In fact he had stubbornly refused to be overwhelmed by 'the spirit of Vatican II'. At the time, their differences had only enhanced their friendship: they had often stayed up late into the night, arguing about the implications of the different decrees. Already the rules had been relaxed: the young seminarians were allowed to drink wine in one another's rooms, and it was no doubt the effect of the wine— unexpected because it was novel . . .

Had it not been for *that*, would they have remained friends? *That*, which Doornik could now think about with a certain dispassion, had been at the time an emblematic *praxis*—a gesture which had symbolised for Doornik the new way of looking at things in the light of Vatican II. It had been wrong, of course, because it had not been welcomed and, had he not been tipsy, Doornik would have seen that this would be the case. The wine had fuelled his fantasy and obscured his judgement. It had, in the old order, led him to succumb to temptation, and, in the new, to acknowledge an aspect of his humanity which had hitherto been obscure. He had thought he loved his English friend because he was intelligent and had the ineffable grace of a gentleman—the quality, Doornik imagined, that would have characterised those English Jesuits who had gone to England in the seventeenth century to be hanged, drawn and quartered for their faith. Scott had also been handsome. Was it a sin, even under the old order, to delight in a man's pleasing appearance? What he had not anticipated was the sudden impulse to take his friend's hand and to move to embrace him, his body *on fire*.

The sins of the flesh. The sin of Sodom. In the Catholic catechism, following Scripture, it is a sin that 'cries out to Heaven for vengeance', but, in the cases of those priests who had succumbed among the Augustinian friars, that vengeance had been postponed. When Doornik was a pupil in the school, it was known that there had been 'incidents' in which certain friars had 'taken advantage' of their pupils, subjecting them to 'inappropriate gestures', sometimes of a gross kind. The friars, the novices, even the boys in the school had known of which priests they should be wary: it was even joked about among the boys. 'Don't bend over to tie your shoelace with Father Jan behind you.' And when Father Jan was suddenly posted to minister in a parish rather than to teach in the school, no reason was given but everyone knew why.

Later in his life, as a superior, Doornik had had to deal with such cases himself. It had been hard to judge harshly when he himself had been subject to the same temptations and had, on that one occasion, succumbed. Were such sins *peccados* or *peccadillos*—mortal or venial sins? It was hard to judge. They were so common in all-male institutions. Was the damage done really so severe? Or was it the lure of lucre that led to the torrent of lawsuits, particularly in the Anglo-Saxon world?

Remembering that night in Rome forty years ago, it is clear to Doornik that he had been caught up in the turmoil of the times. Their Jesuit teacher of ethics was openly dating an American nun and was not only impenitent at the breach of his vow of celibacy but even contemptuous of those who, in the words of *Gaudium et Spes*, wallowed in 'a merely individualistic morality'. He had ridiculed the remorse of the young man who had succumbed to self-abuse or the young woman who had slept with her *fidanzato*. With all the poverty and hunger and oppression in the world, was it credible to suggest that God cared about such trivialities? Was not the only commandment that mattered the commandment to love?

Almost word for word, Doornik now remembered, he had repeated the Jesuit's *apologia* in hot whispers into his friend's ear, only to see an expression of disgust come upon those patrician features and to feel his body pushed away. His body pushed away and his friendship rejected. From that day on, Doornik and his friend Scott had gone their separate ways.

Africa

The smell of Africa. Is it the earth or the vegetation or the detritus of nature rotting in the hot damp air? As she is driven from the airport at Entebbe into Kampala, Kate feels enlivened and alert. Beside her, at the wheel of a Toyota Land Cruiser, is the tall young man who met her at the gate. He introduced himself as Joshua. Kate now asks him if he comes from Kampala. He laughs and, seeing the smaller, darker men and women sitting outside their shacks or sauntering beside the road indifferent to the traffic, she realises that Joshua is taller and, though black, has lighter skin than the native Ugandans. 'I am from Eritrea', he says when he has stopped laughing. 'I worked for Misericordia *there*, and now *here*.' Kate blushes. She must sound like she thinks that all Africans look alike. A bad start.

If Joshua does think that, he does not seem to hold it against her. 'Bats!' he says pointing up at the large black pods that hang from the acacia trees lining the road. Kate shudders. 'But they are not the blood-sucking variety.' He laughs again.

They drive into the centre of Kampala and stop outside the Lions Hotel. 'This is a nice place', he said. 'Very central. Mr. Juan thinks you will like it here. You can walk out into the street.' He leads her into the hotel. Kate registers, and a porter takes her suitcase from Joshua.

'Mr. Juan says he will come to fetch you at about seven; you have time to rest a little, if you like.'

'Thank you.'

Joshua looks heavenwards—a gesture she does not understand. 'Good-bye. I will see you again, perhaps.' He laughs again and is gone.

A simple room—clean, adequate, comfortable. Kate lies on her back on the bed but does not sleep. A long flight leaves the body confused: it has been sitting still for many hours yet is fatigued. The mind too is tired yet alert in strange surroundings. How would she describe her mental state? Apprehensive? Excited? What is the source of the dis-satisfaction that nags her? She had hoped—no, she had expected that Uriarte would meet her at the airport and so had been disappointed to see the strange young man holding up a card bearing her name.

Another bad start, like her assumption that Joshua was from Uganda. She is not on holiday: she is there to write about Uriarte and the work of Misericordia. It is a mistake to think that all human contact should necessarily lead to friendship. She is using Uriarte for a good story; he is using her to promote his work.

At half-past six Kate takes a shower and changes into a shirt and skirt. She brushes her thick shoulder-length hair and considers pinning it up behind her neck. This is not a date: she must look the part of a professional journalist; perhaps a bun would make her seem severe? She lets her hair hang loose but applies no mascara or eye shadow.

The call comes from the desk: Mr. Juan awaits her in the lobby. A last look in the mirror: neat, sensible, dressed to work, not to kill. She takes the stairs—she has no confidence in the jolting lift—and sees Uriarte standing beside the desk studying a copy of the hotel's brochure. She feels . . . she feels what? A jolt—a small twinge of something. Relief, perhaps, at the sight of a familiar face?

'Kate', he says in his lilting Spanish accent. 'You're here. Well done.' They shake hands. 'Is it all right?' he asks, holding up the brochure. 'It's a little better than the place where we usually put our visitors.'

'It's fine', says Kate.

'If the paper is paying, you might like to have stayed at the Sheraton, but in a hotel like that you could be anywhere . . . in Europe or America or Asia. Here you will hear the sounds of the street in the morning. You will know you're in Africa.'

'It's fine', says Kate again.

'Also, when we go up-country tomorrow, things will get rougher, so it's best not to start on a feather bed.'

They go out into the street. 'That is the Aga Khan mosque', says Uriate, pointing to the building facing the hotel. 'The Muslims are a minority here—around 16 percent of the population. But money pours in from Saudi Arabia and the Gulf.' He walks quickly, gesticulating as he speaks. 'There is a great struggle going on in Africa between Christianity and Islam. We are strong here in Uganda—around two-thirds of the population is Christian. The Church flourished on the blood of its martyrs—forty-five Bagandans, both Anglican and Catholic—slaughtered by the Kabaka, Mwanga. They were burned, castrated, dismembered, eaten by dogs. Two Christian pages had repulsed his advances. That started the persecution. Others were killed simply for affirming their faith. It was like the early days of the Church. The twenty-two Catholics were canonised by Pope Paul VI.'

'Aren't the Anglican martyrs in Heaven?'

Uriarte smiles. 'I dare say, but the Church of England doesn't make saints. They don't have a pope.'

He leads her through an archway and across a yard to a cluster of tables on wooden planks under a thatched roof. 'This is simple, too,' he says, 'but it's the real thing. In some of those air-conditioned places, the food's been flown in from Europe.'

The smiling proprietor comes up to them. 'Mr. Juan!'

Uriarte greets him in halting Ganda, then changes into English to introduce Kate.

'You seem well known', Kate says after the waiter has taken their order.

'I was here for seven years before I went to Sudan. It's a wonderful country with great potential but also many problems. People criticise Museveni for his dictatorial tendencies, but it's hard to rule a country with eighteen different ethnic groups with their own languages and dialects. And its recent history is steeped in blood. Since independence, around a half million people have been killed in different civil wars. You're too young to remember Idi Amin . . .'

'I know who he was.'

'He exterminated three hundred thousand of his opponents; Milton Obote, around a hundred thousand more.'

'It makes the persecution of Christians under Mwanga seem small beer.'

'Small beer?'

'Small in comparison.'

'Mwanga had no Kalashnikovs. Now everyone has a Kalashnikov. There are militias loyal to different tribal factions, gangs of bandits and, in the north, the Lord's Resistance Army—as barbarous as anything ever seen in Africa. There are over a million DPs—displaced persons—in the country and many more have fled into Rwanda and Sudan. And on top of all that there is malaria, sleeping sickness, bacterial diarrhoea, typhoid and Hepatitis A.'

'And AIDS?'

Uriarte frowns. 'And AIDS. Over four percent of the population, that's a half million people, are HIV positive. In 2002, around 80,000 died of AIDS. That's the equivalent of 175,000 in the United Kingdom or three-quarters of a million in the United States. It's a pandemic leaving tens of thousands of orphaned children.'

Uriarte speaks with great intensity. Kate wishes she had brought her notebook so she could write down some of what he is saying.

'So you can see that we have our work cut out. We run two camps for displaced persons in the north—one near Gulu, the other near Arua. I'll take you to the first, but I don't know about Arua: the LRA—that's the Lord's Resistance Army—raid the camps, just as the Janjaweed do in the Sudan.'

'I don't mind . . .'

'But *I* would mind if you didn't get back to write your article. They've been known to attack aid workers and even the UN. Some of the LRA fighters are just kids—kids with machine guns and grenade launchers. And the discipline ... well, there isn't any discipline, so you can't be sure.'

The waiter returns with several dishes and lays them out on the table before them. 'That's fish from Lake Victoria', says Uriarte. 'And that ...' He looks up at the waiter. 'Is that beef or goat?'

'Beef, Mr. Juan.'

'And *matoke*—mashed green bananas; and *posho*—something like polenta; and there—well, you can see, rice and beans.'

'Is it ... safe?' asks Kate.

'Here, yes. But don't buy food from the street vendors or drink anything but bottled water, and avoid adding ice.'

Uriarte puts spoonfuls of food from the dishes onto her plate. Kate, who had not been hungry, feels her appetite grow at the sight and smell of these strange foods. Advised by Uriarte, she drinks Bell lager.

'The Lord's Resistance Army', Uriarte goes on, 'is one of the nastiest but also the most intractable rebel forces in the region. The civil war in southern Sudan was easy to understand: it was Arab Muslims against African Christians. In Rwanda, too, it was clear: Hutus against Tutsis. But no one quite knows what the LRA want. Kony, their leader, says he wants to overthrow the government of Museveni and rule Uganda according to the Ten Commandments. What does that mean? No one knows. Most of the rebels are Acholi, the tribe living around Gulu and Kitgum, but it is the Acholi themselves who suffer most at the hands of the LRA. What is so bad about the LRA is the way they kidnap children, forcing the boys to become killers while the girls are raped and enslaved.'

'But how can they survive if their own tribe doesn't support them?'

'Their bases are in the Sudan.'

'The Sudanese support them?'

'Until now, yes, because Museveni was supporting the People's Liberation Army in the Sudan.'

'The Christians?'

'Precisely.'

'But aren't the LRA rebels Christians?'

Uriarte raises his arms in despair. 'Who knows what they are. They attack the Ugandan army and government officials, NGOs, humanitarian convoys, Catholic missions, priests, nuns. They are crazed murderers, nothing more!'

'Couldn't you use Sarin against *them—their* horses and camels?'

Uriarte stops; his fork, laden with food, hovers for a moment in front of his bent head. Then, after only a few seconds, it resumes its trajectory towards his mouth. The food goes in: he murmurs something indecipherable as he chews and finally, when the food had been swallowed, says: 'They don't have camels. Or horses. They have jeeps. And there are the children.'

'Of course. It was only ... well, I remember what you said about tactical deterrents. It's a pity that there isn't some way ...'

Uriarte wipes his mouth with his paper napkin. 'It is a pity, yes. But the LRA and the Janjaweed are quite different. Only from London might they seem the same.'

Reminding Uriarte of his trial seems to put him off his stride, and the vigorous flow of history, analysis and statistics slows to a trickle as the evening wears on. He calls the proprietor to clear away the plates, offers Kate a choice of ice cream or fruit salad and, when she says that she has eaten enough, speaks quickly to his friend in Ganda. Kate assumes that Uriarte has asked for the bill, but the Ugandan returns a few minutes later with a pack of Marlboro Lights and a box of matches.

'Do you smoke?' Uriarte asks her, opening the packet.

'From time to time.'

He holds out the packet. Kate takes a cigarette. Uriarte takes one for himself and, after lighting hers, lights his own. 'Africa is a challenge to all one's preconceptions', he says, sighing as he breathes out his first lungful of smoke. 'It was colonised by the more developed countries of Europe, oppressed, exploited and finally liberated only to find, on the whole, that things got worse. This is the only continent where people are poorer than they were fifty years ago. And with that poverty comes all the other evils—fighting for the scarce resources, reckless with life because they have so little to lose. Yet, for all that, it sometimes seems that they are more beloved by God than the affluent in the Western world. They suffer, and suffering brings them closer to Christ.'

'But does that make it ...' Kate hesitates.

'What?'

'Good to suffer?'

'No.' Uriarte shakes his head. 'No, it is not good to suffer, and it is not good to cause people to suffer or, when we see them suffer, to pass by on the other side of the road like the priest and the Levite in the parable of the Good Samaritan.'

Uriarte escorts her back to her hotel, smoking a second cigarette. He is silent, following a train of thought of his own. Kate does not interrupt him with further questions. When they reach the hotel, he puts out his cigarette, tells Kate that he will come to fetch her at nine the next morning, shakes her hand and says good-night. Kate returns to her bedroom, takes her notebook from her suitcase and writes down what she can remember of what Uriarte had said about Uganda and the Lord's Resistance Army, ending with an observation that might go into the article: 'It would not be difficult to guess, if one did not know it already, that Juan Uriarte was once a Catholic priest.'

Paget

On his return from Rome, David Kotovski reports to his boss, Brian Butler (BB). He can see at once that BB now finds the whole business of Juan Uriarte tiresome. He listens to what Kotovski has to say, frowning as Kotovski describes the inadequate response of Commandante Franchetti. Then, when Kotovski has finished: 'We seem to be back to square one.'

'There's another factor which may or may not be relevant', says Kotovski.

'What's that?'

'I saw Kate Ramsey going into the apartment block where Uriarte lived.'

'The journalist?'

'Yes.'

'Are you sure?'

'Yes.'

'She's onto a story. The heroic aid worker.'

'So it would seem.'

BB sighs.

'I have a gut feeling that he's up to something', says Kotovski.

'A gut feeling . . .' BB repeats the words in a sceptical tone. Then: 'You'd better go and see Paget. Tell him about the Italians and see what he says.'

Paget is at the Italian desk of the Secret Intelligence Service, MI6. He has been sent the papers on Uriarte. Kotovski crosses the Thames to the post-modernist headquarters at Vauxhall Cross. While BB is gruff and untidy, Paget is elegant and suave. His father was a professor of Sanskrit at Oxford. Paget himself went to Winchester and Cambridge, gaining a first class degree in modern languages. He is unmarried.

'You saw Franchetti in Rome?' he asks as he greets Kotovski in his office overlooking the river. 'A waste of time, I am afraid. A time-server from the *Carabinieri*. Side-lined some time ago and given the job of dealing with tiresome requests from abroad. I'm surprised that the Embassy didn't warn you. You didn't see our man at the Embassy, Tim Eagar? I believe he was on leave at the time. He's back there now.'

'My boss wouldn't be keen on another trip to Rome.'

'I can see. Joy-riding on his budget.'

'No one wants to waste any more time on this man Uriarte,' says Kotovski, 'but no one wants to take the responsibility for closing the file.'

'He should really be a matter for the Italians', says Paget. 'You are right about that. But SISMI is a mess—riddled with factions and conspiracies. DIGOS . . .'

'DIGOS?'

'*Divisione Investigazioni Generali e Operazioni Speciali*, the internal investigative unit of their Intelligence Services. It recently discovered that a group of senior officers in their anti-terrorist units had set up a secret and unofficial anti-terrorist unit known as DESSA—*Dipartimento studi strategici antiterrorismo*.' Paget glances at Kotovski. 'Do you speak Italian?'

Kotovski shakes his head. 'No.'

'Eagar would have filled you in if he had been there. There is a rift between what one might call the Atlanticist and the nationalist factions. There are some in SISMI who believe in cooperating with the Americans in their war against terror, and some who do not, and one of the unfortunate by-products of this split was the recent shooting of

Nicola Calipari, a major-general in SISMI, by an American soldier at a checkpoint at the Baghdad airport. You probably remember the case. Calipari had secured the release of an Italian hostage and was bringing her in. His shooting has really fired up the anti-American faction: arrest warrants have been issued for CIA agents for abducting an Al-Qaida suspect off the streets of Milan.'

'Which side is Franchetti on?'

'Oh,' Paget waves his hand dismissively, 'Franchetti isn't a player in that sense. He'll do whatever he's told.'

'Is either side going to show an interest in Uriarte?'

'Not if they think he belongs to ETA. They'll leave him to the Spanish police.'

'This goes round and round', says Kotovski, 'and we always come back to the same place. The Italians aren't interested because, so far as they are concerned, he's not up to anything in Italy. The Spanish aren't interested because their sources tell them that Uriarte has nothing to do with ETA.'

'Perhaps ...' Paget begins. He looks down at a sheet of paper on which he has scribbled some notes. 'I have discussed the case with a colleague from Langley, and he thinks that perhaps the ETA connection is a red herring.'

Kotovski frowns. 'How so?'

'Neither Etchevarren nor O'Brien was an active terrorist. Etchevarren was simply doing a favour for his friend. O'Brien was out to make money. It was Uriarte, and only Uriarte, who wanted to obtain the poison gas. My friend suggests that perhaps he never intended to use it *against* the Janjaweed, but in fact was acting *for* them.'

'Isn't that ... improbable?' asks Kotovski.

'Certainly, the Americans are obsessed with Islamic terrorism and think all roads lead to Al-Qaida. But when there is an unknown, you have to consider the improbable and either establish that the improbability is in fact an impossibility or see if the improbable can become probable and, possibly, certain.'

'Of course.'

'My friend read the transcript of the trial and noticed a brief exchange which with hindsight seems of some interest.' Paget looks down at a stapled pile of type-written pages beneath the piece of paper with his notes. 'The director of Uriarte's charity—or was it the doctor from

Médecins Sans Frontières?—tells the court that, among Uriarte's many qualities, is *his ability to mediate between warring factions.*' Paget's finger settles on a block of typescript. 'Here, I have it. It was the director of Misericordia, Cesare Bianco. He says: "Mr. Uriarte was trusted with the most difficult negotiations with the Janjaweed." "Negotiations?" asks the Treasury Counsel. "He worked to reconcile the two sides of the conflict at great risk to himself." "He was in contact with the Janjaweed?" "Yes, with their leaders in Khartoum."'

'There is another point raised by our American friends', Paget goes on, 'which may or may not be relevant: the silence of Khartoum. One would have thought that where it was established in a major trial at the Old Bailey that a Western aid worker had planned to use nerve gas in Sudan, some kind of protest would have been made at some level. But there has been silence. This would seem to suggest that the people in Khartoum who know our friend Uriarte do not believe his story about killing camels any more than we do.'

'Does this mean', asks Kotovski, 'that Uriarte was somehow working *with* the Janjaweed?'

Paget shakes his head. 'No. We have to accept at its face value the evidence of Cesare Bianco and the French doctor that Uriarte was primarily interested in the well-being of the people in his care. But if you study the profile of our friend Uriarte, you find that he shares some of the antipathetic attitudes of Islamic fundamentalists towards the Great Satan: the imperialist, materialist, capitalist West.'

'That's true of half the Labour Party', says Kotovski.

'Of course. But the most they would do is vote against the government or demonstrate in Hyde Park. Uriarte is different. Remember, he was a priest, and a priest is someone who believes that God has chosen him for a particular mission. Next, he becomes an insurgent. He takes up arms. He kills. Now he is an aid worker—but those two facts remain from his past. The divine mission. The willingness to kill.'

'The two elements of *jihad*.'

'Precisely.'

'But are you suggesting ...?' Kotovski begins.

'I am suggesting nothing', says Paget. 'Nor are our friends from Langley. We are merely ... speculating.'

'Is your speculation, then, that Uriarte might have been recruited by Islamic terrorists?'

'It is not impossible. Or that, when negotiating in Khartoum, he offered something as a quid pro quo.'

'Nerve gas in exchange for a truce?'

'Something like that.'

Misericordia

From the smile on Uriarte's face as he meets her in the lobby of the hotel, Kate knows that the safari suit is a mistake—a divided skirt and khaki shirt as if she were Grace Kelly in *Mogambo*. Uriarte is wearing jeans and a T-shirt. They set off in the Toyota Land Cruiser, crossing the Nile at Jinja, then head north towards Mbale and Soroti. Uriarte drives, Kate sits next to him and Joshua occupies the seat behind them. Joshua is silent and his expression is inscrutable; it is impossible to guess what is going through his mind. Kate, too, is mostly silent, content to absorb the sights and smells and to listen to Uriarte.

They stop for lunch at a roadside eating house; again, the owner welcomes Uriarte as if he were an old friend. They drive on. Kate grows sleepy. The bumpy roads do not stop her from dozing off. A jolt wakens her for a moment; she glances sideways at Uriarte, wondering how he can keep awake. His eyes are wide open and alert. In the mirror she can see that Joshua is sleeping. The drone of the diesel engine is like a lullaby; her eyelids droop. Oblivion.

Kate is woken when they stop at a roadblock. She gives Uriarte her passport, which he hands, together with Joshua's and his own, to the soldier at the window. He switches off the motor. They wait as the passports are scrutinized in a tent beside the road. The passports are handed back. They drive on. Mile upon mile of unchanging landscape. They stop for fuel in Lira. Outside the town, there is a second roadblock, but here Uriarte is recognised and they are waved through.

By the time they reach the Misericordia compound in Lbala, it is growing dark. There is the sound of a generator, and a row of naked light bulbs hang from the veranda of a single-storey building with a corrugated iron roof. Kate steps out of the air-conditioned Land Cruiser into the still-baking heat of the evening. She can just make out a number of bodies lying supine on the veranda. Uriarte stands on the other side of the vehicle, bending backwards to stretch his spine after the long drive. There is a cry from one of the recumbent figures: 'Mister Wan!' It is a man who rises and comes shuffling towards them. All at once, others come to life and from the three sides of the compound a wave of black men, women and children moves towards them, many of them shuffling like the first, some hopping on crutches. 'Mister Wan, Mister Wan', they shout, followed by a babble of words in Ganda. The wave of people laps against the Land Cruiser and then swirls around its passengers. 'Mister Wan, Mister Wan . . .'

A group of old women with leathery, wrinkled faces gather around Kate, cackling incomprehensibly. Kate looks towards Uriarte, who raises his hand cheerfully, then turns to lead the crowd away. Kate finds that Joshua is at her side with two or three young men holding their bags. They follow in the wake of Uriarte and see, coming towards them, three whites—two men and a woman.

'As you can see, you've been expected', says the first man to Uriarte: he is older with close-cut white hair and speaks with an Irish lilt.

Uriarte turns to Kate. 'This is Brendan. And Mickey and Dorothea, who are in charge of the volunteers.' He turns to the blacks who have followed them from the Land Cruiser. 'This is Akello, this is Jimmy, this is Kaikara . . .' He seems to know the names of them all, and, as he introduces them, they stretch to shake hands with Kate. For a moment Kate hesitates—one arm ends in a calloused stub—but then, as if plunging into a dark pool, she clasps indiscriminately the hands held out to greet her. She glances at Uriarte and, from his expression, judges that she has passed some kind of test.

They eat supper at a long trestle table with the aid workers and volunteers. Kate sits next to Brendan, the compound's director and a Jesuit priest. She judges that he is around sixty years old. In a gentle Irish voice he tells her about the work of Misericordia in the region and gives details of the budget and staffing levels of his camp. 'We do what we can', he says apologetically, 'but the problems here are overwhelming.'

After supper, they pass through into a common room where Uriarte shows her how to help herself to coffee from an urn. 'Coffee is one of their main crops,' he says, 'but I'm afraid the best stuff goes abroad.'

Kate sips the milky brown liquid—very different from a Starbucks latte. She senses that Uriarte is waiting and watching for her to crack, and she is determined to frustrate him.

'We'd better move on quite soon', says Uriarte, glancing at his watch.

'Move on?'

'We've booked you a room at the government guest house in the town.'

'Can't I stay here?'

'There's no guest room as such.'

'What about the volunteers?'

'They sleep in a dormitory. It's a little rough.'

'I don't mind sleeping rough.'

Uriarte laughs. 'You'd have a bed, but there isn't much privacy.'

Kate feels annoyed. 'I'm not as soft as I look.'

'I'm sure you're not.' Uriarte glances down at the divided skirt. 'It's just that ...'

'The dormitory will be fine', says Kate sharply.

Uriarte shrugs. 'Very well.'

The dormitory for the female volunteers has eight beds, five of which are in use. It has a concrete floor. Down the passage are three lavatories and a shower. One of the young Africans brings Kate's huge suitcase and lays it flat on the floor beside her bed. 'I am afraid there are no wardrobes', says Dorothea, the German woman in charge of the volunteers.

'It doesn't matter', says Kate quickly. 'I don't suppose I'll need many clothes.'

'*Kein Abendkleid, bestimmt*',[2] replies Dorothea. Kate does not ask what she means.

Dorothea departs. Kate quickly extracts from the bowels of her suitcase her jeans, a couple of T-shirts and underwear for the next day. She bitterly regrets bringing designer jeans rather than her old Levis but hopes that Dorothea and the other volunteers will be too unworldly to notice. The Canadian girl, Laurie, shows her how to

[2] No evening dress, certainly.

puff insecticide powder from a plastic container into the nooks and crannies of her mattress. 'No one's been sleeping here for a while,' she says, 'so I guess the bedbugs may have migrated.'

Though Kate is exhausted, she finds it hard to sleep. The room is hot and airless. Kate feels, or imagines she feels, the fleas and bedbugs feasting on her fresh white body. She still hears the throb of the Land Cruiser's diesel engine and feels the vibration of the ride. She drifts into sleep and then out again. One of the volunteers snores. She wonders where Uriarte is sleeping, and if he snores.

After breakfast the next morning—more watery coffee—Uriarte takes Kate on a tour of the refugee camp, a city of tents built on a ten-acre site around a mile from the compound. It is the day for the distribution of food: thousands of men and women have formed a queue at a table, where Father Brendan checks their ration cards, and then re-forms behind the back of a truck from which a team of aid workers empty scoops of grain into sacks. The men and women then trudge back to their tents and begin cooking gruel over small fires. 'We can provide them with food', says Uriarte, 'but not with fuel.' They walk down into the camp. Once again, no sooner do the refugees recognise Uriarte than they leave their tents to greet him, smiling, laughing and clasping his hand. It is a triumphal procession: Kate thinks of Christ's entry into Jerusalem. All that is missing are the donkey and the palms.

From the camp Uriarte takes Kate to the clinic in an adjacent compound. 'This was set up for the refugees,' he tells her, 'but in fact the people come from Lbala itself. The government hospital can't cope. There are not just the usual endemic diseases you find throughout Africa—TB, meningitis, elephantitis, some leprosy and of course AIDS—but there are also the casualties from the war with the LRA.'

They go into one of the men's wards—a clean room with two rows of beds on a wooden floor—but already, at ten in the morning, the temperature in the room is stifling, and there is a putrid stench that makes Kate want to retch.

'It takes a bit of getting used to', says Uriarte.

They leave the ward and walk through to a second compound that houses the women and children. Here, too, patients are sitting out in the shade of a veranda which runs along the front of the adobe building. They stop by a girl with an amputated leg. 'Now I haven't met you before', says Uriarte kindly.

She looks up timidly.

'What is your name?'

'My name is Miremba.' She speaks slowly, carefully enunciating the three syllables of her name.

Uriarte crouches to look at the dressing on her bleeding stump. 'Was that changed this morning?'

She shakes her head. 'No, las' night.'

'I'll ask Sister if it should be changed again.'

'Sister say she come.'

Uriarte and Kate walk on. 'Probably a landmine,' said Uriarte, 'or simply caught in the cross-fire.'

They go into one of the wards: the same stench and the same spectacle of mute suffering. Some of the women recognise Uriarte, and those who can come to greet him. 'Mister Wan ...'

'They all seem to know you', observes Kate.

'I was here for quite a time. And I paid visits from Sudan.'

'Did you hand the mission over to Brendan?'

'I did.'

'And now?'

'For the time being, they've given me a roving brief. I'm to report back to Rome.' They come out into the compound again. 'That's why it's good to go around with you. A new eye can spot things that an old eye might miss.'

Kate is silent for a moment, then says: 'Would they let me work here?'

'Work at what?'

'As a volunteer.'

'But you're here for only two days.'

'I could stay longer. How long are *you* staying?'

'I'll be here for two or three weeks.'

'Can't I do something useful for those three weeks and go back with you?'

Uriarte frowns. 'Your job is to write.'

'Of course. But to see all this suffering and doing nothing but gawp ...'

'Gawp?'

'Observe. Watch. Stare at these poor people as if they were animals at the zoo.'

Uriarte thinks for a moment. 'It might give some depth to your reporting', he says.

'It would also ...', she hesitates, not knowing what she wanted to say. 'It's not just to help them', she says. 'It would help me.'

The first five days are hard. Never before has Kate had to face the reality of human suffering. She works with the Canadian girl, Laurie, and under the supervision of Dorothea, who is a trained nurse, tending the patients in ways that require no medical expertise. She sponges down women too weak to wash themselves and coaxes them to sip liquid nutrition when thrush in their mouths makes it difficult for them to eat anything solid. There is a girl paralysed from the waist down who has to be carried to the lavatory, and then her body has to be sponged clean. Dorothea teaches Kate how to clean a wound and change a dressing, easing off the gauze when dried blood has glued it to the abrasion. She shaves heads so that the fungal infections on the scalp can be treated and sprinkles open sores with antibiotic powder.

Frequently, the best Kate can do is take the patients' minds off their condition. Laurie teaches her how to massage their aching bodies and play games to raise the spirits of the children. Kate finds crayons and encourages the children to draw pictures in her reporter's notebooks, and she delights the adolescent girls by painting their toenails with scarlet varnish she has brought from England. Though she has only five toenails to paint, this particularly pleases Miremba, the girl with the amputated leg. Kate had thought she was around ten but is told by Dorothea that in fact she is fifteen; malnutrition has stunted her growth.

It has also lowered her resistance. The lesion left by the amputation will not heal. Pus oozes from the flaps of skin which the surgeon had folded over the sawn bone. It is hard to judge whether to pull the skin back to treat the flesh beneath or to leave it in the hope that it will heal. There are also sores on Miremba's emaciated body; while treating one on her buttocks, Kate is horrified to see the exposed bone of her hip. She cannot eat: her mouth is sore with thrush. On Kate's fifth day working as a volunteer, it becomes clear that the girl has not long to live.

Kate goes to Uriarte. 'Miremba must go to a proper hospital', she says. 'Her leg is not healing. She seems to have blood-poisoning.'

'It wouldn't make any difference.'

'Surely something more can be done.'

Uriate shakes his head. 'I am afraid not', he says. 'You see, it isn't the leg that is the problem. Miremba has AIDS.'

Kate returns to the children's ward and sits cradling Miremba in her arms. She reads her a story. The girl listens silently. When she finishes, thinking Miremba asleep, Kate begins to lift her onto the bed. The girl's grip on her hand tightens: she wants her to stay. It grows dark. Kate, no longer able read the words on the page, retells the stories from memory. The time for the volunteers' supper comes and goes. Shortly before ten, when Miremba seems to be sleeping, Kate eases out from behind her body. Miremba is not sleeping. She is dead.

The death of Miremba would have upset Kate more if she had time to reflect and if there had not been others demanding her care. She not only tends the men and women in the clinic, but also goes out with Dorothea and Laurie to visit the sick in the tents of the refugee camp—a woman with a breast tumour so advanced that it has burst out from beneath the skin, an excrescence of blood and pus; another of exactly Kate's age, disabled from birth and left for those thirty-odd years on a pallet, has such terrible sores on her body that there is hardly a patch of sound flesh. Kate looks back on her own life of comfort and privilege and feels ashamed.

There are children with burns that have been treated but, no sooner treated, are infected by the filth of the camp latrines. There are cases of elephantitis—legs so swollen that the skin has cracked, leaving infected wounds on ankles and feet. These she treats with antibiotics and Whitfield's Cream. Kate becomes adept at shaving the heads of those with fungal infections, scrubbing scalps with soap and water, and removing with tweezers dried scabs and large patches of dead skin.

Perhaps the most tormented and tormenting are the patients with AIDS. Many have been abandoned by their families: they find one woman who had been lying for days in the slime of her diarrhoea. Besides the lassitude induced by AIDS itself, there are the painful by-products of the disease—eczema, herpes and thrush: even when the victims have the will to eat, it becomes too painful to swallow and their bodies wither into mere packages of skin and bone. And beyond the physical suffering, there is the mental anguish of the dying mothers fearing for the fate of their children who, even if healthy, will be left defenceless to be abused or even enslaved.

Kate comes to feel a sober admiration, amounting to awe, for those who work for Misericordia, particularly her mentor, Dorothea. She is brisk and sometimes dour, but after supper in the evening she takes out her guitar and sings hymns and German *Lieder* with the younger volunteers. As she joins in the singing, Kate feels she has become a quite different person; Fleet Street, Barney, Charlie and her parents seem to belong not so much to another world as to another life. Her family now are Dorothea, Laurie, the other volunteers, the Swedish doctor, Peter, Father Brendan, Joshua and, of course, Uriarte.

She sees little of Uriarte during the day; he is engaged in work of another kind. But in the evenings he is there—kind, solicitous, always zealous and yet detached, just as he was in the dock at the Old Bailey. No doubt one learns to be detached, working among such misery year after year. Detached and yet, every now and then, a look of anger flashes from his eyes, as happens one evening when she asks him why those with AIDS have not been given retroviral drugs.

'Retroviral drugs!' he snaps back at her. 'Do you know what they cost? Do you think those *bastardos* in the boardrooms of Roche or Pfizer will do something for nothing? Retroviral drugs are for rich pederasts in Los Angeles and New York!'

'Condoms are not so expensive', says Kate timidly.

'No, condoms are cheap, but they are forbidden by the Catholic Church!'

'But does Misericordia ...' Kate begins but, before she can complete her question, she feels that her bowels are about to explode. She stands. 'I must just ...' She flees.

Retreat

A week or so after his return from Rome, Father Luke Scott drives his Volkswagen Golf to visit a small community of contemplative nuns near Chichester. He is to give a retreat—a series of talks during two days of silence and reflection. He is standing in for a Dominican from the Priory on Haverstock Hill who is unwell. The sisters' resident chaplain is away tending his dying mother in Swansea. 'We tried *everywhere* to a find a priest', the Superior, Sister Elisabeth, says as she greets him. It is clear that Luke is their last resort.

Sister Elisabeth shows him where he is to sleep—a sparsely furnished room in the former servants' quarters, well away from the enclosed area used by the nuns. He unpacks his small suitcase and then goes down to the calefactory—the convent's living room—for tea. *The Guardian, The Tablet* and *Priests and People* are laid out on a sideboard.

The talks are given in the library. Six bentwood chairs form a semi-circle facing a moth-eaten armchair. Luke sits in the armchair. The six coifed women who look down on him span the age spectrum: two are young, two middle-aged, two old. Sister Elisabeth, who sits at the edge of the semi-circle, is one of the middle-aged.

Luke takes as the theme for his retreat the predicament of Christian women in the modern world. It is a stand-by topic: he has used it for retreats of this kind for a number of years, and it usually goes down well. The first talk is on women in the Bible. He starts with the second chapter of the Book of Genesis: God creates Adam and then decides 'it is not good that man should be alone. I will make him a helpmate.' He creates and Adam subsequently names 'all the cattle, all the birds of heaven and all the wild beasts.

> But no helpmate suitable for man was found for him. So Yahweh God made the man fall into a deep sleep. And while he slept, he took one of his ribs and enclosed it in flesh. Yahweh God built the rib he had taken from the man into a woman and brought her to the man.

Luke then asks, 'What are we to make of this passage? Was it man who rejected an animal or a bird as a helpmate? Or was it Yahweh God who decided that they were unsuitable? Were those men who described their dogs as "man's best friend" suggesting that God may have made the wrong decision?' No one laughs, nor even smiles. Luke moves on. 'Does the creation of woman as man's helpmate mean that women are somehow *inferior* to men? Or perhaps *superior*?' He then repeats the old joke that in creating woman God had learned from the mistakes he made in creating man. This produces a slight smile on the face of one of the younger nuns. 'No. Woman might be *subordinate* or even *ancillary* in the order of creation but nowhere in either Jewish or Christian thinking is it suggested, as some Islamic scholars did, that women are without souls. Quite to the contrary: in the whole story of the Fall, it is quite clear that Eve as well as Adam is able to choose between right and wrong. Nor are the women portrayed in the Old Testament as mere doormats. Eve is shown as a prime mover in the Fall. Abraham's wife, Sarah, is a considerable figure: so also Rahab, Deborah, Esther, Bathsheba, Judith and Jezebel. Further, while we know less about them, there were many women among Jesus's followers—Martha; Mary, the reformed prostitute who washed Jesus's feet with her tears and dried them with her hair; and Mary of Magdala (the last two women have been conflated in a sermon by Pope Gregory the Great).

'For the Christian, of course, the prototypical woman is Mary, the Mother of God. Again, we are told little about her: she is not mentioned at all in the earliest Christian writings, the epistles of Saint Paul. But much can be gleaned from the role she plays in the Gospels. She is modest, receptive, obedient—"Let it be done unto me according to thy word." She has decided views on social justice: God "has pulled down princes from their thrones and exalted the lowly. The hungry he has filled with good things and the rich sent empty away". And she has great influence over her son: she persuades him, against his will, to turn water into wine at the wedding reception at Cana.'

The rule of silence prevents any discussion during lunch after this first homily. The nuns eat vegetables, bread and water; Luke is given two undercooked sausages. As they leave the refectory, Sister Elisabeth whispers to Luke: 'I think you should know that most of us are graduates.' Luke nods to acknowledge receipt of this information. Nuns with B.A.'s, M.A.'s, perhaps Ph.D.'s. Has he pitched his talk too low?

It is too late, now, to re-work what he had prepared. His afternoon talk considers the example of women saints throughout the two millennia of the Church's history. He hopes that this talk might be better received than the first. There are, after all, some formidable women among the religious—Saint Teresa of Avila, Saint Teresa of Lisieux and Edith Stein, now Saint Teresa Benedicta of the Cross, the epistemological philosopher who died at Auschwitz, who was surely a patron saint, if there was to be one, of nuns with university degrees.

However, despite flattering references to these Carmelite saints, Luke does not feel that he is carrying his audience with him. He normally gives retreats to communities of old nuns with traditional views on the Catholic religion. Here he seems to have stumbled on a nest of holy feminists. He prays to his guardian angel for some help and presses on. Contrary to what is generally believed, he says, the Catholic Church has done much to raise the status of women, particularly through its insistence on monogamy and the indissolubility of marriage. There is no evidence that women were discontented with their domestic role at a time when life for men was hazardous and demeaning. Feminism was the invention of bored blue-stockings from the middle classes who had cooks, maids and nannies . . .

At six Luke sits in the chapel while the nuns sing Vespers. They are invisible behind the screen. Their thin voices combine like plaited silk to sound strong, the words of the Psalms rising pleasantly towards Heaven through the shafts of the dusty evening sun. Should he have been a monk? There was something audacious in the idea of a hermit, a man or woman who withdraws from the world to converse with God. And to struggle with temptation. Luke thought of Saint Anthony in the fourth century living in a cave in the Egyptian desert tormented by visions of lascivious women—this before Hollywood and the advertising industry put such women on every screen and billboard. He had fasted and abstained from eating meat in order to master his animal instincts: weeds that throttle the life of the spirit, or guard dogs that frighten off the angels. Is mortification of the flesh a sure path to holiness? Surer than the pseudo-social work of a parish priest? Or is it a cop-out?

After Vespers, Luke waits in the library to hear confessions. There is no grill to screen the face of the priest from the penitent, but only a prie-dieu facing a crucifix on the wall and a bentwood chair. The first to enter the room is one of the two older nuns. She hesitates between the chair and the prie-dieu and then chooses the prie-dieu. It is a month since her last confession. Since then she has had uncharitable thoughts about other members of the community, particularly the Superior, Sister Elisabeth. Sister Elisabeth looks down on her because she has no university degree. So, too, do Sister Anne and Sister Joan and Sister Ruth. The catalogue of this penitent's uncharitable thoughts, Luke realises, is in reality a list of the sins of the other members of the community. He thinks of Jouhandeau: 'My wife goes to confession to confess *my* sins.' When the litany of complaints ends, Luke speaks of the virtue of humility and gives the sister a decade of the Rosary as penance. She makes her act of contrition. Before she leaves, to raise the old lady's morale, Luke says that she should feel privileged to be subject to temptation. Satan does not bother with souls he does not want.

The second penitent, one of the two younger nuns, chooses the chair. She moves it so that she and Luke are sitting at an angle to one another, not face-to-face.

'I'm Sister Ruth.' She speaks with an Australian accent. 'It's quite a while since my last confession.'

'A month? A year?' Luke has no idea what a modern nun would mean by 'quite a while'.

'Oh, six weeks or so. Perhaps two months. I don't get much out of Father Tim—that's our regular chaplain. I mean, it's bad enough having to confess to a man who's got about as much understanding of the religious life as a Koala bear. It's just ridiculous!'

'Few communities now have a resident priest.'

'Do we need one? I mean, why can't Sister Elisabeth or Sister Dorothy forgive my sins?'

'They are not ordained into the ministerial priesthood', says Luke.

'They'd make better priests than Father Tim.'

'A priest has to be a man.'

'Because Eve was made from Adam's rib? Is that what you were trying to tell us?'

'Because Christ was a man. And because Christ chose only men as his apostles. The Church is not authorised to ordain women.'

'So says Karol Wojtyła.'

'He is the Pope.'

'Not for much longer.'

'No, not for much longer.'

'Another pope might take a different view.'

'Cardinal Ratzinger has explained that the teaching is infallible.'

'Another pope might sack Cardinal Ratzinger.'

Luke sighs. 'Are you here to debate the question of the ordination of women or confess your sins?'

'Is it a sin to disagree with the pope?'

'Catholics are not automatons. If, after careful consideration, you find you cannot assent to a particular tenet of the Church's teaching, then it cannot be considered sinful to disagree.'

'And what about contraception? Or gay sex?'

'The Church would never ask you to go against your conscience in thought, word or deed, but there would come a time when someone who rejected some of the Church's fundamental teachings should ask herself whether or not she is a Catholic.'

'So dissenters should leave the Church?'

'The Church is a community of belief. If I were to decide, for example, that women were inferior to men, or blacks to whites or that might is right, then however sincere I might be in holding those beliefs, I would not feel that I could call myself a Catholic.'

The nun is silent for a moment. Then: 'I swore at Sister Carmella.'

'That was wrong.'

'I was provoked.'

'How?'

'We were gardening. She walked all over the seedlings ...'

And so on. The petty sins of women in community. An act of contrition. Firm purpose of amendment. Penance. Absolution. 'Those whose sins you forgive, they are forgiven.' What is this young woman from Australia doing in rural Hampshire? What are any of them doing? Neurotics escaping from some predicament, or spinsters struggling to be saints?

At ten the next morning, Luke says Mass in the chapel. At eleven he gives his third and last talk on the predicament of women in the modern world. He rattles through it: virginity ridiculed, chastity derided, motherhood demeaned; women liberated and empowered but also exploited. Work. Sex. Romantic love. False expectations. Disappointments. Sex detached from procreation—that mystical joint venture with God. Children avoided. Children aborted. Children neglected. Innocence destroyed.

After that, lunch—roasted root vegetables and bread and cheese for the sisters, a lamb chop for the priest, a glass of wine for all to celebrate the Sabbath, enough to make some of the sisters tipsy. Then coffee in the calefactory: talking is allowed. Sister Ruth, the young Australian, takes him aside. 'Be frank, Father Luke. Shouldn't we be out there in Africa helping the sick and the needy instead of singing and praying here behind our walls?'

'No.' He shakes his head and again says: 'No. The world needs prayer.'

After escorting him to his car, Sister Elisabeth hands him an envelope: his stipend of £50. 'Thank you', she says.

'I hope you were not disappointed', says Luke.

'Not at all. It has been most instructive for our younger sisters to hear a voice from the past.'

Malindi

Jésus, le fruit de vos entrails, est beni—'blessed is the fruit of thy womb, Jesus.' Kate lies on crumpled sheets on a single bed in the government guesthouse at Lbala. All that comes into her mind is this one phrase from the Hail Mary in French: she must have learned it during her French foreign exchange program when she was thirteen. *Entrails.* Entrails. Never before has she been so aware of her entrails; she has been unable to eat or drink anything without it pouring out of her body an hour or so later as a murky brown liquid. Occasionally she laughs at the irony of her condition—the investigative reporter getting more than she bargained for, experiencing what she has come to observe. Laughing causes a spasm of pain in her ribs; she turns her mind to more sobering things. Is she going to die? She has seen three people die since she came to Africa. Miremba died in her arms. Had Uriarte deliberately left her with the dying? Had he thought that seeing life leave an emaciated body was essential for an understanding of suffering? No. She had volunteered. She had stood in the compound and volunteered to work in the hospice to exorcise her embarrassment, her shame—over her neatness, her good health, even the clothes she was wearing, the divided skirt and khaki shirt.

When Kate is well enough to move, Uriarte and Joshua come to collect her in the Land Cruiser. They drive to Entebbe. At the airport Kate and Uriarte leave Joshua with the Land Cruiser and fly first to Nairobi, then on from Nairobi to Malindi. Uriarte leaves Kate at Walker's Hotel on Malindi Beach. She is to remain there to convalesce. He returns to the airport. He does not stay the night.

The next morning Kate has breakfast in her cabin, then walks out into the bright sunlight. She is thin and weak and at first feels embarrassed to lie in her bathing suit on the beach by the Indian Ocean. She walks away from the hotel and pitches camp with her towel, parasol, suntan lotion, book and bottle of Evian away from the other guests. The parasol is unnecessary: she is sheltered from the sun by a palm tree. She returns to the hotel for lunch at mid-day. Uriarte must have told the staff that she is convalescent; the chef comes from the kitchen to ask if there is something she might like that is not on the menu. The hotel staff are particularly kind.

Kate is to be there for two weeks. Uriarte had said he would not let her return to Europe in her present condition and promised to return to Malindi in five or six days. She can wait; she is happy to wait; she wants to recover her strength and see her figure fill out after the weeks of starvation and dehydration. She wants to look good again—not so much for herself as for him.

The other guests are all white, some Americans, but most are Europeans—Italians, British, French. There are two families; the rest are couples. She is the only one on her own. They are well disposed towards her; the ten-year-old daughter of a French family takes a liking to her and follows her along the beach. Kate has a drink with the parents before supper at the bar. The couples, too, say 'hi' when they first see her in the morning. She can tell from the way the men look at her that her makeover has a way to go.

Kate is glad that Uriarte is not there and glad that no one else she knows is there either. She likes spending the days on her own with only the characters in novels for company. She eats big breakfasts of yoghurt and mango, croissants and apricot jam. At lunch she loads her plate with meat and salad from the buffet. She savours her return to good health. On the second day she swims in the sea, her thin body floating in the salt water, the sun on her face. Her eyes remain closed. No sharks, she thinks, will be tempted by a bundle of skin and bones.

At times Kate thinks back to the camp and the refugees who cannot convalesce on a beach at Malindi, but she feels no sense of guilt. This puzzles her. Was compassion something one felt only from a position of strength? Did victims ever feel sorry for other victims? It was a pity that others could not come to recuperate at Walker's Hotel, but it was not as if she were taking the place of someone else. If she had not been occupying her thatched hut with its satellite television, mini-bar and private bathroom, then it would have gone to a European tourist, not an Ugandan with AIDS.

Kate has been content to put her conscience into Uriarte's keeping. She cannot work, he said, unless she is well—her work being to publicise the work of Misericordia. This is unquestionably true. After dysentery, not only the body is weakened but also the mind. She finds it hard to assemble the few words to e-mail her parents.

Kate is in love with Uriarte. This too does not ignite a sense of guilt. Why should it? He is no longer a priest; he is not married; he is 'available', as her friends might have put it—though she is embarrassed by her use of the word. Uriarte does not belong in the same universe as the kind of young men who would be described in that way in London. Nor is he available in that sense. He belongs to his calling. He is not looking for a wife. All she means by the use of the word in her ruminations is that it is not immoral to imagine him as her lover. She does not anticipate that he *will* be her lover; his behaviour towards her has been that of a friend. But she sees no harm in inventing romantic narratives in her head.

There are paradoxes and inconsistencies in her thoughts: if it is only because she has been sick that Uriarte has been solicitous, she might well lose him when she gets well. Yet she has to get well to regain a measure of lustre that would incite his instincts as a male of the species— like any woman, Kate can combine ethereal emotions with a base practicality. In the late afternoon of her third day in Walker's Hotel, she takes a taxi into Malindi and buys two brightly coloured T-shirts, a linen skirt and three sets of white lace-trimmed underclothes.

Kate is not scheming; she feels wholly passive when it comes to Uriarte. Again, phrases returned from her convent education. 'Let it be done unto me according to thy word.' If Uriarte wants her, she is his, body and soul. If he does not want her body, he need not know that her soul is his. Whether he wants her or not, she will never burden him with her longing: she will not, like Dido, Queen of Carthage, try to stop her Aeneas from sailing off to found Rome.

Uriarte does not return to Malindi on the sixth day of her stay as he had said he would. Nor on the seventh. Nor on the eighth. There is no telephone call or fax or e-mail to explain his continued absence. Kate does not mind. Indeed, she is relieved that a real Uriarte has not appeared to oust the Uriarte of her imagination. She is happy to wait, to anticipate, for another day, another week, another month. She also feels that each day that passes makes her body more appealing. Her hair has regained its lustre; her skin is turning brown. In the evenings she now eats with the French family and during the day is followed around by their daughter, Claudine. They go looking for shells on the beach.

They return to the hotel in the late afternoon of her eighth day, the shadows already lengthening, and there Uriarte sits reading from a typescript—minutes of a meeting, perhaps, or a report. As he looks up, his face, after a brief look of puzzlement, takes on an expression of delight. 'I hardly recognised you.'

'I've been leading such a lazy life ...' Kate sits down beside him. Claudine hovers, half-frowning at the unwelcome presence of a rival for Kate's attention. 'This is Claudine', Kate says to Uriarte, wanting to keep her with them.

'Hello, Claudine', says Uriarte. 'Come and sit down. What would you like to drink? A Coke?'

'*Une Orangina, si'il vous plait.*'

'And you?' Uriarte asks Kate.

'What are you drinking?'

'Iced tea.'

'I'd like that too.'

The waiter comes to their table. The drinks are ordered. Claudine sits with them at the table, dangling her legs.

'I am sorry not to have returned when I said I would', says Uriarte. 'I could not get a flight.'

'From Nairobi?'

'From Cairo.'

'You've been to Cairo?'

'Yes. There was a meeting.' He looks down at the typescript on the table.

'Interesting?'

Uriarte shrugs. 'I get impatient with the bureaucratic protocols, but I suppose they have to be there. And there are real dilemmas facing the work.'

Kate turns to Claudine. 'Juan's job is helping poor people and sick people.'

'But it is complicated because sometimes people don't want us to help the poor and the sick people in their countries because we are Christians and they are Muslims.'

Claudine nods. Her English is good enough for her to understand, but she seems uncomfortable being addressed directly by Uriarte. Uriarte therefore turns to Kate. 'Our mission is to aid anyone in distress, but, like Caritas or CAFOD, we are clearly a Catholic charity, so the Muslims regard us with great suspicion. They know that their people benefit from our work—a quarter of all aid work in Africa is done by the Catholic Church—but they fear it is a kind of covert proselytism, and many devout Muslims would rather see their people die than come under the influence of Christians.'

The waiter returns with Claudine's Orangina, Kate's iced tea, a bowl of peanuts and another bowl of olives.

'What is the answer?'

'Dialogue.'

'Is that what you were doing in Cairo? Talking to imams?'

'Unofficially.'

'But . . .' Kate hesitates. She has noticed before that Uriarte does not like to be reminded of his trial. 'Are you the best person, given . . .'

He waves his hand in a dismissive gesture. 'That doesn't matter to them. They regard the Janjaweed as an embarrassment. We engage at a much deeper level.'

A bubbling noise comes from Claudine as she sucks the last drops of Orangina through a straw.

'You had better tell your mother we're back', Kate says to her.

'OK.' The girl jumps off her chair with a look of relief.

'And tell them that I will be having supper with my friend this evening.'

'OK.'

Kate looks back at Uriarte. 'A deeper level?'

'I try to convince them that the struggle today is not between Christianity and Islam but between secularism and religious belief. It is hard for them to distinguish between George Bush and the Pope, or USAID and Misericordia. And this is rebounding on the wretched Copts. I spent quite a bit of my time with them.'

'The Copts are Egyptian Christians?' Kate asks tentatively.

'The original Christians, converted by Saint Mark at the time of the Emperor Nero. From the third to the seventh centuries, Egypt was a Christian country. It remained so even after its conquest by Islam. The Prophet Muhammad had a Coptic wife. Only in the Middle Ages did Islam become the dominant religion. The Copts became second-class citizens. They were persecuted. They are still persecuted today.'

'By the government?'

'No, by Islamic extremists such as the Al-Gama'a al-Islamiyya, but the police turn a blind eye. Converts from Islam to Christianity are threatened with death. Christian girls are raped and forced to marry Muslims. Churches are burned. This goes on throughout the Islamic world. Christians are seen as the enemies of Islam. The Muslims see the Palestinians humiliated by the Israelis and the Israelis supported by Christian Americans, so they take it out on the wretched Copts. And it's all so absurd. We worship the same God, after all.'

Uriarte goes on—fired up, as he always is, by his sense of mission. Kate listens and nods obediently when he says she must read this or that and, as she does so, wonders if he ever relaxes, ever lets go, ever enjoys himself as other men do by lying motionless on the beach or getting slightly tipsy or making love.

Dusk descends. The lights on the terrace usurp the setting sun. First one, then a second family take their places at table.

'I must take a shower', says Uriarte.

'What about a swim?'

He looks uncertain. 'Tomorrow, perhaps.'

They agree to meet again at eight. As they go towards their bungalows, Kate introduces Uriarte to her French friends. The mother looks quizzical: Is this a friend or a lover? Kate cannot answer; she does not know. Claudine has the blank expression of a child who realises that there are things she cannot expect to understand.

Uriarte has taken a shower and wears a clean short-sleeved shirt, but he stands out, nonetheless, from the other men dining with their wives or girlfriends on the terrace of Walker's Hotel. The shirt is white, his trousers are grey: his simple attire proclaims as emphatically as a sermon his contempt for worldly values.

Kate, by contrast, is wearing her new skirt, her new underclothes and a top she had brought from England. Studying herself in the mirror in her bungalow before leaving, she is pleased with what she sees. Understated elegance. Eye shadow and mascara imperceptible to the untrained eye. A skirt that falls modestly to below her knee yet manages to cling to her long flank. A cotton top a little too big, now, that she was so much thinner and thus, when she leans forward, showing more of her brown breasts than before.

As they are shown to their table, Kate turns to the waiter and asks for rum punch. 'Why don't you have one?' she says to Uriarte. 'They're delicious.'

'Why not?'

She turns back to the waiter. 'Two rum punches.'

There is a burgeoning amaryllis on their table—bright, luxuriant, thick-stemmed. The air is scented; the only sound, other than the murmurs from other tables, is the hypnotising thud of the waves breaking on the beach.

Uriarte returns to the topic they had been discussing before—the similarities and differences of the world's great monotheistic religions. 'We are all the children of Abraham', he says, 'and our Muslim friends have to be made to understand that. Christianity and Islam are both in essence Jewish heresies: Jesus always insisted that he came not to contradict the Law of Moses but to fulfil it. And the Koran . . . Have you read it?'

Kate shakes her head.

'It includes many of the teachings from the Old and the New Testaments. The ethical differences are small. However, since there is no one source of authority in Islam, it doesn't have the same flexibility as Christianity. The Church has moved on since Vatican II and, as a result, Catholicism and Islam have less in common than they did before. Muslims are shocked that we fast so seldom, and, of course, by the liberation of women. You won't remember but women used to wear veils when they entered a church. We regard women's liberation as a great achievement, but to Muslims it leads to sexual permissiveness among Christians and non-Christians alike.'

To get someone to think about love, Kate has read, you should talk about love. But perhaps not quite yet. Uriarte has yet to drink his rum punch.

A waiter brings two tall glasses with little paper parasols sticking into the fruit that floats on the top. He then takes their order. Uriarte shows no interest in the menu and accepts the choices Kate makes for them both—cold consommé and seafood shashlik: skewered squares of white fish interspersed with peppers and king prawns. He also defers to Kate in the choice of wine, indicating to the sommelier that he should give her the list. He shows equally little interest in the food that is laid before them—elegantly presented with a small mound of caviar on the consommé and a baroque tracery of piquant sauce around the shashliks. He eats what he is given, just as he had on the roadside eating places in Uganda and in the canteen at the camp. He also drinks what is in his glass. After the rum punch there is a reddening of the skin on his neck, and after the first glass of South African Chardonnay, his talk loosens up. 'You know', he says, 'I was afraid, really afraid, that you were going to die and I had to think— what will I tell her parents? How will I face her mother and her father?'

'Haven't other volunteers gone down with the squitters?'

'The squitters?' Uriarte laughs. 'Is that what you call it? Squitters. Yes. There have been others, but they usually respond more quickly to the medicine.'

'Well, I've e-mailed my parents to say that I'm very much alive.'

'Thank God.'

'Should we really thank God?'

'For everything ...'

'Did you pray that I'd recover?'

'No.'

'You don't think that God was interested? Or that he wouldn't want to waste a miracle on a Western journalist?'

'I thought ... I think ... don't you have a saying—"the Lord helps those who help themselves"?'

'You don't believe in divine intervention?'

'Not like that.'

'No miracles at Lourdes?'

'Auto suggestion leading to spontaneous remission, perhaps.'

'And what about Jesus in the Gospels—walking on the water? Turning water into wine?'

Uriarte hesitates. 'A narrative method for conveying the extraordinary effect Jesus had on those who met him—the power of his personality, the natural authority behind what he said.'

'But not literally true.'

'No. Few theologians now believe that they are.'

'But the older generation ...'

'Of course.'

'Your parents?'

'Yes. And for them it was hard to adapt to the new thinking.'

'They are dead?'

'Yes.'

'Have you brothers and sisters?'

'A brother, yes. He is an engineer in Bilbao.'

'With a family?'

'Yes. A wife and five children.'

'Do you ever see them?'

'When I am in Spain.'

'But you said that you hardly ever went to Spain.'

'When?'

'At your trial.'

'Of course. The trial. No, well, it is true. I do not see much of my brother. We have a different outlook. He belongs to Opus Dei.'

'So he *does* believe in miracles.'

'Of course. And many other things besides.'

'He must admire the Pope.'

'He does.'

'And Cardinal Ratzinger.'

'*Ciertamente.*'

'And is against the use of condoms to stop the spread of AIDS?'

'You can understand, perhaps, why it is better that I keep away from him.'

'To keep your distance?'

'*Precisamente.*'

'What about his wife?'

Uriarte shrugged. 'Also Opus Dei. *Kinder, Küche, Kirche.*'

'Not the kind of wife you would have wanted?'

'No.'

'If you had wanted a wife.'

'If I had wanted a wife.'

'Did you never want a wife?'

Uriarte laughs. 'Is it too late?'

Kate blushes. 'No. But perhaps, if you had wanted to marry, you would be married by now.'

'It would be difficult because of my work.'

'Perhaps.' Kate sounds uncertain.

'As Saint Paul said, a man who is married has to think of his wife.'

'A wife might have made Saint Paul less of a misogynist.'

Again, Uriarte laughs. 'Was he a misogynist?'

'Didn't he say that it was good to be married but better to be celibate?'

'Something like that.'

'Which is why the Church has always mistrusted women and denigrated sex.'

'Not just Saint Paul but also Saint Augustine.'

'Right down to Cardinal Ratzinger and Pope John Paul II.'

'But that is changing.'

'Is it?'

'Most progressive theologians do not share their position, and Catholics now use contraception with a good conscience.'

'And sex?'

'Sex?'

'Sex outside marriage used to be considered a mortal sin.'

Uriarte becomes pensive. 'Sex is a human need', he says. 'Man has need of a woman and a woman of a man. To fulfil that need cannot be sinful.'

'What about a man who has need of a man?'

Uriarte laughs. 'That used to be considered a sin "crying out to Heaven for vengeance". No longer, thank God, even in the most traditionalist circles.'

'Even among cardinals', says Kate.

'Among cardinals?'

'My uncle, who is a priest, said that when he was studying in Rome a Dutch seminarian made a pass at him.'

'And he is now a cardinal?'

'In charge of some department or other in the Vatican.'

'Doornik?'

'He didn't say his name.'

'Doornik is the only Dutch Prefect.'

'Is he gay?'

Uriarte shrugs. 'It's sometimes hard to tell, unless the cardinal has a mistress.'

'Surely not in this day and age.'

'You know, the Church points to certain ideals. But the lives of most people are not ideal. We all live in an imperfect world. It is no good telling people that they should not be gay or divorced or remarried or living with a partner. They are where they are. And there are particular situations in which everything must be provisional. For example, the guerrilla army in El Salvador, the FMLN, no one knew if they would live beyond the next day, but the men had their needs and those needs were met.'

'By the women?'

'Of course. Not by the men! It was clear that it was inconsistent to fight for the rights of the poor while denying the needs of your *compadres*.'

'Did the women agree?'

'You know, they had been indoctrinated by the Church and by their mothers to see sex not as a need but as something to barter for a lifelong commitment—like bait on a hook or cheese in a mousetrap. But when the situation was explained to them, they understood.'

'They met the needs of the men?'

'Of course.'

'And you?'

'I was a man.' He says this simply, without either embarrassment or bravado.

'But as a priest ...'

'I was no longer a priest.'

'And you never fell in love?'

'The conditions were not suited to Hollywood romances.'

Kate blushes. 'No. Of course. But since?'

'Not then. And not since.'

Kate's blush deepens. She feels that she has sunk in Uriarte's estimation by talking about falling in love.

They rise from the table and walk along the beach. Uriarte takes her hand. When they reach the palm tree beneath which Kate pitched camp on her first morning, they stop and Uriarte kisses her. He smells of soap. They then stroll back towards the hotel—a forced saunter because she can sense that his body, like hers, is so taut it might snap.

'Your place or mine?' she says, cringing as soon as the words have left her mouth.

Uriarte says nothing, but the hand that had let go of hers as they had reached the hotel now comes to rest on her shoulder and, after unlocking the door of his bungalow with his other hand, guides her in.

12 Gyle Street

Kotovski and Ashton are summoned by e-mail to a meeting with Paget at Vauxhall Cross. Ashton picks up Kotovski at Thames House in an unmarked Ford Focus: he is wearing a pin-striped suit. 'These wretched Jihadis', Ashton says as he drives over Lambeth Bridge. 'They're driving us mad. The IRA were at least serious gangsters and Black September knew what they were doing. But we're expected to infiltrate a lot of bored losers in Halifax and Bradford whose dads run chip shops or dry cleaners. There really ought to be professional qualifications for terrorists. It's a nightmare dealing with hopeless amateurs.'

From the grunt of its exhaust, Kotovski realises that Ashton's Ford Focus is not the base model that its markings suggest. There is also a SatNav system and, no doubt, some sophisticated communications equipment behind the dashboard. Ashton shows a pass at Vauxhall House, and they drive down into the subterranean car park.

Paget greets them in the same feline manner as before. 'Please take a seat', he says, pointing to the chairs in front of his desk. Then, sitting down himself, he looks at the two younger men and asks: 'Any developments at your end?'

Ashton shakes his head. 'Our man's been out of the country.'

'In Uganda', says Paget.

'The girl has been with him', says Kotovski.

Paget glances at the papers on his desk. 'The girl?'

'The journalist who covered the trial.'

'Kate Ramsey.'

'Yes.'

'Do you happen to know if he has been in Cairo?'

The two younger men shake their heads. 'Why Cairo?' asks Kotovski.

'It would seem that a man—either European or American—was seen in Cairo last week talking with certain parties within the orbit of the Muslim Brotherhood.'

'Within the orbit of the Brotherhood?' Ashton looks puzzled.

'A new faction. The Mukhabarat have a mole, but the mole did not identify the man. Nor could he discover what he wanted. But it seems that our friend Uriarte flew to Cairo at around the same time for a conference of NGOs in Alexandria. The man might have been him.'

'If it was he,' suggests Kotovski, 'he may have been re-establishing his credentials with the people he was negotiating with in Darfur.'

'But he's no longer involved in Darfur', says Ashton.

'Precisely.'

'So what was he up to?'

Paget looks at Kotovski. 'Any ideas?'

Kotovski hesitates, then says: 'If it was Uriarte, the most innocent explanation would be that he was simply keeping open the channels to the Islamic extremists that he had established before.'

'And the most guilty explanation?' asks Paget.

'That he was looking for Sarin from another source.'

For a moment, the three men are silent. Then Ashton turns to Paget: 'Do we know if the Egyptians are capable of manufacturing Sarin?'

'It's a complex chemical process,' says Paget, 'extremely dangerous if you try it in your kitchen. But there are labs and chemists in Egypt. It could be done.'

'But why would the Jihadis want to give Sarin to our friend Uriarte?'

'Let's take it step by step', says Paget. 'Uriarte, at his trial, claimed that he wanted to deploy nerve gas in Darfur to deter attacks on the refugee camps by Janjaweed militia. Now he goes to the Janjaweed's friends in Cairo and asks them to supply it. Let us suppose that they can—that they have the capability. Why would they want to collaborate with this public enemy of Islam?'

'Because they know', says Kotovski, 'that the story he spun at his trial is false.'

'Precisely', says Paget. 'But even so. Why would they want to help Uriarte?'

'Perhaps he has persuaded them that their interests coincide—that the real war is not between Islam and Christianity, but between the God-fearing and the secular, materialistic nations of the developed world.'

'The Great Satan', says Paget. He uncaps his Montblanc pen to draw a diagram on a sheet of paper on his desk. 'Let's say that Uriarte is planning Atrocity X for purposes of his own. He puts it to the Muslim Brotherhood in Cairo—friends of Osama or whatever. They like the idea of Atrocity X; they might even like to claim credit for Atrocity X, so they might well decide to help our friend Uriarte get hold of the gas.'

Kotovski shakes his head. 'I cannot believe that Al-Qaida would trust someone who isn't Muslim. How are they to know that Uriarte isn't a plant?'

'Perhaps the trial convinced them', suggests Paget. 'He stood to go down for a very long time.'

'And they may know him better than we do', says Ashton.

'Even so', says Kotovski.

'And the girl?' asks Paget. 'Do you think she has any role in this affair?'

Ashton looks at Kotovski.

'From her profile, I'd say no', says Kotovski. 'Her background is about as Middle England as they come.'

'Perhaps you should dig a little deeper', says Paget.

'Pull her in?'

'For what?' asks Ashton.

'Just dig a little deeper', says Paget again, without elaborating on what he means.

'We'd better take a look', says Ashton as they leave Vauxhall House.

'At what?'

'The girl's house.'

'That means a warrant.'

'Does it?'

Kotovski sighs. He knows that sometimes Ashton does not bother with the niceties of the law. He himself prefers to play by the rules. 'I'd rather get a warrant.'

'On what grounds?'

'Terrorist suspect.'

'What evidence?'

Kotovski shrugs. 'Our say-so should be enough.'

'It would take time,' says Ashton, 'and we don't know when she's getting back.'

Kotovski is persuaded.

'Where does she live?' asks Ashton.

'Brook Green. 12 Gyle Street. W.14.'

'Punch it in.'

Kotovski sets the SatNav system, and the digitalised voice of a woman directs them down Kensington High Street, then through a complex of one-way streets behind the Olympia Exhibition Hall to Gyle Street.

No. 12 is a small, late Victorian terrace house with wisteria growing over its white stuccoed facade. Ashton parks the Focus in an adjoining street; the two men then walk back and ring the doorbell. There is no answer. Without so much as a glance to the left or right to see if they might be observed, Ashton takes out a bunch of keys to pick the mortise lock. Kotovski stands behind to shelter him from prying eyes. In a little more than two minutes—long minutes for Kotovski—it is done. The second Yale lock is opened in a matter of seconds. The two men enter the house. There is no alarm.

A narrow hallway leads to a kitchen, which looks into a garden. To the left, a door opens into two interconnected rooms. The front looks out onto the street and is arranged as a sitting room with waist-high bookshelves in the recesses on either side of the fireplace and a television with a DVD player placed at an angle in the corner. There is a beige sofa with its back against the wall and, on the mantel, candlesticks, a Wedgwood figurine, two silver-framed photographs and a stack of cards. One wall of the back room is lined with books; against the other is set a desk and a filing cabinet. The window looks out onto the small garden.

Ashton takes two pairs of surgical gloves out of an inside pocket of the jacket of his pin-striped suit and hands one to Kotovski. 'Better safe than sorry.' Kotovski takes the gloves and puts them on. He goes to the mantel and studies the framed photographs. One is of an old couple—presumably her parents; the other of a young man—a brother, perhaps, or boyfriend. He sifts through the cards: they are invitations— some to private viewings in small art galleries, others to parties, two to weddings. One of the wedding invitations is a thick white card with engraved copper-plate writing: 'Brigadier James and the Hon. Mrs. Grayson request the pleasure of your company at the wedding of their daughter Everilda to Thomas Statchley ...' There was nothing in Arabic—no 'Osama Bin Laden at Home'.

The room is furnished in contemporary good taste. There is a wooden floor with a kelim rug in front of the fireplace; bright cushions are laid neatly on the plump beige sofa. On the coffee table in front of the sofa are a pile of magazines and reviews—*The Week, The New Yorker, The Spectator, The Economist*—but nothing Islamic or even liberal: no *Prospect, TLS* or *London Review of Books*. The pictures on the walls seem dull to Kotovski—two original oils with an amateur look, perhaps by friends; a modern etching, perhaps bought at the Affordable Art Fair; a small nineteenth-century portrait, perhaps of an ancestor, probably lent to her by her parents.

Kotovski turns. Ashton is rifling through the filing cabinet beside the desk. 'She's well-heeled, all right. No sign of an overdraft or a mortgage. BACS transfers from an employer; regular credits from a stockbroker; irregular payments from the Alfred Ramsey Discretionary Trust.'

'Nothing from bank accounts in Saudi Arabia?'

Ashton shakes his head. 'No.'

While Ashton continues to study the bank statements, Kotovski turns to look at the bookshelves against the wall. Again, there is nothing to suggest anything beyond a general interest in politics and current affairs, and a taste in fiction that tracks the Booker short lists— novels by Julian Barnes, Ian McEwen, Martin Amis, Margaret Atwood— together with some American best-sellers by Updike, Roth and Wolfe. There is a Penguin Classic edition of the Koran, but it is clear, when Kotovski takes it from the shelf, that it has not been read. Several of the more serious books such as Paul Hollander's *Understanding Anti-Americanism: Its Origins and Impact at Home and Abroad* and *Power, Politics and Culture* by Edward W. Said remain in pristine condition, no doubt for the same reason—the aspirational purchases of someone too tired after a day's work to do anything but flick through the *Evening Standard* and watch TV.

Kotovski leaves Ashton at the filing cabinet, looks into the kitchen, then goes upstairs. There is a bathroom on the mezzanine and a small single bedroom at the back overlooking the garden. Kate's larger bedroom is at the front of the house. There is a double bed covered by a patchwork bedspread and two sets of pillows—ready for a lover but, to judge by the look of the pillows, used only on one side. In the wardrobe are a pair of shiny leather boots, shoes stacked on a shoe rack and a neat row of suits and dresses, around half of which are still covered with dustcovers from the dry cleaners.

Kotovski moves to the chest of drawers. A pleasant odour of lavender comes from her neatly stacked underclothes. He looks briefly beneath them and through the shirts and jerseys in the drawers below. The dressing table is equally unrevealing until he comes to the bottom drawer where, beneath a jewel box, he finds three packets of letters held together by elastic bands. Kotovski hesitates, caught between propriety and duty. Are old love letters likely to contain any clues? More likely, perhaps, than her bank statements. He takes the first and fattest bundle of letters—hand-written notes under the letterhead of a the Modern Languages Faculty of Oxford University signed 'Clive'. Requests for rendezvous, guarded declarations, evasive explanations ending with a dismissal—'my children must come first'—the whole story from start to finish taking only a matter of months.

The second bundle is thin—a series of notes from an Alec, later 'Al'. They are cursory—one ending 'yeah, yeah, love and all that'. In another is the sentence—'I really think you're still hung up on your dad or those nuns, which is why you won't go in for things like that.' Like what? S&M? Three in a bed? Kotovski dislikes Alec, and he does not think much more of the third correspondent, Barney. The writing on the few hand-written notes is not just slapdash but infantile: one did not have to be a graphologist to see that this was someone who had yet to develop a character of a decided kind. Most of the others are not letters but e-mail messages that the girl had printed out—dull travelogues from far-off places. The expressions of affection are tepid: nowhere does Barney say he misses Kate or wishes she was with him in Vientiane or Kandahar or Timbuktu.

There is a waist-high bookshelf running across one wall of the bedroom with a small flat-screen television and a collection of thrillers—

P. D. James, Sarah Padewski, Henning Mankell—clearly the kind of books that Kate enjoys reading. There are also more novels—by Kazuo Ishiguro, Sebastian Faulks, Peter Carey, Salman Rushdie. Stacked on top of one another are three photograph albums. Kotovski sits down on the end of the bed and glances through them: group school photos, pictures of Kate with ponies and numerous holiday snaps—some skiing, others in the Third World—no doubt the record of a gap year between high school and college.

Kotovski has had enough: the mild distaste he has felt at looking through Kate's personal effects has now grown into outright disgust. Certainly, scruples are out of place where terrorism is concerned, and he is responsible for bringing Kate Ramsey to the attention of the security services. But to date they have found nothing to implicate her in anything, and the more innocent she appears, the more unpleasant is this violation of her privacy. Kotovski also feels welling up inside of him a sense of frustration that he does not understand. Kate is intelligent, cultivated. Why has she been drawn to such losers as Clive, Alec and Barney? Why not someone who would love and respect her . . .

'A classy bint', says Ashton, coming into the bedroom behind him. 'Everything neat and tidy and top of the line.'

'Did you find anything?' asks Kotovski.

Ashton shakes his head. 'Nope. I'm afraid it's a case of what you see is what you get. A Sloane with attitude.'

Kotovski gets up off the bed and puts the photograph album back on the shelf in the place order as before.

'We'd better scarper', says Ashton, straightening the bedspread to lose the indentation left by Kotovski.

'Yes.' Kotovski follows Ashton onto the landing but then, before going down stairs, stands for a moment looking back through the bedroom door, which he has left ajar.

Happiness

Kate has read somewhere that happiness is absorption—being so lost in some task that you are unaware of anything else and so unable to ask the question 'Am I happy?' Lying beneath a huge, slow-moving fan in a musty bedroom in downtown Cairo, she decides that she would go along with that definition if the task was *embodied*—in her case embodied in a man. She does not say: I am happy because I love and am loved by Juan Uriarte, or I am happy because he made love to me last night and this morning and will no doubt make love to me again this afternoon, but I am happy because I do not even ask if I am happy. She turns over onto his side of the bed and buries her head in his pillow. She longs for him to come back.

It was Uriarte who had suggested that they return via Cairo: he had said it was a fascinating city not so much for the pyramids and sphinxes and archaeological museums, but as one of the few great, teeming cities that had largely escaped the hegemony of American culture. 'Baghdad, of course, was the seat of the Caliphs at the height of Islamic civilisation, but it never recovered from being sacked by the Mongols. Damascus still has something, but Cairo really is what the Germans call a *Weltstadt*—one of the great cities of the world.'

Uriarte knew his way around. A travel agent in Nairobi had changed their tickets without Kate incurring any extra cost, and, rather than stay at one of Cairo's Americanised hotels, Uriarte had booked them into the guesthouse where he always stayed—a huge, rambling flat with dark corridors and dim lights but bright bedrooms looking out over roofs to minarets and a tangle of television aerials and telephone wires. The furniture and the carpets could have been there for eighty years. The bathrooms, too, which were shared by the guests, had old-fashioned tiling and huge pewter taps from which brownish water coughed and spluttered and then came in a gush. There was no restaurant, but breakfast was served in a panelled room where daylight entered only from the ceiling, filtering through a coloured glass art nouveau dome. Or breakfast was brought to your room. Uriarte had been put in a small single room next to Kate's; hers was larger and had a washbasin and a double bed and was at a discreet distance from the other guests at the end of a corridor at the back of the flat.

This morning Kate's breakfast is brought to her on a large bronze tray by a shuffling old man in a caftan. She does not rise until ten and then goes along the corridor to take a shower. She returns to find that Uriarte has returned. He is lying on the bed playing with her organiser: one of his more endearing characteristics is his interest in the gadgetry of her mobile office—her laptop, her cell phone and her Palm Pilot.

'Who are all these people?' he asks.

Kate goes to the bed and leans over him to look at the screen, a pink-steamed thigh protruding from her dressing-gown. 'Oh, friends.'

'You have a lot of friends.'

'Some of them are contacts.'

'Of course.'

When Kate is dressed, they go out together into the streets. At every corner, a booth sells glasses of freshly squeezed orange juice. Distinguished-looking men courteously intercept them to offer their services as guides. Uriarte declines their offer with an equal courtesy. Sounds and smells swirl around them; Kate delights in the colourful chaos, wondering how people who are so poor can be so cheerful. What a contrast to the gloomy faces of those waiting at the bus stop outside Argos at Shepherd's Bush.

All at once they are in the cool oasis of the Egyptian Museum. As they walk from room to room, Kate leans on the arm of her lover while he tells her about the religious beliefs of the ancient Egyptians. 'On the whole, they were polytheists—they had around seven hundred different gods—though there was an interesting period when the Pharaoh Amenhotep IV decided that there was only one god, Aten, the sun god.'

Kate only half listens. Amenhotep, Akenaten, Amen-Re—meaningless names relating to dull artefacts; Memphis and Thebes, she decided, could well have been designed by Hitler's architect, Albert Speer.

'Of course, all religions have many things in common', Uriarte continues. 'There are similar Creation myths, and the belief that there are gods who control our destiny and have to be placated through intermediaries, the priests. The Egyptian priests, like the priests of Israel, were the only ones allowed to officiate in the temples, which they believed were the homes of the gods. But they were not a special caste; a priest would have another job and perhaps serve in rotation with other part-time priests.'

'Worker priests?'

Uriarte looks surprised. 'You know about the worker priests?'

'A little.' Kate's memory is hazy. 'A French Dominican in Marseille went to minister in factories alongside the workers . . .'

'Father Jacques Loew. And after the war, hundreds of priests followed his example. They exchanged their cassocks for overalls and became manual workers. They involved themselves in the lives of the workers and committed themselves to the workers' cause. The Vatican became alarmed. Priests in trades unions! Priests in politics! Priests cooperating with Socialists and Communists! So the Pope said, *Basta!* They were ordered back into their churches. A wonderful opportunity to evangelise the French proletariat was lost.'

'The liberation theologians of their time', says Kate.

'*Precisamente!* And they suffered the same fate. One man, Pope Pius XII, a narrow, cautious man with the mentality of a civil servant, *un burócrata*, having lacked the courage to condemn Hitler, condemned instead the most dynamic development in the Catholic Church at that time. And thirty years later, we have Pope John Paul II and Cardinal Ratzinger—one the son of an army officer, the other the son of a policeman—rigid men afraid of audacity, afraid of adventure! They condemn Gutiérrez, Segundo and Boff!'

To Kate, the names Gutiérrez, Segundo and Boff mean little more than those of Amenhotep, Akenaten and Amen-Re, but, having hoped to impress Uriarte with her pinch of knowledge about worker priests, she does not now want to disillusion him by betraying her ignorance of liberation theologians. Nor does Uriarte seem to expect her to make a knowledgeable response: he is thinking aloud.

'That is the tragedy of the Catholic Church. It could be—it *could* be—the most powerful, the most effective agency for bringing justice to the world, but always the charism of thousands is thwarted by the *diktat* of one or two old men.' Uriarte stops in front of a gilded wood statue of the Pharaoh Tutankhamun wearing the *khephresh* crown and *uraeus* with the insignia of Osiris in its hands. 'It is quite extraordinary to think that thousands of years after this statue was made we still project onto our popes a concept of divine kingship like that accorded to the Pharaohs by the ancient Egyptians. Pope John Paul II may not be a god, but like the Pharaohs he claims to be the *pontifex maximus*, the bridge between God and mankind, the infallible interpreter of God's will on matters as abstruse as the Immaculate Conception and as banal as condoms!'

Uriarte had used condoms when making love to Kate, and Kate did not want to tell him that it was unnecessary because she was on

the Pill—largely to regulate her periods but also, well, just in case ...
It might have given him a misleading impression.

'Perhaps people are drawn to the Catholic religion precisely because
of the claims made for the popes', she says to Uriarte. 'Perhaps they
like the idea of a *pontifex maximus.*'

'*Claro!* And others are put off the Catholic Church for the same
reason. But we cannot escape the fact—those of us raised in the Catholic faith—that our Church has a huge influence in the world, for
good or for evil, and that influence depends on the mentality of one
old man who puts another old man in charge of the Holy Office and
appoints other like-minded old men as cardinals who in turn will
choose another old man who thinks like them to be the next pope! *It
is an unending cycle of senility and reaction that brings misery to the world!*'

In writing her profiles of captains of industry, Kate would never
use the phrase 'his eyes flashed', which belongs to clichéd romantic
fiction, but she sees something in Uriarte's look, as he spits out those
last contemptuous words, that might properly be described as a flash—
a momentary glimpse of a frightening fury that she has not encoun-
tered before.

'Is there no way to break the cycle?' she asks timidly.

Now there is another flash of the eyes, but this time it is a look
directed at her to see if perhaps, in that moment of frightening fury,
he has let something slip. Her blank look seems to reassure him. 'Of
course, if one could break the cycle ...'

'The next pope ...' Kate begins.

'Will be as bad as this one', says Uriarte.

'How can you be sure? The Holy Spirit, after all ...'

'The Holy Spirit!' Uriarte laughs as they move away from the statue
of Tutankhamun. 'If you knew the lobbying and intrigue that goes
on behind the scenes at a papal election, you wouldn't talk about the
work of the Holy Spirit. The truth is that Pope John Paul II has quite
deliberately appointed cardinals who will choose a successor in the
same mould. Not an easy task, as it happens, because most of the best
bishops want a change. He has had trouble finding men as reactionary
as he is. He has to fall back on Opus Dei.'

'So if by chance, during the next conclave, the roof of the Sistine
Chapel were to collapse, killing the whole College of Cardinals', says
Kate, 'they would have to appoint a whole new batch.'

'It's an interesting conjecture', responds Uriarte, his eyes no longer flashing, his tone of voice calm. 'The members of the College of Cardinals, after all, are qualified to vote not as cardinals but as priests and deacons of the Diocese of Rome: each cardinal belongs nominally to the Roman clergy. Your Cardinal Murphy O'Connor, for example, is the Cardinal Priest of Santa Lucia Sopra Minerva. So, if there were no cardinals, the choice of a new bishop of Rome would theoretically fall on the Roman clergy, but in reality there would have to be a gathering of all the bishops.'

'A Third Vatican Council?'

'Something like that. Perhaps with the addition of members of the laity as there was at the Council of Constance, which chose a new pope after the Great Schism.'

'And they might elect someone unexpected?'

'Certainly, if that roof collapsed, there would be fewer of those geriatric reactionaries to choose from. And that, of course, is what the Second Vatican Council intended. A collegial Church—not the absolute rule of a pope.'

They make love after lunch and at around four in the afternoon take a taxi to a suburb of the city. Uriarte wants her to meet his Coptic friends. They reach a recently built house. It is surrounded by a wire fence. A concrete mixer remains in the drive. The hallway still smells of wet concrete. In the living room there are five or six people—an extended family, perhaps, or simply a group of friends. Uriarte introduces her first to an older woman, then to a man—her husband perhaps. They speak English, but not well. Kate is seated on a sofa and offered tea and sticky cakes. She looks around. There is a crucifix on the wall, and brightly coloured pictures of Jesus and the Virgin Mary. A young man with a heavy face and dun-coloured skin comes to sit next to her. He tells her about the Copts: Saint Mark the Evangelist introduced Christianity into Egypt. He was martyred at Alexandria, Egypt. Saint Mark is the first leader of the Coptic Orthodox Church. There is an unbroken succession of leaders of the Coptic Orthodox Church from Saint Mark to the present Pope Shenouda III. He is the 117th successor of Saint Mark.

Kate feigns interest. Her mind has not yet recovered from the morning's visit to the Cairo Museum.

'The Nicene Creed was written by a Copt, Anastasius. He saved the Church from the Arian heresy. Origen, too, was a Copt. It was he who translated the Bible. But then came Islam. Egypt was conquered by Arabs. The great library at Alexandria—the greatest in the world—was burned down by the Arab general Amer ibin Alass on the orders of Caliph Omar ibin Alkhatab. It took them six months to burn all the books.'

'How awful', says Kate.

'Awful, yes, it was awful.' The young man repeats the word as if it was not one he would have used. 'And the persecution has continued ever since—some periods better than others, but always they find small ways to oppress and discriminate so that we have now become a small minority in our own country.'

Kate nods: her mouth is filled with a treacly cake.

'They need us because we are well educated. Many of the most successful Egyptians are Copts. Do you remember the UN secretary general Boutros Boutros-Ghali?'

'Of course.'

'He was a Copt. We are like the Jews in Russia. They hate us, but they can't do without us.'

'What do you do?' asks Kate.

There is a brief hesitation. The young man glances across the room towards Uriarte, but Uriarte is talking to someone else. Their eyes do not meet. He turns back to Kate. 'I am a chemist.'

'Here in Cairo?'

'No, in Alexandria. I am at the university.'

'Do you teach?'

'Sometimes.' He seems uncomfortable talking about his work. 'I have worked in the United States but returned to Egypt to be with my parents.' He nods towards the woman who greeted Kate when she first came in.

'And how do you know Juan?' asks Kate.

'He met my father through the Patriarch. Misericordia has done much to help our community.'

The mother approaches them to offer Kate more tea. She smiles down at them. Was she trying to match-make? Kate accepts more tea and another *bacclava*.

The young man is momentarily silent.

'Have you any brothers and sisters?' Kate asks.

He scowls. 'I *had* a sister', he mutters.

Kate has asked the question simply to make conversation, but it seems to have touched a nerve.

'I am sorry.'

'Yes.'

'When did she die?'

'She is not dead.'

Kate is flummoxed.

'It is part of the persecution.'

She waits.

The young man lowers his head towards hers. 'She is married to a Muslim. She was raped. She had no choice.'

'But the police ... wasn't there a prosecution?'

'The police ... the government ... they do nothing.'

'That is terrible', Kate says. 'There should be protests.'

'By whom? The Americans? They don't want to make life more difficult for Mubarak. It is the same all over the Middle East. A combination of Zionism and militant Islam means that the Christian communities are almost extinct. There is a conspiracy of silence regarding the true nature of Islam: its intolerance, its bigotry, its ...' He grasps for a word. 'Its *stupidity*.'

'But surely', says Kate, remembering what Juan had said in Malindi, 'all religions worship the same God?'

'Oh, perhaps', says the young man, his voice hoarse with caustic irony, 'if you mean something vague and abstract and undefined. But as soon as you give God a nature, then it is *not* the same God because their God speaks through a primitive, murderous, self-serving brigand of the seventh century whose ramblings in the Koran *can never be changed*, whereas our God speaks through Christ and the apostles and the early Fathers of the Church like Clement of Alexandria whose faith is fused with the reason of the Greeks ...'

'But surely Jesus said that we must love our enemies', says Kate.

'Yes, but he also said that he brought *fire and the sword*, and it is with fire and the sword that Christianity must be defended.'

'A crusade!'

'If there are any Christians in the world today', says the young man, 'it is thanks to the crusaders who expelled the Muslims from Spain and Portugal and stopped the Turks at the gates of Vienna! And it was only because they were at the gates of Vienna that the Christian nations rallied to defeat them!'

'The problem is', responds Kate, 'that the West is no longer Christian.'

'There are a billion Catholics throughout the world. We must open their eyes to the iniquity of Islam! And we will!'

'I should certainly like to write about the difficulties faced by your community', Kate says.

'The pen is all very well,' he replies, 'but it is no substitute for the sword!'

Kate feels uncomfortable sitting next to this fanatic. 'Juan', she says softly, 'thinks that Islam and Christianity should come together to take on the secular world.'

The young man looks towards Uriarte and smiles. 'Of course. He has to say that.'

Kate blushes, annoyed that the young man should seem to know Juan better than she does.

'Juan is an extraordinary man', he says.

'Yes', says Kate. On that they could agree.

In the taxi on their way back into Cairo, Kate starts to say something to Uriarte about her conversation with the young Copt, but Uriarte nods towards the driver and raises his finger to his lips. It is not until they are alone in their room, resting on the bed, that she tells him how the young man seemed to want a revival of the crusades.

'Don't quote him', says Uriarte. 'It could land him in trouble.'

'Has he said the same sort of thing to you?'

'Yes.'

'It is not very Christian.'

'The rape of his sister is hard to forgive.'

'Yes, I can see that.'

'It is the same with Christians throughout the Middle East. They become the scapegoats for everything done by the Americans, and the United States, a superpower and supposedly Christian, does little to help them.'

'Can *nothing* be done?'

Uriarte shrugs. 'Yes. They can buy protection. But that is expensive.'

'And they are poor?'

'Yes.' He hesitates for a moment, then continues: 'Their Church is so desperately in need of money that the Patriarch has sold one of the Nag Hammadi scrolls.'

'Are they the same as the Dead Sea Scrolls?'

'Not quite. They're ancient parchments found in a tomb in the 1950s in Upper Egypt. The problem is that, while they have a good offer from an American museum, they can't get an export licence.'

'Can't it be smuggled out?'

'It would be difficult for a Copt to do it. Their baggage is always searched. But an aid worker might get away with it.'

'You?'

'I made the suggestion when I was here before, and now they've taken me up on the offer.'

'But *you* might be searched.'

Uriarte shrugs. 'They need money. They need it desperately.'

'Isn't it possible that the Egyptian police know you've been in contact with the Copts?'

Uriarte laughs. 'More than possible. Highly likely.'

'Then they'll search you.'

'Not necessarily. They didn't search me last time.'

'You were flying to Nairobi.'

'That's true.'

Kate hesitates, then says: 'Wouldn't it make more sense if *I* took the scroll through customs?'

Uriarte shakes his head. 'No. It would be too risky. You've no reason to become involved.'

Kate frowns. 'You don't have a monopoly on compassion', she says.

'I didn't mean that.'

'There are many people—people like me—who long to do something but don't know what or how.'

'Of course.' His tone is kindly but dismissive.

'Will you at least admit that I am less likely than you to be searched by the customs officer?'

Uriarte ponders. 'As a tourist? Yes.'

'Will you admit that after all that business in London, your baggage may be searched not just when you leave Cairo but also when you arrive in Rome?'

'It's possible.'

'If you really do want to help your friends', says Kate emphatically, 'then you must let me take the scroll.'

Uriarte still seems reluctant. 'I don't know. It could land you in trouble.'

'I could feign ignorance.'

'That's true.'

'And I'm a journalist. There would be a fuss if I were detained.'

'Perhaps.'

'They don't know that we're together. We're booked into separate rooms. If we check in separately and don't sit together . . .'

Uriarte looks uncertain. 'Perhaps.'

'You can't do everything on your own', she says. 'You must let others help.'

The fragment of the Nag Hammadi scroll is delicate. It has been sealed in an airtight flask and that flask fitted into a thermos that is three inches around and eight inches tall. It has an outer casing of blue-ribbed plastic, a black plastic stopper and over the stopper a black cup. Uriarte handles it carefully as he hands it to Kate. He reminds her of the fragility of the parchment. It is oddly heavy. Kate asks why. Uriarte explains that there is an inner lining of lead to protect the scroll from the radiation at 33,000 feet. He cannot show Kate the scroll because opening the thermos would break the vacuum. Perhaps there will be an opportunity for her to see it after it has been delivered to the dealer in Rome.

They are booked onto the same flight, but, to allay suspicion, they travel separately to the airport. Uriarte dithers about whether or not they have made the right decision—whether, as he said before, he is being irresponsible to let her take such a risk; or whether, as she insists, he owes it to his friends to follow the course of action most likely to succeed. In the last half hour before their departure, Kate becomes increasingly exasperated by his hesitation. She snaps at him: 'For God's sake, Juan. It's been decided. Now *go*.'

Uriarte leaves to take the bus to the airport. Kate packs her suitcase, then carefully places the thermos on its side on top of a pullover that she has laid at the bottom of the holdall she always carries into the cabin of the plane. She would normally have taken a bottle of mineral water but thinks it would be inconsistent, if asked about the thermos, to have two sources of in-flight hydration. She does not forget the fragility of the scroll and carries her holdall gently. As she pays her bill, she asks the owner of the guesthouse to call a taxi. He accompanies her to the door. A taxi is waiting. There is an exchange in Arabic between the two Egyptians as the driver places her suitcase in the boot. Kate keeps her holdall beside her on the back seat.

Kate stands in the queue at the Alitalia check-in desk, fighting back a sense of elation. By nature she is cautious and law-abiding, yet here she is risking . . . what? Incarceration in an Egyptian jail? A heavy fine? A criminal record that will blight her career? For whom? The Copts—people who twenty-four hours earlier she had not known existed. Was she doing it for them or to impress Uriarte? No, not to impress him but to earn his esteem—to show him that she is more than she seems.

Kate's suitcase is checked in. She goes to the security barrier and, guided by bored-looking airport staff, carefully lays her holdall on the belt. With nothing in her pockets, she steps through the frame without setting off the alarm and waits for her holdall. It comes out of the X-ray machine but, instead of trundling on rollers towards her, is redirected on a turn-table towards a bench. She walks over, identifies it as hers, and watches an irascible middle-aged security guard rummage through its contents. He takes out her keys and lays them on the table, then a bag containing her cosmetics, which he opens with a look of disdain. He takes out an eye-lining pencil and touches its point with his finger as if it might be construed as a weapon. His attention then moves to a pair of nail clippers with a hinged metal file. Again, he feels the point, but decides that this, too, would hardly enable Kate to hijack the plane. He returns the pencil and the nail clippers to the bag and zips it closed.

Now he takes out the thermos. 'What is this?'

'Iced water.'

He takes off the black cup that covers the stopper. 'It's heavy', he says.

'It's full', Kate replies.

He snaps the black cup back onto the top of the thermos and returns the thermos to the holdall. 'Very well. Have a good journey.'

Kate takes her holdall and sets off for the departure lounge. Her legs feel weak; for a moment she thinks she will swoon. She stops at a shop selling tacky Egyptian jewellery and steadies herself by holding on to the counter. She recovers and walks on to the gate. The waiting area is already crowded, but Kate catches sight of Uriarte sitting next to the soft-drink dispenser. She takes a seat facing away from him. She does not look to see whether he enters the plane in front of her or behind, but, walking up the aisle to her seat, she sees him already seated in the central set of seats. He is reading *Time Magazine*. She is obliged to stop beside his seat while those in front of her stow their baggage. She does not look down at Uriarte, nor does he take his eyes off his magazine.

Kate puts her holdall under the seat in front of her, afraid that the thermos might roll around in the overhead locker. She takes out her book, opens it on her lap but cannot focus on the words. After the plane has taken off, her eyelids close. The adrenaline seeps from her veins. She dozes off and odd thoughts pass in and out of her mind. Scrolls. Money. Persecuted Copts. Uriarte. Radiation. She had once interviewed a director of British Nuclear Fuels. He had talked about public ignorance on the doses of radiation they received from sources other than nuclear power stations. Boron gas in Cornwall; the granite in Aberdeen; or flying. The higher you fly, the less protection there is from the radiation that emanates from the sun. Rays go straight through the skin of the fuselage. Only lead offers any protection. How prescient of Uriarte to have realised this. Or was it the Copts?

She sleeps. She eats. She sleeps again, her book open on her lap. And then, sooner than expected, the Airbus slows and dips and the passengers are told that it has started its descent towards Rome.

The Death of a Pope

'We pray for our Pope, John Paul . . .'

When it comes to that routine intercession during the Mass in his private chapel, Cardinal Doornik stops, then repeats the prayer, asking God to bring an end to the suffering of Karol Wojtyła, who, the night before, had been taken to the Gemelli Hospital. What physical suffering this, the most vigorous of all pontiffs, has had to endure in the course of his life! Shot twenty-five years earlier by Turkish assassin Ali Agca—three bullets hitting his body: one tearing into his intestines, another lodging in his forearm, the third shattering the bones in his left index finger. Then, a month later, returning to the

123

Gemelli—his right lung inflamed with a herpes-type of viral disease—traced to contaminated blood used during the operation after the attempted assassination.

Ten years later, a tumour the size of an orange was removed from his bowels and, while they were at it, the surgeons removed his gall bladder because it was filled with stones. Already the malfunctioning of his nervous system—Parkinson's disease—had led the former athlete to fall while getting out of his bath and break his hip; to fall again during his trip to Poland in 1999, requiring three stitches in his scalp; and thereafter to give up walking down the aisle of Saint Peter's but instead sit on a mobile platform and say Mass seated on a hydraulic wheelchair. His words, too, were becoming harder and harder for him to enunciate until in October 2003, at the beatification of Mother Teresa of Calcutta, Pope John Paul II had been unable to preach even the opening lines of his sermon: it was left to another to speak his words for him.

But with what audacity has the man's spirit defied the failings of his flesh to the point where his suffering becomes a more eloquent witness to the truth than all his convoluted encyclicals, homilies and exhortations put together. Improvisation. Had he learned that as an actor in Warsaw? If you can't speak the lines, mime the meaning. He had always been a showman—an intellectual, of course, a phenomenological philosopher whose writings were often incomprehensible even to other phenomenologists. But he was also a performer—a man who staged a photo op at Assisi standing with a Muslim mullah, a Jewish rabbi, an Orthodox bishop, a Hindu monk, and an American Indian Medicine Man to show solidarity with the world's other religions while still insisting in the small print that his was the *spes unica*—the one true faith. He is confident that God has chosen him to be pope because he is a Pole, thereby hallowing Poland's uncompromising brand of Catholicism, a faith preserved in amber by Communism, but also giving the divine imprimatur to the idiosyncrasies of Karol Wojtyła—an almost idolatrous devotion to the Virgin Mary; an intransigence on the question of birth control; and, of course, a definitive prohibition on the ordination of women as priests.

A twinge in his stomach reminds Cardinal Doornik that he has not yet had breakfast. He gets on with the Mass. As he turns to give the final blessing, he sees that the two Dutch nuns who serve as his house-keepers are both in tears. They, too, no doubt, have been praying for the dying pontiff.

The Cardinal eats a Dutch breakfast: prunes and yoghurt for the sake of his bowels, a slice of rye bread with cheese and sausage, a second slice with butter and jam, orange juice and coffee. However, during Lent—and it is Lent—he gives up sausage and butter, small mortifications of the flesh. His coffee is also Dutch, Douwe Egberts, as Doornik finds Italian coffee too bitter and strong. *La Republica* and *L'Osservatore Romano* are laid on the table. He always chooses to read the first at breakfast on the grounds that he can learn more about what is going in the Vatican from the secular press than he can from *L'Osservatore Romano*.

The Pope is dying. After his death there will be ten days of mourning, then a funeral, and finally a conclave to elect a new pope. A new pope ... For all his disagreements with John Paul II, and the hopes that the progressive wing of the Church hold for a new pontificate, Doornik finds it difficult to envisage anyone else in the Chair of Saint Peter. John Paul II has reigned for more than twenty-five years—a large part of Doornik's adult life. Doornik has often resented the way he exercised his authority, but he never questioned it. When John Paul II summoned him to Rome as Cardinal Prefect of the Congregation for Catholic Culture, he obeyed despite knowing that the promotion was not a reward for loyalty but rather an acceptable way of removing a thorn in the flesh of the universal Church. As a bishop, Doornik's tolerance of theological dissent in his diocese was well known; his own silence on some of the rulings made in Rome—on women priests, on intercommunion with the Lutherans, on admitting remarried Catholics to the Eucharist, on the sinfulness of homosexual relations and above all his views on collegiality and the autonomy of each bishop in his own diocese—made him persona non grata to Pope John Paul II and his closest advisers, namely, Cardinal Ratzinger, Cardinal Sodano, Cardinal Arinze. The Pope could hardly dismiss him—Doornik was popular in his diocese—but he could emasculate him by denying him a diocese. So Doornik was called to Rome. His successor as bishop was not one of his coadjutors but a monsignor who had been working with Cardinal Ratzinger in the Holy Office. A member of Opus Dei.

It was this move, of course, that had made Doornik a hero to the liberal wing of the Church. Everyone knew that his 'promotion' was a move to eject him from his power base, and the very fact that he was considered a danger enhanced his standing among liberal Catholics. Martyrs become leaders and, while Doornik was hardly under house arrest in his apartment in the Vatican, he came to be seen in progressive circles as an Aung San Suu Kyi, confined to her home in Burma, or even an Ayatollah Khomeini, exiled in France.

Over the past ten years, Doornik has grown into this role. Publicly, his statements have been limited to condemning pornography on television or ruling on whether churches could be used as concert halls, but privately, when giving retreats or in 'off the record' talks given in seminaries or Catholic universities, he has been able in an oblique way to let it be known that his views on those litmus-test issues have not changed. He has talked about 'a too exclusive emphasis on tradition' and has asked, 'Are we afraid of dialogue within the Church?' He has said that the emancipation of women 'poses a challenge for a Church that excludes women from its priesthood'. He has quoted the moral theologian Alberson: 'God is not interested in commandments but freedom.' And he has said that the Church must come to terms with a younger generation who believe that no one has the right to interfere in their private lives.

Doornik's delivery has always been quiet and persuasive: he has eschewed strident polemic. He brings into his talks historical anecdotes, but also reflections on the meanings of words, their etymological origins. He is unquestionably learned but also humble: after a display of erudition he confesses to some human frailty—a passion for chocolate, his support for Ajax—to show that he is a man like any other. His manner is modest, patient, kind; he looks holy with his Dürer-etched face, and his lean body suggests fasting and the mortification of the flesh. In fact, Doornik works out twice a week in a gym. *Mens sana in corpore sano*: a healthy mind in a healthy body. Had not Pope John Paul II built a swimming pool in the Vatican Palace?

Doornik has received many invitations to speak in different parts of the world—particularly the developed world—and the area of his apostolate has spread from his native Netherlands to France, Germany, England and the United States. Doornik speaks some French, Spanish and Italian and is fluent in German, English and, of course, Dutch. He has addressed crowded auditoriums in Catholic universities such as Leuven in Belgium or Notre Dame and Georgetown in the United States. He has developed bonds of friendship with like-minded diocesan bishops, and fellow cardinals such as Daniels in Malines, Hume in Westminster and Bernardin in Chicago.

Hume, it was said—and he confirmed this to Doornik in a private conversation—had gone through a 'dark night of the soul', a period of spiritual aridity, in his last years as Abbot of Ampleforth. This consoled Doornik because he too often has the sense of *Deus abscondicus*, of God being absent, even indifferent—God, who in his youth had seemed so close. He knew, of course, from his spiritual reading—from Thomas à Kempis and Ignatius Loyola—that this is a common experience for even the greatest saints; that it is God's way of showing that nothing could be done without him; that the Christian life is not following a code of conduct laid down by Jesus or striving to please, let alone placate, an almighty deity, but rather opening our hearts to the grace of God so that our thoughts and acts and prayers are not ours but those of Jesus—'not us', as Saint Paul had said, 'but Christ in us'.

Cardinal Hume's 'dark night of the soul' had ended when he had been chosen, quite unexpectedly, to be the Archbishop of Westminster, and now Doornik wonders whether the spiritual staleness that he has felt now for a number of years might also be coming to an end. Karol Wojtyła, Pope John Paul II, is dying and with his death will pass all the exceptional strengths but also the stubborn prejudices that pertained to the man. The cardinals will have to choose a new supreme governor of the Catholic Church: a man who will bring back the spirit of *aggiornamento* that animated Vatican II; a man who can read the signs of the times; a man who *embodies* the signs of the times; and a man who can alter the world's perception of the Catholic Church as something rigid, authoritarian and out of touch to something joyous, compassionate and understanding—a man like Bernardin or Hume, had either been still living; or like Cardinal Martini, had he been in better health or like Daniels, had he been younger; or even, possibly, a man such as the Prefect of the Congregation for Catholic Culture, Cardinal Doornik.

Doornik does not pray 'Oh God, make me pope.' Quite to the contrary, he has seen close at hand the intolerable demands made of the spiritual leader of more than a billion Catholics. However, true humility, to Doornik, is not self-denigrating but recognising what talents one has been given by God and how they might best be used. Who should now lead the Catholic Church? Not, certainly, a cardinal associated with the intransigent policies of Pope John Paul II such as Ratzinger or Sodano. An American pope would be unacceptable to the cardinals from the Third World. A majority of Catholics are now to be found in Africa, Asia and South America, but who among their bishops is *papabile*? Cardinal Arinze is black but as reactionary as Ratzinger. The South Americans strike poses but have no substance. Inescapably Doornik feels obliged to conclude that, with the possible exception of Cardinal Daniels, no one is better qualified than he to step into the shoes of Saint Peter, and should the call come from the cardinals in the conclave, he will obey. 'Not my will but thine be done.'

Kate's Return

Soon after Kate returns from Africa, Father Luke Scott spends the weekend at Peacock's Farm. He can see at once that his sister is anxious: she tells him that, in her view, Kate has not fully recovered and asks him to persuade her to go for a checkup at the Hospital for Tropical Diseases in London. She says this in a muted voice—almost a whisper—as she makes a pot of tea for her brother in the kitchen.

Luke does not see Kate until she comes into the living room, shortly before supper. It is clear from her appearance that she has been ill. She is very thin—a good twenty pounds lighter than when he last saw her. The skin on her face is taut over her cheekbones and there are deeper shadows under her eyes. This does not detract from her beauty but rather enhances it, making her seem older, wiser, more interesting. Something has happened in Africa that has changed Kate in ways that have yet to become apparent. Is it what she has suffered or what she has seen?

Luke senses at once that the change in Kate affects her attitude towards him. The look she directs towards him when she enters the room is one of enmity. She quickly recovers her self-control, kisses

him as she has always kissed him and says with a conventional polite-
ness how nice it is that he has come to stay.

As the weekend proceeds, Luke is reassured that he is not the sole
object of Kate's antagonism. Her mother's ministrations clearly irri-
tate her, and she seems exasperated whenever her father opens his
mouth. She spends long periods in her bedroom. It is clear to them
all that Kate wishes she were elsewhere. Luke recognises at once
what he calls 'First World re-entry Syndrome'—the impatience, iras-
cibility, even revulsion those who have been immersed in the poverty of the Third World feel on returning to their affluent, complacent
mother-country. He had felt it himself after he had served in the
missions in Africa. After witnessing the courage and good humour
of those with nothing but a mat to sleep on and a bowl for gruel,
the clutter of affluence—all the paraphernalia of the good life in
the developed world—leads to a mental nausea that takes weeks to
subside.

Charlie comes down on Saturday morning and teases his sister over
lunch. 'Ah, the Kate Moss look. Nothing like squitters for losing weight.
Do you remember Patsy? She went to India, ate the salad, drank the
water, practically licked the dung off the waiters' fingers, but failed to
get anything. . . . Solid stools from Kerala to Rajasthan. Came back as
fat as ever and in a rage. She wanted to sue the tour company.'

Kate tries to ignore Charlie's jibes and for the most part succeeds,
only occasionally saying 'shut up, Charlie' or 'do grow up'.

'Do tell us more', her mother says to her daughter. 'Wasn't it dangerous in Uganda? We read such terrible things.'

Kate tells her story. They listen. 'At first you think you cannot bear
to be among all this suffering, but then you see how the other aid
workers just get on with doing what they can, and how even the
smallest gesture—finding some felt tips and paper so that a child can
draw a picture, letting disabled girls play with your makeup, that kind
of thing—can actually make them forget their condition for an hour
or two, and that is better than nothing. But then I came down with
amoebic dysentery that wouldn't respond to the usual antibiotics, and
I became part of the problem rather than the solution.'

'It wasn't your fault, dear', says Caroline.

'No. But it was a distraction that Juan could have done without.'

'Juan?' Kate's father looks puzzled.

'The camel killer', says Charlie.

'Juan Uriarte,' says Kate, 'the man from the charity Misericordia who was showing me around. He felt responsible.'

Caroline turns to her husband, George. 'We really must thank him . . .'

'You don't have to thank him', says Kate, a trace of irritation showing on her face.

'We could at least make some contribution to the charity', says George.

'They do need money', says Kate.

'Yes', says Charlie. 'Charity doesn't come cheap.'

'What do you mean?' asks Kate sharply.

'Well, they have to pay the salaries of their workers for a start. It's the same with NGOs as it is with UN agencies or government. They have priorities, and at the top of the list are their own salaries and pensions and subsidised housing.'

'That's such nonsense', says Kate.

'I'll bet your Mr. Uriarte doesn't live in a mud hut.'

'He lives in a shed.'

'In Rome?'

Luke notices Kate blush. 'No, in Uganda.'

'In Rome, I dare say, he lives as the Romans do.'

'The charity puts him up. There's a flat. He has to live somewhere. But you really talk such rubbish, such ignorant rubbish!'

'Look at the UN', Charlie goes on. 'Tens of thousands of unaccountable bureaucrats paid lavish tax-free salaries to work at the World Health Organisation or the World Food Organisation . . . and the life expectancy in Africa is lower than ever before. It's an industry—aid, charity, whatever you like to call it—which pays good money for those who work in it to salve the conscience of the affluent in the developed world.'

'That's not true of Misericordia', says Kate.

'Maybe not. I'm sure your friend the camel killer earns a modest salary, but I bet he has benefits of another kind—travel, adventure, drama, the glorious feeling of doing good. No one will face up to the fact that the corporate lawyer in the city who buys coffee at Starbucks or cotton shirts from Harvie & Hudson is doing more good than the charity worker by providing proper work for those who grow the coffee and the cotton.'

Luke sees that his niece is about to explode. 'The word "charity"', he says to Charlie, 'means love. It is not an industry or an economic system but a sign of solidarity with the poor to show precisely that human relations are *not* just a matter of buying and selling, that men are not just donkeys who move only if hit by a stick or enticed by a carrot.'

'The Good Samaritan . . .' George Ramsey begins.

'He had money', says Charlie. 'He could pay the innkeeper.'

'That's true,' says Luke, 'but he could have chosen to spend his money on other things.'

'Like the ceiling of the Sistine Chapel or the Vatican Palace!' says Charlie, a mild mockery in his tone of voice.

'Monks take vows of poverty, not priests.'

'And *individually* monks may not own property, but *institutionally* they are as greedy and ostentatious as anyone else. They start out as hermits living in caves and end up with palatial monasteries like Cluny or Melk or Monte Cassino!'

Luke lowers his head. 'It is true. The original simplicity is rarely sustained.'

The cook, Mrs. Spurling, has made a Queen of Puddings that Charlie gobbles up as he is talking before he rises for a second helping. Kate has put some on her plate, but, after one or two mouthfuls, lays down her spoon. Her mother looks plaintively towards her. 'Oh, do eat up, darling. You're so thin.'

'I'm not hungry, Mother.'

'But Mrs. Spurling cooked it especially because she knew you liked it.'

'I know. But you can't suddenly stuff yourself.'

'Of course you can't', says George Ramsey, standing even though Charlie is still eating. 'And anyway, we all eat too much.'

The Walk

The family disperses. Luke goes to his room. He lies on his bed and opens a book but after reading half a paragraph falls asleep. He dreams.

He is one of the acolytes standing behind Pope John Paul II as he tries to speak, croaking out his blessing from the balcony of Saint Peter's. He turns back in his wheelchair and looks angrily at Luke as if he were responsible for his condition. There is white foam on the corner of his mouth. Luke leans forward to wipe away the foam with a white cloth, but to his dismay he sees that the cloth is a corporal, the white square of linen placed beneath the chalice during the Mass. Is it sacrilegious to use it to wipe away spittle? He turns. Smiling cardinals urge him on. He looks back at John Paul II. The bristles on his ill-shaven upper lip make a rasping sound as Luke wipes the corners of his mouth. The Pope grasps his sleeve. He draws Luke towards him. He tries to whisper something in his ear. . . .

Luke wakes. What had the Pope said? What had he wanted to say? Luke dislikes dreaming because dreams are usually meaningless—rubbish tipped out of the subconscious mind—yet sometimes so powerful that they preoccupy him for the rest of the day. The source of this dream is clear enough. The pitiful condition of Pope John Paul II over the preceding weeks and the painful spectacle of his last appearance at the balcony of Saint Peter's has affected Luke deeply. He has loved and admired Karol Wojtyła, and he saw his election in 1978 as providential, bringing to an end the covert apostasy that had been foisted on the faithful in the wake of Vatican II. Would the new pope be as steadfast? Or would he be weak like Pope Paul VI? No doubt that was the anxiety behind the dream.

Luke goes to the washbasin in his bedroom and splashes his face with cold water. After he has dried it with a hand towel, he leaves the bedroom and goes downstairs. It is a quarter to four, time for a walk before tea. He goes through to the cloakroom to borrow a walking stick, a Barbour and some boots. Once through the back door, he looks up at the sky to see if it might rain. There have been moments of sunshine followed by showers all day, and always a cold wind. As he stands there, the door behind him opens and Kate comes out—also dressed for a walk. Their eyes meet.

'Are you going for a walk?' asks Luke.

'Yes.'

'Perhaps we could go together.'

Kate hesitates. 'If you like.'

Luke pays no attention to her reluctant tone but leads her towards the gate into the woods behind Peacock's Farm.

'It must be difficult to reacclimatise to an English spring', he says.
'Yes.'

'And to the old routine.'

'It ...' She gropes for the right words. 'You feel that ... I don't know, that while in Africa, though you couldn't understand the language, you somehow knew what people meant; while here, everyone speaks English, but what they say is incomprehensible.'

'Charlie?'

'Yes, and ...' She waves her hand to signify others besides Charlie.

'He likes to argue. He doesn't always mean what he says.'

'I know. He does it to put me down.'

Luke waits for a moment, then says: 'Possibly he's a little jealous of you?'

'Jealous?'

'Jealous of the attention and perhaps jealous, too, that you have found a cause.'

Kate thinks for a moment. 'Perhaps.'

'Sibling rivalry is an odd thing', says Luke. 'Brothers and sisters will die for one another yet are constantly competing.'

'You and Mum?'

'We're beyond that now.'

They walk on for a moment in silence; then Kate says: 'It's difficult when you find you don't speak the same language as the people you love.'

Luke senses that Kate is not just talking about Charlie. 'Do *we* not speak the same language?' he asks her.

'Not really, no.' Her voice is cold—almost hard.

'I feel', he begins, choosing his words carefully, 'that perhaps what you hear is not what is being said.'

'Oh, what is being said is clear enough!' Kate says, the anger now out in the open. 'Sex is sinful unless it is open to the creation of human life. So it is a sin to use condoms and, as a result of that teaching, hundreds of thousands of Africans contract AIDS, which is bad enough when you see it on television but when you hold dying children in your arms, as I did in Uganda—see and *smell* the dreadful sores and fungal infections—when you understand that what little life they had to enjoy is snatched from them because in the Middle Ages a fusty old friar called Thomas Aquinas saw a way for the Church to

133

hijack the Renaissance by adopting Aristotle's concept of natural law! Really, Uncle Lolo, it is cruel and heartless and *criminal*, and those who defend it are *evil people*.'

Luke says nothing. He rehearses in his mind all the arguments put forward by the Church: that condoms are no solution; that they may offer some protection in the short term, but in the long term they encourage the very promiscuity that leads to an increase in HIV infection; that condoms, anyway, are not foolproof—that they have a limited effectiveness even in preventing pregnancy, and this despite the fact that a woman is only fertile for three days of her cycle, and so for a man who is HIV positive to use a condom when making love to his wife is like playing Russian Roulette, pointing a revolver with a bullet in one chamber, not at his own heart but at hers. Should he articulate these thoughts to Kate? No, because the premises from which their two lines of reasoning depart are themselves so different—hers being the well-being of the body, his the well-being of the soul.

'It cannot be evil to do the will of God', he says.

Kate has been waiting like a terrier outside a rabbit hole. She pounces. 'And does God really want people to suffer like that? Should they regard it as a privilege, perhaps, to have so much to "offer up" and feel sorry for yuppies like Charlie who have so little!'

Her voice is scornful. Luke looks down at the muddy path that runs alongside the wood. He feels a chill dismay at the thought that the human being he cares about more than anyone else—for whom, without hesitation, he would sacrifice his own life—has come to despise him, not because of who he is but what he believes.

'We have a body and we have a soul', he says. 'Heresies such as Manichaeism have tried to divide them: they taught that the soul was created by God and was good, while the body, created by the devil, was evil. Today we tend to believe the opposite: that the body is good and the soul, well . . . no one talks much about the soul. And the body *is* good, but the nature of that goodness is misconstrued. It is much more than the sum of our thoughts and sensations, which will cease when we die. The body will be raised *immortal*. "He who eats my flesh and drinks my blood will live forever." God, a being of pure spirit, so mysterious and awe-inspiring that the Jews dared not speak his name, became a man—a two-legged *homo sapiens*—who accepted torture and death as the scapegoat for our sins. And he left us not just his teaching but also his flesh. You may find the idea gruesome, even preposterous. So did many of those listening to him at the time. They started arguing with one another: "How can this man give us his flesh to eat?" And many of his disciples left him. Only a few remained. "Where else are we to go?" asked Saint Peter. No doubt he was as baffled as the others by what Jesus had said, but he trusted that in due course all would be made clear. And it was. At the Passover supper in the upper room, Jesus took a piece of bread in his hands and said, "*This* is my Body", and then a cup of wine saying, "*This* is my Blood". The full audacity of God's plan of salvation was now clear. We are no longer dust that will return to dust, but by receiving God in the Eucharist, we become divine. The body of Jesus rises from the dead. So will ours. This is why the human body is something sacred, something holy—what Saint Paul describes as "the temple of the soul"—and so what we do with our bodies is not simply to be evaluated in terms of appetite, pleasure or feeling. A Christian must make sure that everything he does is in accordance with the will of God, and it is this that contradicts the modern cult of self-abandon—the satanic *nostalgie de la boue.*'

Luke looks at his niece. She avoids his eyes. In so far as he can see any expression on her face, it is determined, almost cruel. 'I have to say, Uncle Lolo,' she says, 'that all that sounds no more likely to me than *The Chronicles of Narnia* or *Harry Potter*, which would be fine if it had no more effect on the world than any other fairy story, but as a basis of a system of ethics that condemns a couple who take an elementary precaution against infection by a fatal disease when they have sex seems actually pernicious.'

'But don't you see,' asks Luke, unable to prevent desperation coming into his tone of voice, 'that it is also the system of ethics that sets our species apart from all the others, and makes each human life of equal worth? *The Church cares desperately for the well-being of humanity in this world*—it does more to care for the sick and the displaced in Africa than any other single institution—but it cannot put the well-being of the body over the well-being of the soul because Jesus himself warned that if you do, both may suffer eternally in Hell.'

Kate snorts. 'Hell! No one believes in that anymore, Uncle Lolo, except you. Not even Catholics. I don't think I've ever heard it mentioned in a sermon when, if it really did exist and we might go there, we would be warned about it every week.'

Luke cannot contradict her. He says nothing. They change the subject. They talk about George, Caroline, Charlie, Mrs. Spurling, the weather. When they reach the house and go their separate ways, it is Luke who avoids looking at Kate for fear of seeing a glint of triumph in her eyes.

Inquiries

Kate is offered a lift up to London on Sunday night by both her brother and her uncle, but, unable to face any more of Charlie's banter or another homily from her Uncle Lolo, she stays at Peacock's Farm until Monday morning. Her mother begs her to remain longer, but Kate has had enough of her parents' solicitude and of being told how thin she is by Mrs. Spurling. She is also aware that she has behaved badly. Her illness—or perhaps it was the experience of Africa—has taken its toll: she has been constantly on edge, snapping at everyone and irritated at almost everything anyone says, yet at the same time she is annoyed at herself for showing her irritation. It is not the fault of her family, after all, that they have remained the same while she has changed, finding their affluence somehow offensive and their opinions intolerably self-serving. If there really is a Hell, as her Uncle Lolo believes, then surely the entire Western bourgeoisie is damned.

Kate is miserable without Uriarte. After landing at Fiumicino on the flight from Cairo, she had taken a taxi into the city and checked into the Hotel Novali close to the Piazza Mazzini. There she had taken a shower, put on some clean clothes and then waited. Two hours later there was a tap on her door: she had opened it and there was Uriarte. They had embraced; then Kate had triumphantly produced the thermos from her bag. Rather than take it from her, Uriarte had simply glanced at it saying, 'Excellent. It was just as well . . .' His baggage *had* been opened and inspected at the Cairo airport and again when he had reached Rome. Indeed, at Fiumicino he had been strip-searched by a plain-clothes policeman while uniformed customs officers looked on.

'They must have been tipped off, probably by someone in the Patriarch's curia. They were hoping to catch me red-handed.'

'And the Italians?'

Uriarte had shrugged. 'I don't know. That may be something to do with my troubles in London.'

Kate had made another attempt to give him the thermos, but he had waved his hand dismissively saying: 'That can wait. Wouldn't you like some supper? Or did you eat the *porqueria* they served on the plane?'

'No, I'd love some supper.'

They had gone out to a small restaurant then returned to the hotel and made love. How different are the ways in which a man can make love. That night Juan had seemed wild, triumphant, yet when they awoke the next morning in one another's arms, he had nuzzled her and caressed her and then made love to her in a gentler, lazier way. He had then looked at his watch and, muttering *'per dios'*, leaped out of bed, taken a shower, dressed quickly and, leaning down to give her a quick kiss, said: 'I must get back to work. And you must get back to work. Write. Write something—something *muy brillante.*'

'I will.' She had smiled up at him, concealing the trace of disappointment she felt that they should part so abruptly. Of course, he could not take her to the airport—she understood that—but they might have had breakfast together, she did not have to leave until eleven.

'Ah, the scroll', said Uriarte. 'I mustn't forget that.'

'No, most certainly not. It's there, in my bag.'

Uriarte transferred the thermos carefully from Kate's holdall into his own. 'I will not tell my friends,' he said, 'that it was you who brought it into the country. It is better that no one knows you are involved. But if they knew, they would be eternally grateful.' He hesitated for a moment, as if pondering what he had just said. 'Yes, *eternally* grateful. I think that for once that is the right word.'

Kate finds it hard to go back to normal life. The train from Petersfield, Waterloo Station, the Underground all seem banal, and her little house in Brook Green, empty for so long, now has a musty smell which somehow seems part of the mustiness of England. Her fridge is empty so she walks to the Tesco on Shepherd's Bush Road, past the playground where mothers, nannies and *au pairs* are pushing children on the swings or chatting to one another as their charges sway on see-saws or climb up steps onto the slides. A couple of old drunks are sitting on the grass clutching cans of beer.

The Tesco store itself is unchanged, and Kate walks down the aisles picking out the items she wants—a baguette, *crème fraiche*, Milano salami, olive oil, tomato paste, vermicelli, a tin of anchovies, butter, apple juice. The list is much the same as it had been in that earlier life—BU, before Uriarte—and it is only when she finds herself staring at a free-range chicken, wondering whether she should have some friends over for a small dinner party, to catch up after her month away, that she realises that she would have to re-ground herself in her own life: she cannot continue indefinitely in a bubble, thinking of Uriarte.

Kate walks back across the Shepherd's Bush Road carrying two bulging plastic bags, along the north side of Brook Green, then up towards Masboro Road. She should ring Barney; he might give her some advice on how to pitch a piece on her trip. She has to decide where she will try to place it and tailor it accordingly. *The Guardian* or *The Independent* are the obvious choices but neither will like the idea of promoting the work of a Catholic charity like Misericordia. The *Sunday Telegraph*, perhaps, or the Saturday *Telegraph Magazine*.

Kate reaches her house. A man is standing at the door. She comes up behind him and asks: 'Can I help you?'

The man turns. It is David Kotovski.

'Hello', she says, surprised but not displeased to see him. 'What are you doing here?'

'I was passing.'

'Come in.'

Kotovski steps aside. Kate puts down one of her bags, takes her keys from her handbag and opens the front door. She turns to retrieve the second bag but sees that Kotovski has picked it up and is now following her into the house. She goes through to her kitchen and puts her bag on the table. Kotovski does the same.

'Thanks. Would you like a cup of coffee?' She takes the chicken out of the first bag and puts it in the fridge.

Kotovski does not answer. He seems uncomfortable. He looks through the second bag for perishable goods and hands her a carton of milk, a packet of butter, the *crème fraiche*. 'What about this?' He holds up a pack of fresh parsley. Kate hesitates. 'No, leave that. I'll deal with it later.' She takes the electric kettle to the tap and half fills it with water.

'Coffee?' she repeats. 'Or tea?' He still looks confused. Kate is not. Though she has hardly thought of him since leaving for Africa, she remembers that he had seemed to like her and now assumes that is why he has dropped by.

'Yes', he says finally. 'I would like some coffee, but I'd better come clean.'

'Come clean?'

'This isn't really a social call.'

The kettle rumbles. She turns to face him, leaning against the kitchen unit. 'Are you selling something?' She smiles.

'It's ... official business.'

'Official business?' She repeats his words with a frown.

'I work for the Security Service.'

'I see.'

She turns and takes two mugs, a spoon and the jar of powdered coffee.

'I couldn't tell you at the time of the trial.'

'I understand.' To her own surprise, a bitter tone had entered into her voice. She had been deceived. So what? It went with his job. Why should she care? 'So all that business about covering the trial for *The Law Review* or whatever it was ...'

'That was my cover.'

'I see.'

'Uriarte ...' he begins.

'He was acquitted', she says sharply.

'I know. But ...'

'You think he's up to something?'

'Yes.'

Kate pours hot water into the mugs, then milk from a carton. She does not understand why she suddenly feels annoyed. 'You know, I assume', she says coldly, handing one of the mugs of coffee to Kotovski, 'that I have been in Africa with Uriarte?'

'Yes.'

She sits down at the kitchen table. After a moment's hesitation, Kotovski does the same.

'Do you want to know why?'

Kotovski waves his hand in the air as if a vague gesture will make up for the lack of an answer.

'I was impressed, during the trial, by what Uriarte said about his work in Darfur', says Kate. 'I thought it would make a good story. I went to see him in Rome. He offered to show me the work of his agency—Misericordia International—in Africa.'

'Not in Darfur', says Kotovski.

'Clearly, he could not go back to Sudan. Thanks to you.'

Kate regrets the last phrase, but Kotovski does not seem put out. 'You went to see him in Rome in March. Is that correct?'

'Yes.'

'And later met him in Kampala?'

'Yes. He took me to the Misericordia refugee camp in northern Uganda. There I fell ill. Amoebic dysentery. I went to Malindi to recuperate.'

'With Uriarte?'

'He took me there but didn't stay.'

'Do you know where he was while you were in Malindi?'

Kate hesitates. She does not want to say anything that might incriminate Uriarte, but it would be futile to deny what Kotovski almost certainly knows. 'I believe he went to Egypt, to a conference of aid workers.'

'That is what he told you?'

'Yes.'

'When he returned to Malindi?'

'He came back to fetch me.'

'To fetch you?'

'I had been very ill. He felt responsible.'

'Why?'

Kate frowns. 'He had invited me to Africa. He wanted the work of Misericordia to be better known. He thought my project was important.'

'He was keen to cultivate you?'

'As I said, he felt responsible.'

'If he had been anxious about your well-being, wouldn't it have been better to have sent you straight home?'

'I was over the illness. The idea was to convalesce in Malindi.'

'And when you left Malindi, did you fly back to London?'

'Juan was going back by way of Cairo. I went with him. He offered to show me the city.'

'Do you know *why* he went back via Cairo?'

'No. It may have been something to do with his ticket. Or perhaps it was to be nice to me—to make up for what I had gone through.'

'Wasn't a luxury hotel in Malindi enough?'

Kate frowns. Kotovski's questions are becoming intrusive. 'What has that got to do with anything?'

Kotovski blushes and looks down at his open notebook. 'What interests us', he says, as if trying to share the responsibility for his line of questioning with others, 'is what Uriarte did, or might have done, while you were in Cairo.'

'We looked at the pyramids and sphinxes and went to the Cairo Museum ...'

'Was he with you all the time?'

'Most of the time.'

'But there were times when he went out alone?'

'Yes. He was more energetic than I was. I was still weak.'

'You stayed in the same hotel.'

'It was more like a guesthouse.'

'Were you in the same room?'

'That's none of your business.'

Kotovski blushes. 'I only ask because if you had separate rooms, you couldn't know when he came and went.'

'He had his own room', says Kate, 'but he slept in mine.'

Kotovski seems taken aback by this admission. Kate's tone is deliberately brazen; her sex life is none of his business, but she is damned if she is going to be coy.

'Do you know', he asks, seeming to choose his words carefully, 'if Juan Uriarte picked up anything from Cairo that he then took to Rome?'

Kate looks away. 'I would doubt it', she says. 'He travelled light.'

'No flask or canister?'

Kate shakes her head. 'No. I would have noticed.'

Kotovski now looks directly into Kate's eyes. 'Did he give *you* anything to take for him?'

Kate looks at him and smiles. 'That's the question they always ask when you check in.'

'And?'

'I packed my own suitcase. I carried nothing for anyone else.'

'Are you sure? Are you absolutely sure?'

'Yes, I'm sure.'

'You see . . .' Now he hesitates and the expression that comes onto his face is not accusatory but anxious. 'There is a danger that you could be an accessory to a serious crime.'

Kate flushes with anger. 'Are you talking about nerve gas?'

'Yes.'

'Won't you people ever give up? Juan was acquitted because it was blindingly obvious that he is not a terrorist or a lunatic but a man who deeply cares about the suffering of others and, unlike the rest of us, is prepared to do something about it.'

'Do what?'

'Do what he does already—and more. If you'd seen him at work in the refugee camps, with the sick and the dying, you would realise that his life's work is to *save* life, not take it.'

'We have been told that a man answering his description made contact with Muslim extremists in Cairo to obtain nerve gas.'

A policeman's expression: 'answering his description'. 'It could not have been Juan.'

'Uriarte was looking for nerve gas before, and we have reason to suspect that he has now obtained it.'

'Juan? Just because . . . What's your source?'

'An Egyptian.'

'Tortured, no doubt, so that he'd say anything. And, anyway, the people Juan saw in Cairo were not Muslims, they were Copts.'

'Copts?'

'Yes. Copts. Christians who are *persecuted* by the Muslims.'

'I know about the Copts', says Kotovski.

'He wants to help them—to raise funds in Europe and America. He'd like me to write about their plight as well as that of the refugees in Uganda.'

'But so far as you know they gave him nothing?'

'Nothing.'

'And he gave you nothing to take to Rome?'

'Nothing', says Kate. 'Nothing at all.'

She was lying. Of that Kotovski is sure. Seventy percent sure. Perhaps eighty percent sure. Lying, anyway, about some things but perhaps not others. She is in love with Uriarte, therefore nothing she says about him can be trusted. When it comes to their children or their lovers, facts become subservient to women's visceral instincts. It is like primitive patriotism: my country, right or wrong. Does that mean that she is complicit in his conspiracy? Only if it involves something like the killing of camels; he cannot believe that she would collaborate in the mass murder of human beings. Even so, she would have been taking an insensate risk if she had knowingly carried a phial of Sarin from Cairo to Rome. The Italians might have searched her as well as Uriarte.

Finding nothing on him had, of course, confirmed the view of the Italians that he posed no threat to Italian security. There was a 'we told you so' tone to their e-mails. And it had been hard for Kotovski to come up with a hypothesis that would alarm them. Certainly, Rome was teeming with people who had come to pray for the dying Pope, creating a perfect gathering for a chemical attack, and it was conceivable that Al-Qaida or some off-shoot could see some value in massacring thousands of Christians in the Holy City. But what would be in it for Uriarte? Killing fellow Catholics does not fit his profile. That is the riddle at the core of their investigation: *What is the Sarin for?*

Kotovski reports back to his boss BB and receives a reprimand for interviewing Kate Ramsey on his own. It is a breach of protocol. Kate Ramsey could accuse him of harassment or worse. However, if he—Kotovski—thinks that she might have acted as a courier for Uriarte, he should report the matter to Paget.

A meeting is fixed for that afternoon at Vauxhall Cross. Once again Kotovski is picked up by Ashton in his Ford Focus. Kotovski tells him about his conversation with Kate Ramsey.

'And?'

'I think she's got herself into something she doesn't understand.'

'You fancy her, don't you?' says Ashton.

Kotovski frowns. 'I think she deserves better ...'

'Better being you?'

'Better than a ten-year sentence for aiding and abetting.'

Paget, like BB, frowns when Kotovski tells him that he has talked to Kate Ramsey. 'Our American friends should have been consulted before making a move like that. If she *is* involved with Uriarte, your visit will have put both of them on their guard.'

'I cannot believe that Ramsey is complicit in terrorism', says Kotovski.'

'Yet you think she lied about smuggling something into Italy for Uriarte?'

'Yes. But she may not have known it was Sarin.'

'*May* not have known.' Paget pauses, as if giving Kotovski time to appreciate the contradiction between the certainty of his first assessment and the uncertainty of the second.

'I would even say it was inconceivable', says Kotovski.

'Whether she did or did not know, why Rome?'

Kotovski shakes his head. 'I don't know.'

'To kill Catholics', says Ashton.

'Why should Uriarte want to kill Catholics?' asks Kotovski.

'Why indeed,' says Paget, 'unless ...' He pauses, following his own train of thought in silence.

'What?' asks Kotovski.

'Let's take Uriarte at face value. Let us assume that he really does care about Africa. Let us speculate further that his concern is not just for the conflict in Darfur but also for the wider pan-African conflict between Christianity and Islam. He has dealt with Muslim extremists; he knows their intransigence and ambition to convert the world with the sword. He knows, too, that the campaign is succeeding. In every country where there is a Muslim majority, Christians are persecuted and oppressed, and if they can, they leave. The Christian communities are dwindling: soon they will be extinct. To him Islam is the enemy, and the enemy succeeds because we in the West accept double standards. Mosques are built in Rome, but no churches are allowed in Mecca. Indeed, churches in Islamic countries are desecrated and burned. Christians are persecuted. Nothing is done. Why? Because the Western democracies, though more powerful than the Islamic nations, are essentially indifferent to religion. They don't really mind if churches are burned in faraway countries. Seventy percent of Americans are Christian, but they are Baptists and Pentecostals who dislike Catholics as much as they dislike Muslims and are too parochial to take a worldview. To galvanize public opinion against Islam, to bring it to a pitch where something *had* to be done, there would have to be something far more dramatic than burning a few churches in Pakistan or imprisoning a priest in Saudi Arabia for saying Mass. There would have to be something on the scale of 9/11. A major atrocity. Something huge.'

'Such as a Sarin bomb in Saint Peter's Square?' suggests Ashton.

'While the crowds await the puff of white smoke.'

'Are you then suggesting', Kotovski asks, 'that Uriarte is bluffing the Muslims in Cairo?'

'Bluffing them? Perhaps. Or maybe he is offering to be the instrument of their *jihad*.'

'But are they so stupid that they don't realise that such an atrocity would be counter-productive?'

Paget shrugs. 'It depends upon one's perspective. The Serbs' slaughter of Muslims in Kosovo precipitated the intervention of the Western powers, and just because it was so obvious that it would do just that, it is possible that it was in fact the Albanians who staged the whole thing. And 9/11? One could not predict that it would lead to the invasion of Iraq, but that it did was a bonus for Al-Qaida. Saddam Hussein, after all, was a Ba'ath Socialist: he made short work of Islamic fundamentalists. Deposing Sadam took the lid off the pressure cooker, and if any group is now benefiting from the post-war chaos, it is precisely the allies of Al-Qaida.'

'The law of unintended consequences', says Ashton.

'For the Americans, perhaps, but for Al-Qaida the law of probable, even intended consequences. The more they can provoke conflict between Islam and the West, the better. And nothing would provoke that conflict more effectively than an atrocity in Rome.'

'Are you suggesting that Uriarte *knows* this?' asks Kotovski.

'For them both it is a grotesque gamble', says Paget. 'For Al-Qaida it is a dramatic demonstration of their ability to mount an attack in the heart of Christendom. For Uriarte it is a sacrifice of a thousand pilgrims that will galvanize the West to mount a new crusade. The conflicting ideologies meet at their extremes. They join hands to throw the dice, both confident that God will ensure that their numbers come up.'

Kotovski takes the Uriarte dossier back to his flat that night, leafing through it as he watches the ten o'clock news on television. Pope John Paul II is dying. He has been brought back to the Vatican at his own request from the Gemelli Hospital, where he had refused the offer of a life-support system. The Last Sacraments have been administered by his faithful secretary, Archbishop Dziwisz. He lies in a coma while tens of thousands of pilgrims pray for the pontiff they love. The via della Conciliazione and the bridge over the Tiber are teeming with people who will remain in Rome for the Pope's funeral and the conlave. Kotovski's eyes flit from the screen to the dossier then back from the dossier to the screen, and, despite his fatigue, he feels a growing alarm that many of those pilgrims may die if he does not do something to save them.

Kotovski rehearses in his mind the known facts to distinguish them from conjecture.

1. Juan Uriarte, a Basque aid worker, has tried to buy nerve gas in London.

2. His defence, that the nerve gas was to deter the Janjaweed in Darfur, was accepted by the jury but not by the prosecuting authorities, the police or MI5.

3. Investigations have proceeded on the premise that Uriarte wants the nerve gas for some other purpose.

4. Uriate's movements since his trial have been consistent with his duties as an aid worker: he returned to Rome, then went to Uganda.

5. He has gone to Egypt—twice. On the first occasion, it was to attend a regional conference of aid workers in Alexandria. On the second, it was to show the city to Kate Ramsey. While he was there, according to Kate, he was in contact with Copts.

6. Reports relayed by the CIA from the Mukhabarat indicated that in Cairo a Caucasian male—European or American—had made contact with Islamic extremists allied to the Muslim Brotherhood. Was the man Uriarte? Was he looking for nerve gas? There is no definitive answer to either question.

7. Juan Uriarte was searched both on leaving Cairo and on arriving in Rome. No nerve gas was in his possession. Thus, if he has

obtained nerve gas in Cairo for use in Rome, someone else must have brought it for him. A sympathetic Egyptian? Likely to be known to the Mukhabarat and so searched. A Western tourist? Unlikely to be searched. Kotovski is back to Kate.

What is known about her? On the face of it, a straightforward Sloane—father in the City, mother a lady of leisure, brother a hedge-fund manager ... The chances of a girl from that background entering into a terrorist conspiracy are remote. And yet she is more than she seems, or is more than she seems to Kotovski. He has looked through her photograph album, read her correspondence, rifled through the clothes in her drawers: there had been nothing unusual there. What he has seen has not led him to change the profile he and Ashton have tentatively established based on the known facts, but, having now seen her and talked to her and even been the butt of her irritation and dislike, he feels doubly sure that she is more than she seems. Her face is different. Kotovski cannot get the image out of his mind. Even when she was irritated—and she was clearly irritated by his enquiries—there was something charming in her expression: the puckered brow, the square-set jaw. Her eyes, though they had met his with a righteous, even brazen, expression, were huge and blue. He had noted—not in his analyst's notebook but in a personal compartment of his mind—her thick brown hair, her slight figure, her long legs and, to his confusion, had felt a surge of a jealous rage when she had said that she and Uriarte had shared a bed.

The facts. Kotovski must not let his feelings get in the way of his professional judgement. Everything suggests that Kate is no different from a thousand other girls from privileged families living in the home counties—posh school, good university, prestigious profession, pretending to be ambitious until they meet the right man; then, after a year or two of going out together, marriage, a mortgage and children winkled into posh schools, good universities, prestigious profession—all predictable except her affair with a middle-aged Basque and that other anomaly that suggested an unconventional gene: her mother's brother was not a banker or a businessman but a Catholic priest.

On Westway there is a steady column of theatre-goers returning to the Chilterns in their BMWs but little traffic going into town: it takes Kotovski only twenty minutes to drive from Acton to Marylebone. He has telephoned the priest, saying that he must talk to him that night. The priest had asked if it could wait until the morning. Kotovski had said it could not.

Kotovski rings the bell at the entrance to the building on Devonshire Street. He speaks his name into the intercom. There is a pause and then the words 'fourth floor' followed by a buzz that enables Kotovski to enter. He takes the lift and finds the door to Father Scott's flat ajar. He pushes it open, enters the flat, closes the door behind him and passes through the small vestibule into the book-lined living room. An elderly man sits on an armchair facing away from the door. He mutes the television—*CSI Miami*—and gets to his feet. 'One moment', he says. He fumbles with the controls of the remote, and the picture of the forensic experts from Florida fades from the screen.

Now he turns and holds out his hand to Kotovski. 'Come and sit down.' He shows no resentment or surprise: priests, Kotovski remembers, expect to be called upon at any time of the day or night. Kotovski sits on an armchair next to the television. The priest, dressed in black trousers and a dark blue jersey over a white open-necked shirt, resumes his seat and, after a brief look of regret at the blank screen, turns to Kotovski. 'How can I help you?'

'I work for the Security Service. We are making enquiries about your niece, Kate Ramsey.'

A look of great sadness comes onto the priest's face. 'Yes, Kate', he says; then again, 'How can I help?'

'She covered a case at the Old Bailey—three men charged under the Prevention of Terrorism Act with conspiracy to obtain toxic substances with the intent to take human life.'

'Yes', says the priest. 'I know about that.'

'The three were acquitted. One, a Basque called Juan Uriarte, works for a Catholic aid agency. Some time after the trial, your niece went to see him in Rome. It appears that she thought that his work would form the basis of an interesting article or series of articles.'

'Yes. She went to Rome, and then on to Uganda. She became very ill.'

'She went to Malindi to convalesce. She and Uriarte established a close relationship.'

'Yes', says the priest. 'I imagined as much.'

'On their way back to Europe, they stopped off in Cairo. They were there for two or three days. They stayed in the same guesthouse, and by her own admission they shared the same bed.'

'What has that to do with national security?' asks the priest.

'Nothing as such. It is only relevant because we have reason to believe that Juan Uriarte, while he was in Cairo, managed to obtain the nerve gas that he had failed to find in London.'

The priest frowns. 'For what purpose?'

'We don't know.'

'To kill camels in Darfur? Wasn't that his defence?'

'Yes.'

'The jury accepted what he said.'

'Yes, but we think they were mistaken.'

The priest nods. 'Yes, of course, the jurors could have been wrong. In which case he wants it for some other purpose.'

'Precisely. And we think—we fear—that he has in mind some atrocity, possibly in Rome.'

'To kill the pilgrims?'

'Yes.'

'But why?'

'We are not sure. Our present hypothesis is that the atrocity would be ascribed to Islamic extremists and so outrage the West that there would be an all-out war against Islam.'

'A crusade. Yes, well, the crusades began for similar reasons. But how is my niece involved?'

'Uriarte may have obtained the nerve gas in Cairo, but he did not bring it back with him to Rome. He was searched. Nothing was found. They were on the same flight but did not sit together. She was not searched. Is it possible that she might have taken the gas for him?'

The priest is silent. He does not seem outraged or upset at the suggestion: priests are familiar with all the vagaries of human nature. He remains silent for a while, and Kotovski does not press him, realising that his question has provoked deep thought.

Finally the priest looks up, as if deciding that his thoughts are sufficiently collected to be shared. 'In my view', he says, 'knowing Kate—having known her all her life—what you suggest is improbable but not impossible. She wants to do good, but there are times when impressionable people come under the influence of charismatic figures and, in the case of women, surrender not just their bodies but also their minds. You are too young to remember, but this was the case with the Baader-Meinhof gang in Germany and the Red Brigades in Italy.'

'Yes.'

'Now as I understand it, this man Uriarte is charismatic in some sense. And my niece, though she seems at first sight to be sane and sensible, has perhaps been looking for something—some issue, some ideal—to take the place of her lost faith. We all have a yearning to do good; it is implanted in our consciences by God. If Uriarte was to offer her a role in some radical plan for the betterment of humanity, then it is possible that she would take it. I cannot say more than that.'

'Even if it means the taking of innocent human life?'

The priest smiles. 'It didn't take much to persuade people that it was right to bomb Hiroshima, or more recently to invade Iraq. Most atrocities are committed by people sure of the righteousness of their cause.'

'If you were to ask her ...'

The priest shakes his head in a way that is both weary and sad. 'There was a time when we had no secrets, but now I am the last person in whom she would confide.'

Interregnum

The Pope is dead. The Polish acolytes who have cared for Pope John Paul II during the last hours of his mortal life now leave his bedside to make way for the Vatican officials whose duties in such circumstances are laid down in the Apostolic Constitution *Universi Dominici Gregis*. First, the Camerlengo of the Roman Catholic Church, Cardinal Eduardo Martinez Somalo, examines the corpse in the presence of the Master of Papal Liturgical Ceremonies and prelates of the Apostolic Camera. He confirms the judgement of the doctors. The Pope is dead. A death certificate is drawn up by the Chancellor of the Apostolic Camera. The body of Karol Wojtyła is removed to be prepared for public display. The doors of the late Pope's private apartments are locked and sealed by the Camerlengo, to be re-opened after the election of a new pope. Then, in accordance with the established procedures, the Camerlengo notifies the Archpriest of Saint Peter's Basilica, the Cardinal Vicar of the Diocese of Rome, the Prefect of the Papal Household and the Dean of the College of Cardinals, Joseph

Ratzinger. Cardinal Ratzinger in turn informs diplomats accredited to the Holy See, the Heads of State of different nations and the cardinals of the universal Church living in the four corners of the earth. They are told of the death of the 264th successor of Saint Peter and summoned to Rome to attend his funeral and to choose a new pope.

Cardinal Doornik is informed of the Pontiff's death just before midnight. With the official notification comes the reminder that, with the death of a reigning pope, all those he appointed to the different Curial departments lose office. Cardinal Doornik is no longer the Prefect of the Congregation for Catholic Culture: his duties devolve during the interregnum on his secretary, Monsignor Perez.

On hearing of the death of the Pope, Doornik weeps. Doornik is a little embarrassed by his tears. Saint John Chrysostom wrote that one should rejoice at the death of a Christian—particularly a Christian clearly destined for Heaven—and, despite his differences with Pope John Paul II, Doornik has no doubt that Karol Wojtyła is a saint. He was wrong on many issues but that had been inevitable, given his background. Wojtyła's father had served in the army of the Austro-Hungarian Empire, and he, like his protégés—the Bavarian Cardinal Ratzinger and Christoph Schönborn, the Cardinal Archbishop of Vienna—thought alike because they came from the same culture of Central European Catholicism. The Iron Curtain had isolated Wojtyła in Krakow from changes in Catholic attitudes in the rest of the world. But God was not a Central European, and the military template had become inimical to the contemporary *zeitgeist*. It was inevitable that the College of Cardinals would choose a pope of a quite different kind.

Just as he was mildly ashamed of his tears on hearing of the Pope's death, Doornik is now mildly ashamed of allowing himself to speculate on who might be the successor to Pope John Paul II. He reflects again on the extraordinary man who was such a signal witness to the Catholic Faith that thousands—hundreds of thousands—had come to Rome to say farewell. Who other than Karol Wojtyła could have drawn such a crowd? Who else, for that matter, could have pulled the Church together after the dithering last years of Pope Paul VI and the short, ineffectual reign of Pope John Paul I? And how else could he have done it than by those dramatic appearances before vast crowds?

At first, of course, he had been considered a reactionary, and some of Doornik's liberal friends had feared a return to the days of Pius X. They had turned out to be wrong. Pope John Paul II had made his own views plain—and he had clearly favoured those who shared his views in his episcopal appointments—but there had been no witch hunt. Pope John Paul II decided that he would govern the Church by example and exhortation, not by discipline and coercion: and, if many of the faithful were not at once persuaded, well, as Saint Peter himself had put it, 'with the Lord one day is as a thousand years and a thousand years as one day.'

Doornik is tired. It is time to go to bed. Wearing pyjamas and a dressing-gown, he goes to his private chapel and kneels to pray before the crucifix made of twisted pewter. He prays fervently for the soul of Karol Wojtyła and thanks God for the gift to the Church of that exceptional man. He then returns to his baroque bedroom, lies down on his narrow bed, sleeps and does not dream.

Monsignor Perez is waiting for him when Doornik arrives at his office at eight the next morning. Perez, too, has been greatly affected by the death of Pope John Paul II; he now kneels before Doornik and, as he kisses his ring, wets the Cardinal's hand with his tears. Doornik lays the hand that remains free on the head of the younger man—a gesture of comfort and also a blessing. Perez rises, brushes away his tears and blows his nose with a silk handkerchief.

'My dear Monsignor,' Doornik says, 'last night, I, too, was in tears.'

Perez lowers his head in grateful appreciation for what the Cardinal has said.

Though Cardinal Doornik is no longer a Prefect and Perez is notionally in charge, Doornik sits down as usual at his desk and Perez resumes his subordinate role. 'As you will see, your Eminence,' he says, pointing to the papers that have been laid out on the desk, 'a meeting of the General Congregation of the Cardinals has been called for this afternoon at four o'clock. All are to attend. There is the ceremonial breaking of the ring—the Fisherman's Ring—by the Cardinal Camerlengo. And the cardinals are to approve the minting of the coins and medals bearing his coat of arms.'

Doornik frowns. 'Is this customary?'

'Since 1521. It is to establish the authority of the cardinals during the interregnum. There is also a special *sedente vacante* issue of Vatican City postage stamps.'

Doornik nods to acknowledge that he has understood Perez' outline of the ancient protocols. 'Postage stamps . . .' he mutters almost inaudibly. He does not expect a reply.

'There are nine days of mourning', Perez goes on. 'The *novandi* as prescribed in the *Ordo Exsequiarum Romani Pontificis*. There will be the Rite of Visitation on Monday and the funeral itself will be on Friday, April 8, conducted by the Dean of the College of Cardinals.'

'Ratzinger', says Doornik.

'Yes, your Eminence. Cardinal Ratzinger. He will celebrate the Requiem Mass and, of course, preach the homily.'

'And the conclave?'

'This is prepared by the Cardinal Camerlengo and three other cardinals who will be chosen this afternoon. One must be from the order of bishops, another from the order of priests, the third from the order of deacons. Every three days, they are replaced by three other cardinals chosen by lot. They will handle minor matters, referring major decisions to the full College of Cardinals.'

Perez has a passion for the archaic customs and rituals of the Holy See—that is plain—and Doornik is happy if this outline of the minutiae distracts the Monsignor from his grief.

'There is of course one change from previous elections,' says Perez with a smile, 'and that is the construction of the Domus Sanctae Marthae, where your eminences will be housed for the duration of the conclave. It will not only be more comfortable than previous accommodation but will also be admirably secluded. There will be no communication with the outside world. Only a restricted group of assistants will be allowed access. . . .' Perez glances anxiously at Doornik as he says this; Doornik smiles and nods to reassure his secretary that this restricted group of assistants will include him.

'Conclave . . . *cum clave*—with a key', muses Doornik, 'to protect us from all influence from the outside world.'

'In fact, Eminence,' says Perez, 'it was a rule established by Pope Gregory X at the Council of Lyons in 1274 to lock the cardinals *in*, not keep others out. The cardinals, meeting in Viterbo to elect a successor to Pope Clement IV, failed to reach agreement. The deliberations continued for weeks, then months, and finally years until the citizens of Viterbo became so exasperated that they walled up the entrances to the palace, leaving only a small gate through which they passed a steadily diminishing amount of food.'

'And?'

'The tactic worked. The cardinals elected Teobaldo Visconti as Pope Gregory X. It had taken them almost three years.'

'God grant that we shall come to a quicker conclusion', says Doornik.

'Indeed', says Perez, lowering his eyes, as does Doornik. Neither wants to read the mind of the other at this stage.

'You will reside in the Domus Sanctae Marthae,' Perez goes on, 'but the deliberations will take place, of course, in the Sistine Chapel . . .'

'With Michelangelo's God the Father looking down on us to make sure we behave.'

'Indeed.'

'And his fresco of the Last Judgement to remind us of what will happen if we do not.'

'It could be said, Eminence, that recent conclaves have been freer of corruption than at any time since the earliest years of the Church.'

'Certainly no one has offered me a bribe!'

'From the time of Constantine to Franz Josef, an emperor might exercise a veto, or the King of Spain, or the King of France; indeed, in the conclave of 1903 Cardinal Rompolla was vetoed by the Emperor of Austria. But you do not have to worry, I think, about who would be acceptable to President Bush or President Putin.'

Doornik raises his hand: enough! Perez' knowledge of the Church's history, rituals, customs and protocols is remarkable, and indeed useful at just this time, but Doornik is being told more than he wants to know. Of course the Church needs priests like Perez who, like the eunuchs in the courts of the Byzantine emperors, keep the show on the road. He is far better suited to the long corridors of the Vatican Palace than Doornik, who still feels ill at ease in his scarlet robes. How Perez would love, one day, to be the Cardinal Camerlengo or the Master of Papal Liturgical Ceremonies. And were Doornik to be pope . . .

'There is one other matter', says Perez, looking decidedly embarrassed as he speaks.

Doornik looks up. 'Go on.'

'It has nothing to do with the funeral or the conclave. In fact, I don't really know what it is about, but that man Uriarte—do you know who I mean?'

Doornik nods. 'Yes. The former priest who works for Misericordia.'

'And was charged in London, you may remember ...'

'The camel killer.'

'A name given to him by the tabloid press.'

'What about him?'

'He came to see me—we were priests together in El Salvador many years ago ...'

'Yes, yes. I remember.'

'He came to see me yesterday to ask for an audience with your Eminence ...'

'With me. Why?'

'He would not say, but he insists that it is a matter of the greatest urgency.'

'But at this time ...' Doornik fights back a tone of exasperation. 'My powers are in abeyance. The new pope may not reappoint me. There is nothing I can do for Uriarte or anyone else.'

'I know. I explained this. But he said it was a personal matter—and most urgent, particularly at this time.'

Doornik throws up his arms as a gesture of resignation. 'Well, if he is an old friend of yours, by all means, I shall see him.' He looks down at the diary open on the huge leather-topped desk. 'Find a time to fit him in.'

Lies

Kate dislikes telling lies. She dislikes it not just for moral reasons but also because it makes life so complicated. One has to hold in one's mind the two versions—the true and the false—and so incessantly scrutinise everything one says before one says it. Having denied to David Kotovski that she had brought the Nag Hammadi scroll from Cairo to Rome, she would have to stick to her story with everyone else. It would now be dangerous even to refer to it to Uriarte, or even speak to him, if his telephone is tapped and e-mails read by MI5. She had wanted to ring him as soon as Kotovski had left her, but she was afraid that she might let something slip that would compromise him.

For a brief, chill moment Kate had considered the possibility that what Kotovski had said was true, that the thermos she had carried in her holdall from Cairo to Rome had not contained a papyrus scroll but a phial of liquefied nerve gas. But the moment had passed. It could not be so because if the thermos had contained nerve gas and had been opened by a security officer or customs official, hundreds, perhaps thousands, of people would have been killed—among them, Kate. Juan would not put her life in jeopardy in such a way; there-fore, Kotovski's hypothesis could be discounted. The only thing that still puzzles Kate is why Kotovski should have put it forward. Perhaps it was a matter of pride. MI5 or the police had felt humiliated by Uriarte's acquittal and so were dreaming up a conspiracy involving the Muslim Brotherhood and, no doubt, Al-Qaida. Why did Kotovski go along with it? Probably to save face for someone above him in the hierarchy at the Security Service. Bureaucracies have their own rules of the game.

Some days after her return to London and the interview with Kotovski, Kate has lunch with Barney at Alastair Little's restaurant in Soho. They have eaten there before: Kate is naturally frugal but knows that Bar-ney and his left-wing friends like eating in expensive restaurants. On this occasion, with the suffering of the refugees in Africa still fresh in her mind, the idea of cosseting her palate seems particularly repug-nant and the sight of Barney in his combat fatigues even more irri-tating than before. One of her reasons for wanting to see him is to impress him with what she has been through, but, as she starts to describe her trip to Uganda and her work at the Misericordia refugee camp, she can see that he is only half listening to what she says. And, as soon as she pauses in her account, he starts to reminisce about *his* last assignment in the same region, describing how he had come within a whisker of getting an exclusive interview with Joseph Kony, the commander of the Lord's Resistance Army.

It is hard to impress an egoist. As grilled monkfish with a lobster *coulis* is placed before her, Kate gives up on her traveller's tales and turns to the real point of the lunch: advice on the writing of her articles—whether to seek a commission before she starts or to write them on spec. It does not matter whether she impresses Barney or not; what matters is meeting Juan's expectations.

Barney affects an interest in her project. He gives his on-the-one-hand-but-on-the-other advice and, when she asks outright whether he will ask *his* paper to commission the articles, he looks embarrassed. 'They might think, well, that it's more of the same; I mean, that it's my territory and why pay a freelancer when they have me on the staff.'

'A woman's eye? The dilemma of a Catholic charity faced with AIDS?'

'Yes, well, with the death of the Pope, Catholicism is the flavour of the week. In fact, now that I come to think of it, we're looking for someone to go out to Rome to cover the conclave. You're a Catholic ...'

'I was.'

'Once a Catholic always a Catholic so far as Fleet Street is concerned. Wouldn't that interest you? They could fix up your accreditation this afternoon.'

Kate frowns. Her mind is set on getting straight to work writing about Uriarte and the work of Misericordia in Africa; that is what Juan wants her to do. But before she opens her mouth to turn down the idea, she realises that if she were to go to Rome she would be able to see Juan and tell him face-to-face about Kotovski's suspicions. The idea that within a day or so she might be with him produces a surge of happiness. She blushes and Barney, imagining no doubt that the blush is caused by his brilliant idea, smiles in self-congratulation.

'I'll tell them that your uncle's a priest with contacts in the Vatican. He's always going to Rome, as I remember. They'll jump at it. This pope thing is far bigger than anyone expected. Prince Charles has had to postpone his wedding because Tony Blair and the Archbishop of Canterbury put the Pope's funeral first—that's extraordinary, really, when you think about it. A humiliation for the Church of England when the heir apparent to its Supreme Governor plays second fiddle to the Whore of Babylon ... And it was fantastic! All those old men with their red robes blowing in the wind; the two Swiss Guards standing motionless in their helmets and striped uniforms ... If you write some good stuff, it'll raise your profile far more than yet another series on starving Africans with AIDS.'

They go out onto Frith Street. Barney calls his foreign editor on his cell phone and nods encouragingly at Kate as he listens to what the man says. 'You're on', he says when the call comes to an end. 'He wants you there now. They can get accreditation by e-mail, but they need your details. Have you got your passport with you? Good. The biggest problem will be finding a flight and somewhere to stay. But the conclave promises to be high drama. The dogmas may be hogwash, but those RCs certainly know how to put on a good show—crowds in Saint Peter's Square, black smoke, white smoke—better than the Changing of the Guard.'

The Skeleton in the Cupboard

In the course of the ten days between the funeral of Pope John Paul II and the start of the conclave to elect his successor, a number of the non-Curial cardinals now in Rome make a point of calling upon Cardinal Doornik. Some are his friends. Doornik has travelled much in performing his duties as the Prefect for Catholic Culture, staying with cardinals and bishops around the world. Others are no more than acquaintances but greet him warmly when they meet in general congregation. There are a few, such as Cardinal Pell, the Archbishop of Sidney, who treat him with a certain reserve, but that is inevitable. Pell is known to be conservative on just those issues where Doornik is known to be open-minded—gays, condoms, inclusive language, women priests.

There is no electioneering—it is specifically forbidden by Church law—but it is clearly important that the Cardinals should have an opportunity to know what is passing through each others' minds prior to the conclave, and it therefore irritates Doornik that, at this extraordinary moment in the history of the Church and in Doornik's own life, he should be pestered by Perez to find time to talk to the Basque, Juan Uriarte. He has agreed to do so as a favour to Perez, but why Perez should insist is a mystery. So far as Doornik knows, Perez has not seen much of the man since they were fellow priests in El Salvador thirty years before. However, Doornik approves of the work done by Misericordia—it is an excellent example of the Church's social teaching in action—and, despite his insane idea of killing camels in Darfur, Uriarte's record in the service of the poor is impressive.

Uriarte is shown into Doornik's office by Perez shortly after ten in the morning. He is not in a suit—it is said that he does not possess one—but at least he wears a jacket and a tie. Cardinal Doornik rises from his desk as Uriarte enters and, with a routine that he has practised now for many decades, he comes round to greet his guest, smiling and extending his right hand at an ambiguous angle so that either it can be shaken or his ring be kissed—an act of obeisance which was by no means extinct. Then, when the right hand is released, Doornik uses it to point to the chair where the guest is to sit, while his left arm comes round and rests on the guest's shoulder—a gesture to denote a pastoral affection but also, through the slight pressure he applies, a way to get things under way.

Uriarte sits down. 'It is very good of you to see me', he says. 'I understand how busy you must be.'

Doornik goes to a second ornate chair facing Uriarte. 'One must always find time for what is important', he says. Again, this is a phrase he developed as a bishop in the Netherlands—it disarms the visitor who, as often as not, has come to complain about something utterly trivial.

'It *is* important', says Uriarte. Then he hesitates, looking around to Perez who is hovering nearby. 'It is also something', Uriarte goes on, looking back at Doornik, 'that I would rather discuss with you alone.'

'Of course.' Doornik looks up at Perez, who is practised at reading his expression.

Perez withdraws.

'He is a good man . . .' says Uriarte.

'Indeed', agrees Doornik.

'We were once close friends. But what I have to say, well, it is better if no one else hears it, and, if you so choose, it can then be as if it were never said.'

Doornik nods. 'Go on.'

'Your Eminence, I am quite aware of rules that apply at this time, between the death of one pope and the election of another. I am aware that the cardinals are forbidden to lobby for a particular successor.'

'That is true, although it is not sinful for private discussions to take place.'

'Of course. There is speculation. That is inevitable. And though there may not be campaigns for one candidate over another, the positions of the various cardinals on certain questions are a matter of public record. It is clear, for example, that Archbishop Martini has distinct views on the question of the use of condoms by married couples when one has AIDS and the ordination of women . . .'

'Yes', says Doornik. 'It is well known that Cardinal Martini differs with the late Holy Father on a number of issues.'

'And for a time, your Eminence, it was the hope of the more progressive members of the Church that Martini would be the next pope. But now he has been ill . . .'

'I think', says Doornik, 'that even if he were quite well, he might be considered too liberal by most cardinals.'

'I agree', says Uriarte. 'And the same is true of Cardinal Daniels because, though many of the cardinals from the Third World may be liberal on social issues, they are highly conservative on doctrinal matters. The late Holy Father made sure of that.'

Doornik inclines his head. 'You may be right.'

Uriarte leans forward, his body taut. 'But would you not agree', he says, 'that the Church needs a pope who will change course?'

'A tilt on the tiller, perhaps', says Doornik.

'Will that be enough?' asks Uriarte. 'Is it not true, your Eminence, that because of its teaching on women, on birth control, on sexual morality, the Church has become marginalised in the developed world?'

'But in Africa . . .' Doornik begins.

'Africa!' hisses Uriarte. 'I have devoted half my life to Africa. It is a continent of *pobrecillos*. The dynamic of the *Zeitgeist* is not to be found in Africa but in western Europe and the United States.'

'In Asia . . .' Doornik interjects.

'Oh, they have nimble fingers—they can manufacture cars and microchips all right. But the dynamic of our times is not found in Asia any more than Africa. Malaysia, Taiwan, South Korea, even Japan: What do they do but cater to Western markets, Western tastes? China? Look at Singapore: that is the prototype of the rising dragon. Dull, dull, dull. There is a greater cultural dynamic in Greenwich Village or on

Paris' Left Bank than there is among a billion Chinese. Yet it is precisely there, among the vanguard of humanity, that the Church is losing its relevance.'

Doornik lowers his head, neither agreeing nor disagreeing.

'Think back to the early Church, your Eminence, to apostolic times. Jesus came to preach to the Jews, the Chosen People, and revealed himself as their promised Messiah. He could only come to Israel and only die in Jerusalem, because it was only there and in that context that what had been prophesied could be fulfilled. But at Pentecost, your Eminence—after the Holy Spirit had descended upon the apostles and flames appeared on their heads—did they go out and preach only to the Jews? No, they went out to preach to men of "every nation under heaven" and spoke to them in their own tongues. And when the apostles set out to preach the gospel, they did not go to the provincial backwaters but to the most dynamic cities of the Roman Empire—Antioch, Athens, Ephesus, Corinth—all caught up in the ferment of the different faiths and philosophies of the ancient world: today's New York, Los Angeles, Sydney, London, Paris, Rome!'

'That is true', says Doornik. 'And Rome, the capital of the Empire, was chosen by Peter to be the Holy See.'

'And the Holy See remains in Rome,' says Uriarte, 'but we cannot pretend that Rome is not now a provincial city; why, even Milan is more cosmopolitan.'

'And was the capital of the Empire at the time of Saint Ambrose . . .'

'And today. Would Saint Peter have chosen Rome or Milan? Or would he have gone to New York or even Los Angeles? Never mind. The place is not the point. What is important is that the Church should read the signs of the times. Wasn't that what Pope John XXIII intended when he called a Church council? Isn't that what he meant by *aggiornamento*?'

'Indeed.'

'And is it not also true, your Eminence—though it is painful to speak of it now, and I would not do so if my conscience did not insist— that the process was stopped, even reversed, by Pope John Paul II? That the Polish Pope, with his experience limited to the Archdiocese of Krakow, a provincial city even within Poland, which itself was a country cut off from modernity by the Iron Curtain, actually turned the face of the Church back towards its past—a glorious past, no doubt, but the past all the same—with the result that the extraordinary spirit of renewal that had followed Vatican II was frustrated?'

Doornik looks up at Uriarte. Where is this leading? Why is this man telling him what he already knows? Is it a trap? How should he respond? 'History will judge,' he says, 'but now is not the moment.'

'But now *is* the moment', says Uriarte, 'because now you must choose a new pope.'

'Not me alone', says Doornik with a feeble smile.

'No, the College of Cardinals meeting in conclave. But you must know, your Eminence, that because of the careful choice of like-minded men by the late Holy Father, there are few in the College who understand that they themselves are the cause of the predicament now faced by the Church. They read the signs of the times and throw up their hands in horror! Relativism! Secularism! And their solution? Withdraw behind the ramparts of dogmatic intransigence. Form exclusive, secretive communities like Opus Dei or Comunione e Liberazione, and hurl anathemas at the modern world.'

'Please God', says Doornik, 'that we shall not elect such an inward-looking pope.'

'But you will,' says Uriarte, his voice suddenly hushed, 'or, rather, *they* will unless they elect *you*.'

Doornik raises his right hand and at the same time opens his mouth to make the usual protestations of his inadequacy, the inappropriateness of the suggestion, the futility of second-guessing the Holy Spirit and so on, but before a word comes out, his eyes meet Uriarte's and he realises that a display of false modesty would be a waste of time. He therefore limits himself to saying what he knows to be true. 'It seems unlikely that I will be chosen. There is a strong feeling that the next pope should be from outside Europe.'

'In theory, yes', says Uriarte, with the swift and certain speech of someone who has considered all the eventualities over and over again. 'But when you come down to it, who among the possible candidates has the stature of a pope? Cardinal Arinze? Black, certainly, but also irascible, unpredictable and not very clever. A South American such as Hummes or Rodriguez? They're big fish in their own small ponds, but far too small to govern the universal Church. They are virtually unknown, and no cardinal will vote for a candidate he knows nothing about. And little *can* be known of the candidates because there are no manifestos. They know the Curial cardinals—Sodano, the Secretary of State, and of course Ratzinger. But Cardinal Sodano is too old and Cardinal Ratzinger would be too divisive. The Italians? Re, Tettamanzi, Martini? Unlikely. The first two, unknown. Martini? Ten years ago, he would have been the ideal candidate for the liberals—even five years ago—but now it's too late; he's a sick man. Daniels? He's burned his bridges by stepping out of line. The truth is, your Eminence, that in the end the cardinals will be forced to conclude that there is only one among them who is fit to govern the Church in the twenty-first century, and that is you.'

Doornik is silent. He does not think of himself as a proud man, but in all honesty he cannot deny the logic of what Uriarte is saying. How many times has he rehearsed all these arguments in his own mind? There were more spiritual cardinals, no doubt, and there were cardinals with more progressive views, but there is none he could think of who sees more clearly than he does what has to be done to fulfil Pope John XXIII's project of *aggiornamento* and the promise of Vatican II.

'If it is God's will', he says eventually.

'It *is* God's will', says Uriarte. 'I am sure of it. But so is the Evil One, and he is determined to thwart it.'

'The Evil One?' Doornik looks puzzled. It was rare these days to hear the devil spoken of as the Evil One, or indeed spoken of at all.

'That is why I am here', says Uriarte. 'I have learned ... information has come into my possession ... that there is a conspiracy to make sure that you are *not* chosen as the next pope.'

'A conspiracy?'

'You must realise, your Eminence, that what is clear to me and to all of those who want an open-minded, forward-looking pope is also clear to those who want a pope in exactly the same mould as John Paul II—even if his name should be Ratzinger! And to achieve their purpose, they are willing to resort to the methods more fitting to the Renaissance than the present day.'

'Bribery?' asks Doornik.

'No. Dirty tricks. Mud slinging. Smear tactics—just as one might in an election for a secular office.'

'But what mud can they sling?' asks Doornik, genuinely puzzled as to what aspect of his frugal and chaste life could be used against him.

Uriarte looks straight into the Cardinal's eyes. 'A tape has fallen into the hands of a British journalist.'

'A tape?'

'A recording of a conversation in which a priest asserts that as a seminarian he was sexually molested by a fellow seminarian from the Netherlands, and that this seminarian is now a Curial cardinal in Rome.'

Doornik was dumbfounded. 'But who ...?'

'The priest is an Englishman—a Father Luke Scott ...' Uriarte pauses, watching Doornik's reaction; Doornik is aware of this and does not allow his expression to change. 'It would seem that he was unaware that a recording of his conversation was being made, but when asked by the journalist to either confirm or deny the remarks imputed to him, he would do neither. The journalist has taken this as confirmation that the conversation was genuine and therefore what he claims to have happened is true.'

Luke! Was it possible that after all these years Doornik's friend from the Gregorian University should remember, let alone speak of, that brief and terrible moment when *eros* and *agape* had become confused? Yet perhaps, just because it had been so terrible, he *had* remembered it, and it was not inconceivable that he had let something slip. But was it possible that something so trivial, so long ago, could influence the judgement of his fellow cardinals when choosing a new pope? He put his thoughts into words. 'I cannot believe', he says to Uriarte, 'that a scrap of scurrilous gossip would weigh in the balance ...'

'In itself, it would not', says Uriarte. 'No prince of the Church would be so ignoble as to ask whether the charge is true or untrue, and whether, even if true, it could affect the reputation of a man whose sanctity and integrity are beyond dispute. But *what is made of it* may lead some to consider whether it is appropriate to appoint a new pope tainted with even a touch of scandal. I have been told that the journalist is ready to offer his story to the British tabloid newspapers. From that small fact—or what he claims is a fact—he has constructed a vast edifice of innuendo, referring, inevitably, to the protection of paedophile priests, homosexuals in seminaries and even the murder of the commander of the Swiss Guard, Captain Estermann, by Corporal Tornay ...'

'But that had nothing to do with me!' exclaims Doornik.

'Of course it didn't', says Uriarte. 'But these British journalists are past masters at innuendo—suggesting things without stating them to avoid the libel laws.'

Doornik feels that he is losing his composure and, to conceal the fact, stands up. 'This is monstrous', he says, stalking across the room to stare out of the window towards the Apostolic Palace. 'It must be stopped. We must speak to the Nuncio in London. He must retain lawyers.'

'It will be too late', says Uriarte, 'and with the evidence of the tape . . .'

'The tape', Doornik repeats. 'After all these years . . .'

'If you were to swear an affidavit that what Father Scott said was untrue or referred to another Curial cardinal . . .'

'But I am the only Dutch cardinal in the Curia!'

'Indeed.'

'There must be another solution.'

Uriarte is silent—a silence that provokes Doornik to turn to him with a look of anguished interrogation.

'Your Eminence,' says Uriarte, 'I have not come here simply to warn you of an impending scandal. I am here because I believe that you and only you can save the Church, and that, as a result, *anything and everything* must be done to prevent this story from being published before the conclave.'

'But what?'

'There is a solution but it is . . .' Uriarte hesitates.

'What?'

'It would, in my view, be the lesser of two evils, but it would be an evil all the same.'

'Money? Buy off the journalist? That wouldn't be difficult. I have friends who could transfer funds tomorrow—many times the fee he would receive for his story.'

'I have thought of that. I have talked to the journalist, but he isn't in it just for the money. He has to have what is called a "scoop" . . .'

'A scoop, yes. I know what that means.'

'He feels his story will make his reputation. It will be the first step in a successful career . . .'

'Did *he* make the recording?'

'No. It was made inadvertently by another journalist who is the niece of Father Scott.'

'And she gave it to the journalist?'

'He came upon it. She told him about her uncle. He deduced the rest.'

'But now—is he prepared to negotiate with us?'

'Yes.'

'What does he want?'

'A tape in return for a tape.'

'A tape of what?'

'The proceedings of the conclave.'

'Impossible!' Doornik turns away from Uriarte again and stares out of the window. Even though he knows he should feel grateful to the Basque for his faith in Doornik's mission to lead the Church and for warning him of this impending scandal, he feels the rage of the Oriental despot who executes the bringer of bad news.

Uriarte says nothing. Doornik is suddenly curious to see the expression on his face. He turns towards him and says again: 'Impossible.'

Uriarte is leaning forward in his chair, his elbows resting on his knees, his head held in his hands. Now he looks up with an expression that Doornik finds hard to interpret—a weariness, a resignation, but behind it determination. '"For God, nothing is impossible ..."', he says.

'Then what?' asks Doornik irritably. 'Shall we pray for a miracle? That your journalist drops dead?'

'No.' Uriarte shakes his head. 'But I believe we must realise that you are not here facing a choice between right and wrong, but between two different evils. On the one hand there is the solemn oath you will take as you take your place in the Sistine Chapel that you will observe faithfully and scrupulously the Apostolic Constitution regarding the election of the Roman pontiff and maintain the strictest secrecy about what takes place. Certainly, you know and I know that sooner or later there *will* be leaks about the deliberations; there always are: who voted for whom, how many votes such-and-such a cardinal gained on the first ballot. Who swung behind whom. So were you to break that oath, you would merely be pre-empting some other cardinal—inevitably one of the Italians who as an Italian takes oaths less seriously than Northern Europeans.'

'Perhaps', says Doornik.

'But on the other hand', says Uriarte, 'there are other less concrete but perhaps more weighty considerations. I cannot think of any other cardinal who, as pope, would have the courage to modify the Church's teaching on contraception. It is not for me to ask you now whether or not you would have such a change in mind, but were such a change to be made, it would not only make the Church's overall teaching on sexuality credible in the developed world; it would also enable Catholic aid agencies such as Misericordia to cooperate in the distribution of condoms to those infected with AIDS in Africa and, in my view, alleviate great suffering and save many thousands of lives.'

Doornik says nothing.

'I cannot think of any other cardinal', Uriarte goes on, 'who as pope would authorise the ordination of women as priests. Again, it is not for me to ask you whether you would have this in mind, but I am sure you recognise, because it is so clear, that the exclusion of women from the Catholic priesthood places the Church alongside the most backward and primitive religions, alienating not just all educated women but anyone sensitive to the implementation of human rights.'

'But to break a vow . . .'

'Yes. To break a vow is a serious matter. But there are sins of *omission* as well as sins of *commission* as you well know, your Eminence. And you must ask yourself now whether, when you die and face God's judgement, keeping one vow will outweigh the good you might have done had you been pope.'

Both men are now silent. Clearly, Uriarte has said all that he has to say and it is for Doornik to speak—but what can he say? That he will take a tape-recorder into the conclave? An hour before, such an idea would have seemed quite monstrous—a heinous betrayal of a sacred obligation. But the line of argument of this Basque is irrefutable. He, Doornik, is quite possibly the only man who can take the Church into the modern world. The Holy Spirit is at work, but so too is Satan. How else does one explain the election of despots, tyrants, murderers and debauchees as the successors to Saint Peter? Was breaking an oath *such* a weighty matter? Had not fifty thousand priests broken their vows by leaving the priesthood after Vatican II—men, for that matter, like Uriarte? Had they been cast into outer darkness? No, they had been given jobs in aid agencies, theological faculties and the bureaucracies of bishops' conferences. Is not the vow he must take on entering the conclave much like the helmets and halberds of the Swiss Guards—a colourful remnant of an earlier epoch in the history of the Church? Is there not something to be said, in fact, for more transparency in the election of a pope? Are not the bishops and priests entitled to know which cardinals have voted for which candidate? Is not open government in the Church as in the state a right of the People of God?

Doornik returns to his chair and leans towards Uriarte. 'How would it be done?'

'It would be possible for me to provide a tape-recorder which would not set off a metal detector ...'

'But I could not be seen carrying it into the Sistine Chapel!'

'No. It would have to be concealed beneath your cassock.'

'You could arrange that?'

'Yes. I could give it to Monsignor Perez, and he could take it to you in the Domus Sanctae Marthae.'

'Perez ...'

'Can you trust Perez?'

Doornik shrugs. 'He would like me to be pope.'

'He need not know what it is.'

'No. I could simply tell him that ... I don't know. I'll think of something. But the journalist ... will he keep his side of the bargain?'

'The difficulty will be to persuade him that you will keep yours. You will have to bring out a tape after the first day of the conclave.'

'Of course.' But suddenly the idea of walking in and out of the Sistine Chapel with a concealed tape-recorder fills Doornik with horror. 'I don't know ... I'm not sure.'

'You do not have to make up your mind now', says Uriarte. 'I will simply tell the Englishman that his proposal is under consideration.'

'Is he in Rome?'

'He is coming.'

'When must I decide?'

'He will wait. I have told him that you must have time to examine your conscience and pray for the guidance of God.'

The Assignment

A reservation has been made for Kate at the Allegra Hotel on the Via Giulio Cesare. Jill, the foreign editor's personal assistant, tells Kate on her cell phone how lucky she has been to secure a room in such a central location, but the paper is famous for its stinginess over expenses, and when Kate checks in, she suspects that the search has been confined to three-star hotels and below. The Allegra has two stars: her room is small with a window opening onto the busy Via Giulio Cesare, but it is close to the Vatican and also to a Metro station, which is useful because taxis are scarce.

Kate unpacks, takes a shower but does not ring Juan; almost certainly, his telephone is being tapped. She will seek him out, but first she must secure her accreditation at the Vatican press centre. She leaves the Allegra Hotel and walks towards Saint Peter's Square. The crowd is benign and cheerfully parts to let Kate through. The police, too, after examining her credentials in an easy-going way, let her through to the press centre behind Bernini's colonnade. There, with impressive efficiency, Vatican officials match her letter of accreditation with the e-mails they have received from London. She is shown the facilities available at the centre for conducting interviews or filing reports and is given an identity tag and an 'info-pack' prepared for foreign journalists.

It is now four in the afternoon. She sits down at one of the desks at the press centre and in less than an hour knocks out a thousand words of waffle about the atmosphere in Saint Peter's Square and the protocols for the conclave—the latter based on the press releases from her info-pack. The paper will not expect anything more that day; therefore, there is no reason why Kate should not see Juan that evening. She leaves the press centre, crosses the Tiber on the Ponte San Angelo, and makes her way towards the Misercordia offices on the via Chieti. She is hungry, as she has had no lunch, and stops off for a salami sandwich and an espresso on the way.

A middle-aged Italian woman—a nun, perhaps, or an ex-nun—sits at the reception desk at the office of Misericordia International. Kate, with her journalist's ID hanging around her neck, introduces herself in broken Italian and asks for Juan Uriarte.

'Is he expecting you?' the woman asks in English.

'No.'

'I will see if he is here.' The woman picks up a telephone and, when it is answered, asks in Italian for Uriarte. 'I am afraid he has not been in the office today', she says to Kate. 'No one seems to know where he is. He may be at home. Shall I call him?'

Kate shakes her head. 'No, don't worry. I have his number. I'll call him from my hotel.'

But she cannot call him and decides to go to his flat on the via Manzoni: even if he is out, his housekeeper might know where he is. There are no taxis. She takes the Metro at Barberini, changes at Termini, gets out at Bologna and walks towards the via Manzoni. She remembers the way but, though that lunch with Juan was less than two months before, it feels to her now as if it had taken place in the long-distant past—indeed, as if the memory is lodged in the mind of a different person. Then she had been curious and uncertain as to what to expect; now she is no longer curious but is still uncertain. She does not doubt that Juan will be pleased to see her: how could it be otherwise? But will he be disappointed that she has left London before finishing her articles on the work of Misericordia? And how will he react when told that the police have him under surveillance? He may think that she is fussing about nothing, that she is using it as a pretext to see him.

Kate reaches 12 via Manzoni and pushes the button for apartment No. 8. She leans forward to speak into the grill of the intercom, but without any interrogation there is a buzz and the door to the building opens. She goes in and takes the lift up to the second floor. She knocks on the door of Juan's flat. Silence. She waits, then knocks again. The door is opened by the housekeeper, Lucia. Seeing Kate, she frowns.

'Good evening', says Kate holding out her hand. 'I am Kate Ramsey. Do you remember me? I came to lunch here some time ago.'

The older woman with her Aztec face clearly does remember her but does not hold out her hand to take Kate's or step aside to invite her in. She looks blankly at Kate, awaiting further elucidation as to why she is there.

'I am looking for Signor Uriarte . . . for Juan', Kate says. 'It's rather important.' Again the woman does not react: perhaps she does not understand English.

'*Juan? Dove è Juan?*' Kate cannot remember whether Lucia had addressed Uriarte as Signor Uriarte or Juan; presumably, because she is part of the team, she calls him Juan.

'*Juan, si.*' The woman understands. She turns and calls over her shoulder: '*Ignacio, ¿donde está tu padre?*' [3]

[3] Ignacio, where is your father?

'*No lo sabemos.*' The voice is that of a young man.

'*No sabemos.*'[4] The woman remains standing in the doorway.

'*¿Quien es?*'[5] comes the voice of the young man.

'*La periodista que estaba con tu padre en áfrica.*'[6]

'*¿La inglesa?*'[7]

'*Sí.*'

'*Madre, sé educada. Invitala e entrar.*'[8]

With her expression still impassive but with a gesture inviting Kate to enter, Lucia steps back and holds open the door. Kate finds herself once again in the marble-floored apartment. The door to the living room is open and, catching sight of her, a young man with long hair rises from the sofa. His skin is as dark as his mother's but his features are unmistakably Basque—or what Kate takes to be Basque because they are Juan's.

'Please come in', he says. His assured English has an American twang.

Kate goes through to the living room and, feeling suddenly dizzy, leans against the arm of a sofa.

'Please sit down', says the young man.

'No, I won't stay. But I must speak to Juan.'

The young man takes a cell phone out of the pocket of his jeans. 'I'll call him.'

'No!' She holds up her hand. 'I need to talk to him ... face-to-face. Not on the telephone.'

'He may be back to eat but we never know ...' He glances at his mother. '*¿Dijo si iba a volver?*'[9]

Lucia shrugs.

Kate takes her notebook out of her bag and writes down the address of the Allegra Hotel. 'When he comes in, would you give him this? I'll be there all evening. But say it would be better not to telephone me.'

'*¿Quiere ella que le haga una visita al hotel?*'[10] Lucia asks her son.

'*Sí.*'

---

[4] We don't know where he is.

[5] Who is it?

[6] The journalist who was with your father in Africa.

[7] The English woman?

[8] Be polite, mother. Invite her to come in.

[9] Did he say whether he was coming back or not?

[10] She wants him to visit her in her hotel?

Lucia gives a snort and for a moment the impassive look gives way to one of fury.

'I am Ignacio', the young man says to Kate, extending his hand. 'As it happens, I have to go out, so why don't I come with you and find you a taxi?'

'That would be kind.'

'*Madre, realmente eres demasiado mayor para estar celosa*',[11] he mutters as he walks past his mother into the hall.

Lucia gives another snort.

'It really is important', Kate says to her. 'For his safety . . . *la seguridad.*'

'Don't worry', says Ignacio. 'We'll make sure he knows.' He opens the front door to the apartment and guides her through. While Kate goes towards the stairs, Ignacio turns back and speaks to his mother: Kate cannot hear what he says. Then he joins her, and together they go down and out into the via Manzoni.

'Are you in a hurry?' he asks. 'Why don't we have a drink?' His manner is precocious, even conceited—and there is something unattractive about his American accent—but Kate could do with a drink.

'That would be nice', she says weakly.

'So dad's ass is on the line once again?'

Kate imagines that he must have learned English from watching TV. 'What do you mean?'

'Didn't you cover his trial in London?'

'Yes.'

'And now he's in trouble again?'

'He might be. I don't know. They never really accepted the verdict.'

'They?'

'The police.'

They come to a bar and sit down at a small aluminium-topped table by the plate glass window. 'What'll you have?'

'A Campari.'

Ignacio shouts towards the bar. 'Toppo! *Un campari ed una birra, per favore.*'

'They know you here?'

'Oh yes. They know me well. I've lived here most of my life.'

'I thought that the flat belonged to Misercordia.'

---

[11] Really, mother, you are too old to be jealous.

172

'Sure. My mother runs it as a place to stay for whoever's passing through. But in the back behind the kitchen there are a couple of bedrooms—servants' quarters I guess you'd call them, but they don't like using words like that. We're all part of "the team".'

'And your father?'

'Well, as you know, he spends most of his time in the bush.'

'So you haven't seen much of him?'

'Enough!' Ignacio laughs. 'No, we get on fine, but he's kind of restless and not easy to live with. I mean, would you want to live with Don Quixote?' He pronounces the word in the American manner: kee-hoté.

Kate smiles. 'No.'

'But you put up with him in Africa?'

'Yes. He showed me round. He was very kind.'

A girl in a short leather skirt brings them their drinks. '*Ciao Ignacio. Perché non sei giù in piazza San Pietro con tutte quelle belle ragazze polacche?*' [12]

'*Dove pensi che stessi andando? Una amica di mio padre mi ha intercettato.*' [13]

'*E' troppo vecchia per te!*' [14] With a disparaging smile at Kate, the girl goes back to the bar.

'Do you understand Italian?' Ignacio asks.

'Enough', replies Kate tartly.

The young man laughs. 'Sex. That's all these Italian girls think about', he says.

'What do you do?' asks Kate.

'I'm studying chemical engineering. I spent a year in the States. Now I'm back at the university here. I designed the delivery system for the Sarin.'

'To kill camels?'

'To *potentially* kill camels. A credible deterrent.'

'You knew what he planned to do?'

'Sure. We cooked up the idea together. We were talking about Pascal and how he discovered vacuums, and we got onto aerosols and how those terrorists in Tokyo could have killed thousands if they had vaporised the Sarin. And dad had just come back from Darfur and said that if he could vaporise Sarin he could hit the Janjaweed where

[12] Hi, Ignacio. Why aren't you down at Saint Peter's Square with all those pretty Polish girls?

[13] Where do you think I was going? A friend of my father's waylaid me.

[14] She's too old for you.

it hurt by showing them that he could kill their livestock—and would, if they didn't desist. So we got to thinking about how he could do that, and I figured out that if you put it under pressure in a small cylinder and laid a charge against the valve, then you would simply have to detonate the charge ...'

'That would kill a herd of camels?'

Ignacio snaps his fingers. 'Stone dead. Of course you'd have to make sure the wind was blowing in the right direction ...'

'If the wind changed?'

'That would be dangerous.'

'It might have killed people?'

'It might. There was always that risk. But people were being killed out there every day. And it really drove my dad crazy that no one was doing anything about it.'

'I know. And well, your father's an exceptional man.'

'Exceptional or crazy. I have yet to decide.'

'You can't have thought he was crazy if you helped him with his bomb.'

'No. I kind of admire him for thinking outside the box.'

'Weren't you worried when he was arrested in London?'

'Sure. And I wanted to give evidence, but he wouldn't let me. And I guess he was right. No one's going to pay much attention to what a son says about his father.'

'Did you do experiments?' asks Kate.

'Sure. I made a prototype. We tried it with ammonium nitrate on some chickens.'

'Did it kill the chickens?'

'They didn't like it, but if it had been Sarin, they would all have died. And we tried it in a barn.'

'A barn. Why in a barn?'

Ignacio shrugged. 'I don't know. Dad wanted to judge how it would vaporize in an enclosed space.'

'Who was going to gas the camels?'

'That I don't know.'

'Wouldn't the Janjaweed have noticed someone approaching their camels looking like a scuba diver?'

Ignacio laughed. 'No. The cylinder was made from a block of nano-composite plastic and lined with Ramex titanium sheeting. That way it wouldn't show up on metal detectors. And it was concealed.'

'Concealed?'

'We enclosed the bomb in a box that from the outside looked like a tape-recorder—an Uher—again, in titanium. Dad imagined someone posing as a journalist getting close to the herd of camels. He probably meant to do it himself. I mean, no one else is going to do something as dangerous as that.'

'Didn't you try to dissuade him?'

Ignacio shakes his head. 'You can neither persuade nor dissuade my dad once he's got something into his head. And, anyway, after the trial he couldn't go back to Darfur, so I guess he found someone else who was prepared to do it.'

'Who?'

'I don't know. But he rang from Cairo to say that someone would come by and I was to give him the cylinder.'

'And someone came by?'

'Yes. A guy. An Egyptian.'

'How did you know he was an Egyptian?'

'He was wearing an EgyptAir uniform. I guess he was a pilot or one of the cabin crew.'

'And he took the cylinder hidden in the tape-recorder?'

'No, in a thermos.'

'You had concealed it in a thermos?'

'Sure.'

'Did your mother know what was going on?'

'No. She doesn't go for individualistic stunts. For her it's class action or nothing.'

'She's a Marxist?'

'Unreconstructed. She's from El Salvador—*una mestiza*—you know, mixed Indian and Spanish? They met fighting for the FMLN. She still believes everything the commissars taught her.'

'Were you born under a tree in the Sierras?'

Ignacio laughs. 'No. I was born here in Rome.'

'So after the civil war ended, they married and came out here?'

He laughs again. 'They came out here but they didn't marry—too bourgeois!'

'But they stayed together?'

'Sure. And I don't think it was just because of me. In a funny way, though they aren't married and though Dad goes off for months at a time, they get on better than most of my friends' parents. They sleep in the same bed, and I'd say they still have sex.'

'What makes you think that?'

'Oh, you can tell. He comes back from Darfur or wherever; they go out for dinner; I go stay with a friend; the next day my mother's in a good mood!'

'You're very observant', notes Kate.

'I'm a scientist', says Ignacio. 'We're trained to observe.'

Alarm

Kotovski is woken at six in the morning by a call on his cell phone. It is his boss, BB. 'You're to go to Rome.'

'When?'

'Now. There's a plane waiting to take you from Northolt. I'll send a car.'

'Who . . . ?' Kotovski begins.

'Your friend Paget has got the wind up. There's some new information from Cairo. He doesn't think that the Italians can handle it. It seems you're the only person who can identify Uriarte and the girl.'

Soon afterwards, while he was only half-dressed, there was a call from Paget. 'I'll brief you at Northolt', he says. 'There's no point in my coming with you. I don't think you'll need Ashton either. Our man Eagar will meet you.'

Kotovski shaves, dresses, packs a holdall with his wash bag and some clean clothes. The car is already waiting by the entrance to his block of flats—a sign that BB, too, has got the wind up and wants to show that he has pulled out all the stops. It is one of the BMWs from the pool, and the driver takes it through the underpass at Hanger Lane at 90 mph. There is no need for a siren: he is past the few cars going out of London before the drivers realise that he is behind them.

Paget is waiting at Northolt. He leads Kotovski into an empty office and closes the door. 'I couldn't speak on the phone. Everything we do must be deniable because if something happens and it emerges that we knew it might happen, then clearly we'd be hung out to dry.'

'We've done our best', says Kotovski.

'That won't wash when the public is baying for scapegoats. We can blame the Italians, of course, but covering our tracks is not our priority at present. We want to stop the thing from happening.'

'The thing?'

'We had a call from Cairo at four this morning. The man being interrogated has come clean. The Mukhabarat confirm that Sarin was prepared in a laboratory in Alexandria and delivered to the European in Cairo. The European was Juan Uriarte. Our American friends are sure of that. The new twist is this. The group that made the gas for Uriarte are not Muslims. They are Copts. They had laid a trail—quite cleverly—back to the Muslim Brotherhood and Al-Qaida, but there are in fact no Muslims involved. The Copt confirms my hypothesis: the plan is to kick-start a crusade by perpetrating an atrocity in Rome.'

'This is Uriarte's idea?'

'So it would seem.'

'Crazy.'

'No crazier than 9/11.'

'Do the Americans want us to pull in Uriarte?'

'They want you to find him. They'll do the pulling in themselves.'

The Artesia

When Luke Scott goes to Rome, he always buys his ticket from a travel agent in Marylebone, but now even this travel agent cannot find him a seat on a plane. The best she can suggest is to go by train: Eurostar to Paris, a taxi to the Gare de Bercy and then a berth on the night train—the Artesia—that reaches Rome's Termini Station at 9:00 A.M. The only available berth is in first class. Luke tells her to book it and goes back to his flat to arrange for somewhere to stay. Here again, he meets with difficulties. The Domus Sancta Marthae is being used by the cardinals; the English College is full; so is the Monastery of San Anselmo. In the end, he telephones his friend the Contessa who can only offer him *una soffitta*—an attic—in the Palazzo Freschi but assures him that he is most welcome to that.

Why is he going to Rome? What does he hope to achieve? The visit of the young policeman has alarmed him. He, too, at the time, had wondered whether the jurors had reached the right decision about Uriarte and now wonders what that wrong decision might imply. He dislikes the idea of Uriarte but fears that this dislike might stem from theological prejudice—his doubts about the theology of liberation. How many young idealists had died in El Salvador for the revolutionary cause, misled by Jesuits like Ellacuria or ex-Jesuits like Uriarte into a belief that Christ's Kingdom was of this world?

Going to bed after the policeman's visit, Luke had slept for a few hours but was woken suddenly with an idea that sensitised every nerve in his body but which he could not at first identify. So wide awake was he that it was as if a bucket of water had been thrown on his face, but ten, perhaps twenty, seconds passed before he identified the thought that had awoken him: it was that Kate, the creature he loved more than any other in the world, was in great danger. He felt oppressed by something powerful, mocking, evil—the residue of a nightmare, perhaps, that had been erased from his memory as he awoke. Never before had he felt so intensely the reality of predatory evil. Had he been watching too much TV? Perhaps. Was it in *Alien 2* or *Alien 3* where Ripley finds men and women trapped like flies in a web, kept alive only to be devoured, begging to be killed? Was Kate caught in a tacky cocoon, waiting to be devoured? He must speak to her and warn her that Uriarte might not be what he seems. Difficult, difficult . . . It is hard to turn a woman against the man she loves, particularly if she senses some kind of perverse jealousy at work.

Luke had fallen asleep again when it was already getting light and only woke finally at eight. Was it too early to telephone Kate? It would be starting off on the wrong foot if he woke her up or spoke to her before she had been fortified by a cup of coffee. He had switched on his electric coffee-pot and put some milk in a pan on the stove but felt no appetite for his usual bowl of cereal or slice of toast. He drank the coffee when it was made, looking at his watch every two or three minutes, waiting for the hands to reach nine. At two minutes past nine he had dialled her number: it rang five times and then was answered by a machine. 'Hi. This is Kate Ramsey. I've gone to Rome to cover the conclave. I don't know yet where I'll be staying, but you can reach me on my cell . . .'

Luke had put the telephone back on its receiver. He would ring her on her cell phone, but only when he, too, was in Rome.

Pique

Kate returns to the Allegra Hotel in a state of stupefaction. Already enfeebled by a long and tiring day that had started by taking a mini-cab to Heathrow at six in the morning, she now feels confused and disoriented like someone who has been poked and prodded and twirled around a thousand times in a game of Blind Man's Bluff. *Has* she been blind? Or bluffed? How could she have imagined that a man of Juan's age wouldn't have some baggage in the form of a child? Why had he not told her? Why had she not asked? No doubt, for the same reason. She had wanted him to be unencumbered; he had wanted her to think he was free. And perhaps he *was* free of any particular emotional attachment or legal commitment; he was not *married* to the Indian woman and though they might share the same bed, Kate couldn't believe that he still had *sex* with her—a woman with thighs like sacks of flour and a moustache! That was surely the son's wishful thinking, though God knows there were plenty of women who had been lied to about this sort of thing by married men.

And the son! He was *so old*—not in an absolute sense, of course. He was more than ten years younger than she was but old to be the child of her lover and an unwelcome reminder that Juan was closer in age to her father than he was to her. Not that she was ageist about lovers; older men were often more interesting and considerate and mature, and no doubt all these qualities had drawn her to Juan. Mature, controlled and considerate enough not to spoil a holiday romance by letting her know that the woman she had thought was the housekeeper was in fact his mistress and the mother of his twenty-two-year-old son! As she sits in the taxi that Ignacio found for her on the Piazza Bologna, she tries to replay the scenes in which Juan had talked about his personal life, but there are no clips in the file. His mind was always on higher things and, when it came to sex, he had somehow made a

179

virtue of nil commitment. The men fighting for the FMLN had their needs met by the women. How noble! How heroic! The *mestiza* slut!

It is after eight when Kate reaches the hotel. She goes to her room and opens the window because it is stuffy, then closes it again because of the noise. She opens her laptop on the small table and tries to write something about the atmosphere in Rome; she does not know how she will send it since the Allegra does not have a Wi-Fi connection. She cannot go to the press centre in case Juan comes while she is out. She writes one paragraph and gives up. She feels a twinge of hunger, but the Allegra does not provide room service either. She lies down on the bed, props her back up against the two pillows stacked against the headboard and switches on the television. She watches pictures of the crowds in Saint Peter's Square on CNN—events taking place a quarter-mile away beamed up onto a satellite and back into her room.

Kate's eyes close; she drifts into sleep. She is awakened by the telephone. She picks it up. It is the desk clerk. A Signor Uriarte is there to see her. 'Send him up.' Without thinking, she has spoken in English but the clerk understands. Kate gets off the bed, goes into the bathroom and splashes her face with cold water. She catches her face in the mirror over the basin: she looks dreadful. It is too late to put on eye shadow or mascara; she takes a brush to her hair but then hears a knock on the door of her room. She takes one last look at her face, purses her lips, then goes back into the room and opens the door.

Uriarte smiles when he sees her. 'So you came back to Rome?' He does not try to kiss her but steps past her into the room. What does that signify? Would not lovers normally fall into one another's arms in such circumstances? The detached smile, the matter-of-fact greeting, is disorientating: is he trying to convey that they were now only friends? Or, knowing what she now knows, does he judge it prudent to make no assumptions and wait to assess her mood?

'I'm covering the conclave', she says, annoyed with herself that she feels she has to explain her presence. But now he turns and, as if to reassure her that she is welcome, opens his arms saying, 'That's good', and—abandoning any feelings of anger or resentment—Kate steps forward into his embrace. 'Oh, Juan!'

Uriarte kisses her neck beneath her left ear, then gently places two fingers beneath her chin and moves her head around to kiss her lips. 'It is good', he says.

'Why didn't you tell me?'

'About Ignacio?'

'And . . .'

'And Lucia?' He waits and then says, in a caressing whisper: 'Because they are in the present only because of the past whereas you . . . *you are the present.*'

Kate presses her face against his chest, inhaling his intoxicating aroma and letting her thoughts be waltzed around her head by his words. 'I didn't know whether you would want to see me . . .'

Again, he raises her chin with two fingers. 'To see you? Oh, more than to see you . . . *tu eres mi muchacha.*'[15]

'And I was so worried.'

'Why?'

'Someone from MI5 came to see me in London.'

'The police?'

'No. The Security Service. I got to know him at the trial. He pretended to be a journalist.'

Uriarte loosens his hold. 'What did he want?'

'He knows that we were in Cairo and wants to know whether I had brought anything back for you to Rome.'

'And what did you say?'

'I said I hadn't.'

Uriarte releases her and turns away. 'What else did he ask?'

'He said . . . oh, I was so angry. They won't admit defeat. They're want to believe that you are planning something horrible to justify bringing you to trial.'

'Planning what?' He sounds curious, not disturbed.

'They don't know. That's what's stupid. He said they had been told that Muslims in Cairo were thought to have sold nerve gas to a man like you—a man "answering your description".'

'Muslims? They were sure it was Muslims?'

'Yes. He said the Muslim Brotherhood, but perhaps he meant Al-Qaida. Why *you* of all people should be in cahoots with Islamic fundamentalists was *not* explained.'

---

[15] You are my girl.

Kate looks at Uriarte: he seems thoughtful rather than indignant. Then suddenly, as if snapping out of a daydream, he looks around and says: 'This is a horrible little room.'

'It's all they could find—or all they felt they could afford.'

'I can find you somewhere much nicer to stay.'

Kate hesitates.

'Quick. Pack your bag.'

'But if the paper wants to get hold of me . . .'

'They can call your cell phone.'

'It's close to the Vatican.'

'This place is not far.'

'Is it a hotel?'

'No, a flat. You can't stay here.'

Kate checks out of the Allegra hotel, and they drive east in Uriarte's Fiat Punto to the Piazza Mazzini, then over the Tiber on the Ponte del Risorgimento, and back into the city on the via del Corso. When they have passed the Piazza Colonna, Uriarte turns right into a narrow street and Kate loses her bearings. They stop in a small triangular piazza. 'This is as close as we can get with the car', he says as he parks the Punto. They start to walk through the dark, narrow streets. Uriarte carries her suitcase. Kate is without any energy; her reserves are spent, and it seems odd, since they are not in a pedestrian precinct, that they did not stop closer to the flat.

Finally they come to a door cut into heavy wooden gates. Uriarte searches by the light of a street lamp for a key on his fob and, finding it, opens the door into an inner courtyard. He leads her up a staircase at the back of the courtyard to the third floor where, with a second key, he opens the door to a flat.

'Is this another Misericordia safe house?' asks Kate.

'More or less', says Uriarte.

They are met by the musty smell of stale air. Uriarte walks straight through the small hall into a living room and throws open the windows. 'Look', he says to Kate. She comes up behind him and sees, through the window and the space between a wing of the palazzo and the side of a church, the dark line of the Tiber. 'It's not as close to the Vatican, perhaps, but it's not that far.' He goes back to the doorway and switches on the lights. The room is ancient and elegant—

white walls, exposed stone jambs and lintels, a stone mantel of the seventeenth or early eighteenth century, a painted wooden display cabinet of around the same period, a modern plate glass coffee table, a beige sofa and two armchairs. On the walls are four prints of views of Rome—by Piranesi, perhaps, or Bellini. It is clear that no one lives in this apartment; it has the air of an expensive rental.

'You'll be more comfortable here', says Uriarte, pushing open the door that leads into the bedroom but not going in and then moving to the small kitchen. 'There is some food', he says, looking into the fridge, 'and of course there are shops and cafés down in the street.'

'It's beautiful', says Kate. She looks round and puts her laptop down on a desk—a black slab of slate on two stainless steel trestles. 'Can I use the telephone?' she asks.

'I don't think it is connected', says Uriarte.

Kate picks up the handpiece: there is no sound; the line is dead. 'It doesn't matter. I can use my cell.' She takes it out. The signal is weak. 'And I can file from the press centre.'

'Of course.' Uriarte is distracted: clearly his mind is on something other than Kate's professional requirements. 'I think,' he says, 'if you don't mind, I will stay here, too.'

'Of course I don't mind', says Kate, turning to go to him, but she sees at once that he has not arrived at this decision for romantic reasons.

'If the English Secret Service is looking for me,' Uriarte says, 'then the Italian police will be looking for me, too.'

'But why would it matter if they found you?' asks Kate. 'You've nothing to hide.'

'Where terrorism is concerned, innocence is no protection. If they have suspicions, they arrest you, they hold you, they interrogate you, they may even hand you to the Americans who fly you to Guantanamo Bay.'

Kate could not disagree.

'But now we will sleep. You are very tired. I will sleep here on the sofa tonight; you must have a good rest.' He comes to her, embraces her, kisses her gently and then carries her case into the bedroom. 'We will talk tomorrow', he says, kissing her again—a brush on the lips—before leaving the bedroom and closing the door.

The Palazzo Freschi

The attic in the Palazzo Freschi is not an attic at all but simply one of the less grandiose guest rooms on the second floor. It lacks the Renaissance furnishings of the huge bedrooms that open off the great corridor on the floor below: the large mahogany bed had been made in the nineteenth rather than the seventeenth century. The wallpaper, the wash-stand, the water jug, the bed, even the blankets and bed linen seem seventy, perhaps even a hundred years old and remind Luke of an Edwardian shooting lodge in Scotland. Incongruous but not uncomfortable. There is a bathroom down the corridor, and he is welcome at any time in the Contessa's drawing room and at her table.

How is he to find Kate? Luke has no cell phone. Will Kate's work outside England? Before leaving London, Luke has learned from his sister, Caroline, the name of the paper for which Kate is covering the conclave, and the paper has told him that Kate is staying at the Allegra Hotel.

Luke goes down to a telephone in the hall of the Palazzo Freschi. He rings the Allegra Hotel and asks for Kate Ramsey.

'*Tutti stanno cercando Miss Ramsey. Non è qui. Non so dove sia andata.*'[16]

Luke leaves the Palazzo Freschi and walks towards Saint Peter's Square. There must be a press centre and perhaps Kate is there. As a member of the Liturgical Committee, he has a Vatican pass; indeed, he has been in and out of the Vatican so often over so many years that he is waved through a number of checkpoints. The press centre is half-filled with journalists presenting their credentials, conducting interviews, filing copy. Luke cannot see Kate. He asks after her at the desk: her name is found on a list, and Luke is given the address of the Allegra Hotel. It is now half-past eleven; Luke decides to return to the Palazzo Freschi for lunch.

Luke sits on the right of the Contessa, a privilege always accorded to the most recent arrival. There are nine other guests, one a distinguished neo-conservative pundit from the United States who, because he does not understand Italian, speaks across the table to Luke. There are three or four churchmen with red or purple piping to their cassocks designating their ecclesiastical rank—among them Monsignor

---

[16] Everyone's looking for Miss Ramsey. She isn't here. I don't know where she's gone.

Perez, whom Luke knows already. Perez is sitting on the far side of the table, too far for the two men to exchange more than a smile of recognition, but every now and then Perez glances at Luke as if to say that, were they within earshot, he would have much to say.

When lunch is over, the Contessa leads the way into her salon where small cups of black, treacly coffee are waiting for them on a silver tray. As Luke takes one of the cups, Perez comes up to him and the two priests go to sit together on two chairs by one of the windows. 'I am so glad that you are here', Perez says, his Spanish accent giving the impression that he has a lisp. 'But not for the meeting of the Liturgical Committee, surely? Everything like that is *en suspension.*'

'It is. I am here . . .'—Luke can hardly say that he was in Rome to find his niece who might be in trouble—'for other reasons', he finishes lamely.

Perez shows no deeper curiosity but talks in an animated, nervous way about the complexities of the interregnum—how the powers of the Prefect for Catholic Culture have devolved on him as Secretary but how, of course, Cardinal Doornik can hardly be expected to stay out of his office and how the non-Curial cardinals finding themselves in Rome still take up some outstanding issues with Cardinal Doornik even though notionally Cardinal Doornik no longer has authority over his department, but then quite possibly taking up the issue is merely a pretext to call on the Cardinal to discover what he is thinking about how things will go in the conclave. 'Now, of course, Cardinal Doornik is shut away in the Domus Sanctae Marthae, but I am still summoned there to see to him about this and that . . .'

Perez, Luke decides, has clearly been under great pressure during the last weeks. Not only does he speak in an almost frenzied way, but every now and then he also looks obliquely at Luke as if trying to read something in his expression or discern a thought that he has not expressed. Luke feels drowsy. He had hardly slept on the train from Paris. He will resume his search for Kate after a short siesta. He puts his empty cup down on the marble-topped table next to his chair, stands and takes leave of Perez. But, no sooner has he left the salon and is half-way across the great hallway making for the stairs, when he hears Perez behind him say: 'Father, one moment.' Luke turns. Perez catches up with him and says, almost in a whisper: 'Father, you must hear my confession.'

Luke is dumbfounded. 'But there must be a thousand priests ...'

'No, Father. You must hear my confession. Only you.' The emphatic tone of the words is accompanied by an intense, desperate, almost aggressive look in his eyes.

Luke shrugs. 'Very well. Come up to my room.' He crosses the remaining half of the hall and starts up the shallow marble steps. Perez comes behind him. Luke can hear his puffing. Has he drunk too much wine at lunch?

They go into Luke's room. Luke takes his stole from the top right-hand drawer of the chest of drawers. He looks wistfully at his bed, then turns to Perez who stands in the doorway. 'Come in. Close the door.' Luke throws a shirt that he has left on the upright chair facing the washstand onto the bed. 'Why don't you sit there?' he says to Perez, pointing to an armchair with frayed loose covers.

'No, I would prefer to kneel', says Perez, falling onto his knees but resting his elbows on the arm of the chair.

Luke sits in the upright chair, says the opening prayer of the Sacrament of Reconciliation, then waits.

'My sin, Father ... it is complicated.'

'Sin is rarely simple.'

'Some days ago ... perhaps it was a week ago, a friend—no, not a friend but a man whom I had known many years ago in El Salvador—asked me to arrange an audience with Cardinal Doornik. He did not say what it was about but that it was *muy urgente*. He was Spanish—or rather Basque—but we spoke in Spanish. I did as he asked. Doornik agreed to see him. He came. He indicated that he must speak to Doornik alone. His Eminence signified that I should withdraw. I withdrew but ... well, because I had introduced this man I felt some responsibility and thought it best if I heard what he was saying to the Cardinal so that I could offer him advice.'

'The Cardinal had not told you to do this?'

'No. But he had dismissed me at the other man's request, not his own.'

'All the same.'

'Yes. *Peccavi*.'

'Go on.'

'There is a private staircase leading from Cardinal Doornik's office with a concealed door set into the bookcase. I went down and round

186

and then up the staircase and found that by opening the door a few inches I could hear clearly what was being said. I heard . . .'

Luke holds up his hand. 'It would compound the sin to repeat what you heard.'

'But you cannot give me spiritual direction unless you know, Father, and it is, I promise you, a matter of great, great importance.'

'Very well.'

'First, he told Doornik that he should be the next pope—that the whole future of the Church depended upon his election.'

'But . . .' Luke is about to say that the future of the Church depended on someone quite *unlike* Doornik being chosen but holds back. 'Go on.'

'Then he said that there were dark forces determined to prevent it. That a British journalist has a story about a scandal in Cardinal Doornik's past. He has a recording in which an English priest asserts that Doornik, when a seminarian, made homosexual advances . . .' Perez pauses. 'That priest was you.'

Throughout his life Luke has suffered from occasional spasms of imprecise dread originating, he thought, from the brutal regime at his prep school where one could be beaten for breaking rules one did not know existed. Now just such a spasm convulses him like a winding blow. A recording? Of an assertion? By him? To whom? So far as he could recall, he has spoken to no one about Doornik's lunge all those years ago—not to the Rector of the English College, nor even to his confessor, since it was not his sin. It has been filed away in his mind as something unfortunate, even disagreeable—it had brought his friendship with Doornik to an end—but not as something significant or relevant to Doornik's position as a Prince of the Church. As the vile sins of pedophile priests had been exposed, it had crossed Luke's mind that Doornik might at some point in his career have been compromised by an inappropriate gesture, a tainted tenderness . . . But he had then decided that Doornik was too controlled to allow a weakness of the flesh to thwart his ambition. 'Who was this man, this Basque?' he asks Perez.

'Juan Uriarte.'

Now a second spasm of dread grips him, for Luke suddenly remembers that in passing he had told Kate about Doornik and perhaps, while she was with Uriarte in Africa, she had told him. There is clearly no other way Uriarte could have known. And Luke also recalls Kate's Spyware pen and watch, and his telling her that to record what a person said without his consent was at worst a venial sin. Had she, for fun or for practice, recorded their conversation as they dined that night at Langhan's Bistro? Could she have told Uriarte that she had done this? Could she have given him a disk or a tape? Or had she passed it to another journalist and told Uriarte what she had done?

'I cannot imagine', Luke says to Perez, 'that the story could be of much interest to the British press.'

'Apparently it is', says Perez. 'A month ago, no one in Britain had heard of Cardinal Doornik, but now he has been named as a possible choice as the next pope.'

'It seems unlikely', says Luke.

'But possible unless, of course, there is a story in a British newspaper about a homosexual incident in his past. Then it would be impossible. The cardinals could not elect anyone tainted by scandal. That was Uriarte's point.'

'He came to warn Cardinal Doornik?'

'And propose a solution.'

'The solution would surely be for the priest in question to denounce the whole thing as a fabrication.'

'The journalist had told Uriarte that the priest had declined to either confirm or deny.'

'That is a lie: it is a lie, that is, if I am the priest. It may be someone else.'

'He gave your name. But whether it is you or another former seminarian does not alter the fact that if the story is published during the conclave, Doornik will not be chosen as pope.'

'In my view, that would be no bad thing', says Luke.

'But in Doornik's view ...'

'Of course.'

'And Uriarte's.'

'Yes. So what did he propose?'

'The journalist could be bought off.'

'How much?'

'Not with money but with a ... scoop?'

'Yes. A scoop.'

'A sensational revelation. An inside story.'

'About what?'

'The conclave.'

'He wants Doornik to tell him what transpires?'

'He wants Doornik to record the proceedings.'

'Record? What? Take a tape-recorder into the Sistine Chapel?'

'Precisely.'

'But that's impossible.'

'Not technically, it seems.'

'But he is asking Doornik to break a most solemn oath.'

'Far worse things have been done at conclaves, and Uriarte was insistent that in this case the end would justify the means.'

Luke shakes his head. 'It is hard to believe that even Doornik ...' But even as he speaks he realises that it is not hard to believe. He could quite imagine Doornik doing what he felt had to be done for the salvation of mankind.

'He has agreed', says Perez. 'Uriarte will provide a tape-recorder that apparently can pass through all security devices undetected, concealed beneath the Cardinal's robes. Uriarte will bring the tape-recorder to the Vatican press centre, and I am to take it from there to the Domus Sanctae Marthae.'

'That would draw you into their sin', says Luke. 'For the sake of your soul, you must have nothing to do with this degrading, corrupt transaction.'

'Would it not be the lesser of two evils?'

'What is the greater evil? A Church without Doornik as pope?'

'Doornik excluded by outside worldly powers.'

'But everything you have said in the past suggests that you are opposed to Doornik's ideas.'

'That is true. But we understand each other. Were Doornik to be made pope, and had I some role in thwarting those who had wished to prevent it ...'

Luke understands. Doornik would be forever beholden to his former secretary.

'Monsignor,' says Luke, 'you must beware ambition.'

'True humility, surely,' says Perez, 'is to have a proper understanding of one's worth. In the parable of the talents: God rewards those who use their talents and punishes the man who makes no profit from what he has been given.'

'Of course,' says Luke, 'and you undoubtedly have talents, and in God's good time he will show you how you can develop them for the good of the Church. But it is always wrong to do evil that good may come of it. That is a fundamental truth of our Faith.'

'If I refuse to deliver the tape-recorder,' says Perez, 'then Cardinal Doornik will find someone else. And he will have no further use for me.'

'Monsignor,' says Luke, 'for the sake of your soul, you must have nothing to do with this blackmail. You must report the matter to the Cardinal Camerlengo.'

Perez looks up at Luke. 'I cannot do that, Father. Cardinal Doornik would simply deny it. *I* have no tape-recording, after all. *You* are the source of this difficulty, Father. It is for you to recall whom you told about the Cardinal's youthful indiscretion, find the tape and then destroy it. If there is no recording, there can be no blackmail, and we will all be saved from sin.'

Dragnet

The BAC-1-11 of the Royal Air Force, with David Kotovski as its only passenger, lands at the Ciampino military airport outside Rome. Three men are waiting for him on the tarmac—the first, Tim Eagar, Paget's colleague in Rome; the other two, Italians from SISMI. They lead him to a helicopter and, as they fly towards Rome, Eagar briefs Kotovski, shouting above the sound of the rotors. 'There's a full alert on, but they can't find your man Uriarte. They've been to his home and his office. He has disappeared. The girl, too. She's not at her hotel. She checked into the Vatican press centre, but no one has seen her since.'

'She may have tipped him off', says Kotovski.

'Is she in it with him?'

'Not knowingly.'

One of the Italians speaks to Eagar; Eagar passes on what he has said to Kotovski. 'They've got a picture of Uriarte and it's been circulated among all uniformed and plain clothes *Carabinieri* in the vicinity of the Vatican. But it's not a good one; it was given to us reluctantly by Misericordia and is around ten years out of date.'

'Nothing in his home?'

'No. No holiday snaps.'

'We have one taken when he was in custody. I've asked Paget to make sure it is e-mailed to the right people.'

The helicopter lands on the roof of the Questura, and Eagar leads him and the two Italian acolytes in for a briefing. A uniformed *Carabinieri*, flanked by the familiar Franchetti, points to all the police posts on a wall map. All are aware of the urgency of the matter; all have a picture of Uriarte; but it is clear that, if he chooses to disguise himself, it would be difficult to pick him out in a crowd of a hundred thousand people. They repeat what Kotovski has been told by Eagar on the helicopter: Uriarte has not been either to his home or to his office for the past twenty-four hours. Kate Ramsey checked in and out of the Allegra Hotel on the same day without saying why or where she was going. A man was with her when she checked out.

'Ramsey sees Uriarte as a victim', Kotovski says to Eagar. 'She refuses to accept that he is dangerous.'

'Then why has she gone into hiding?' asks Eagar.

'They may both be afraid of extraordinary rendition. They wouldn't be the first to disappear from Italian streets.'

'*Non possiamo fare altro che aspettare*',[17] says Franchetti, sidling up to Kotovski with an ingratiating expression on his face.

Ignoring him, Kotovski turns to Eagar. 'I'm wasting my time here. I should be out there looking for him. I know the man. I don't need a picture.'

Eagar speaks to his Italian colleagues, and one of those who had met him at the airport comes forward: 'I take you to Saint Peter's Square.'

'This is Penalta from DIGOS', says Eagar. 'He has a radio. I'll wait here and keep you informed.'

Kotovski and Penalta are driven out of the courtyard of the Questura in an Alfa Romeo, the siren blaring; Penalta leans forward to ask that it be turned off. He is a thin, quiet man—more reassuring to Kotovski than the blustering Franchetti. His English is not fluent but

---

[17] We can do nothing but wait.

good enough. As they reach the thickening crowds towards Saint Peter's, he says: 'It will be like looking for a needle in a haystack, no?'

The car draws up at a police post under Bernini's colonnade. The uniformed officers salute them. Penalta is briefed, then turns to Kotovski. 'All their men are out there ...'

'In my view', says Kotovski, 'Uriarte will want to survive. He is not a suicide bomber. They should keep their eyes skinned for someone leaving a bag or a satchel.'

'"Eyes skinned"?'

'A sharp look out. To watch carefully.'

'*Si, si.* And ... "a satchel"?'

'A bag.'

Penalta turns to the *Carabinieri* and repeats in Italian what Kotovski has said.

From the elevated position under the colonnade, Kotovski scans the crowd of eager, cheerful pilgrims, with their backpacks and bottles of mineral water—religious sisters with beatific smiles, young seminarians in old-fashioned cassocks, black faces, white faces, and many with the high Slav cheekbones and sharp noses of Poles. How would Uriarte stand out in this crowd? He was slightly older, that was all. The chances of picking him out, particularly if he had dyed his hair or wore sunglasses or a false moustache, seem poor.

'There is a line at the entrance to the square', says Penalta. 'We should go there?'

Kotovski nods, and the two men go down into the mass of people. If Uriarte is going to detonate a bomb, he will not plant it in some side street or even on the via della Conciliazione but in Saint Peter's Square itself. It therefore seems best to go to the gap in the crowd barriers at the entrance. When they reach it, Kotovski stands for a moment studying the faces in the crowd. The plain-clothes *Carabinieri* are as easy to identify as those in uniform, if only because they face away from Saint Peter's Basilica and the Apostolic Palace, their eyes not on the chimney from which black or white smoke will appear.

Suddenly Kotovski sees Uriarte. To be exact, Kotovski does not see Uriarte but a face that, seeing him, looks surprised and turns away. Kotovski catches both the look of recognition and the evasive movement only on the edge of his retina. It is enough. When he turns, though, he sees only the side of a man's head: he recognises at once the profile he has studied over so many weeks in Court No. 4. 'There!' he says to Penalta.

'*L' abbiamo*',[18] Penalta says into the mouthpiece of his radio.

Uriate is only around twenty-five or thirty metres from Kotovski, but he is now moving away. Kotovski, followed by Penalta, moves after him. A minute later, the other *Carabinieri* start to give chase, but not knowing who they are chasing, go off in different directions. Penalta, too, is uncertain who they are pursuing. 'What is he wearing?' he asks Kotovski.

'Beige trousers. A blue anorak.'

Penalta struggles to translate the words. '*Pantaloni . . . beige. Una giacca a vento blu.*'

It is like wading through water up to one's waist—weaving in and out of the pilgrims, now catching a glimpse of the blue anorak, now losing it. The *Carabinieri* on the bridges over the Tiber have been alerted, but, as they pass the church of Santa Lucia, Kotovski steps on something soft: it is the blue anorak. The snake has shed its skin. They reach the Victor Emmanuel Bridge. A flow of people is crossing towards them. The officers do not know whether a man wearing brown trousers has crossed the other way. Penalta radios for news from the other bridges, his head bent as he concentrates on the crackling words. The same. Kotovski looks back. Uriarte must have ducked into one of the small streets behind the church of Santa Lucia. They have lost him, the man and his bomb.

The Safe House

Kate wakes late in the wide bed of the strange flat, confused for a moment about where she is and what had happened the day before. Juan. She recalls that he had come to her bed early in the morning, and they had made love with the kind of drowsy rapture that is possible when one is only half-awake. Or has she dreamed it? No. She sighs and turns and buries her face in the pillow, reluctant to leave this state of sleepy

[18] We have him.

happiness and face the complexities of the day. But one cannot fend off consciousness by an act of will, and the anxieties she wishes to avoid stack up in her mind despite her attempts to keep them out.

The first is a professional reflex: she has accepted an assignment, so she must file a story. This is the second day of the conclave and it is not impossible that the cardinals will make their choice today. Pope John Paul II had been chosen on the second day, so, too, Pope Paul VI. Kate goes into the living-room and switches on the television: CNN has a panel discussing the conclave, but there is no breaking news. She mutes the television, takes a shower, dresses and goes into the neat modern kitchen where a pack of Lavazzo coffee and a small espresso machine have been laid out ready for use. In the fridge there is a carton of milk and a pack of butter; in a cupboard is biscotti and a jar of raspberry jam. When the coffee is ready, she takes her breakfast to the dining table in the living room. There she finds a note from Juan. 'I shall be back. Please wait.'

Kate likes to read the paper while having breakfast, and now, since there is nothing to read in the flat, she takes from her briefcase a copy of *The Tablet* which she had bought before leaving London: a Catholic journal might have a better insight into the conclave than *The Economist* or *The Spectator*. Her Uncle Lolo, she remembers, disapproves of *The Tablet*; he thinks it too liberal and disloyal to the Apostolic See. Reading it now, Kate can tell that behind a veneer of respect for the late pontiff is the hope that the cardinals will choose a successor of a very different kind. Who would it be? She should draft two pieces—one speculating on the choice placed before the cardinals, the other as if the choice were made—the second having its own variations based on the election of a liberal, a conservative, a South American, an African . . .

Kate sips her coffee. She must go to work, but first she should ring the paper to say that she has left the Allegra Hotel. She picks up the telephone: the line is still dead. She rummages through her bag for her cell. It is not there. Has she left it in her briefcase? No. What had she been wearing the day before? She goes back into the bedroom to search the pockets of her beige linen jacket, then looks on the bedside table, the dresser and finally under the rumpled duvet on the bed. It is not there. Her cell phone is gone.

Should she go out to a call box? If she does, she might miss Juan. 'I shall be back. Please wait.' It is odd that when she is with Juan she cannot envisage doing anything to thwart him, but, after he has gone and the sense of his presence has gradually dissipated, a flicker of resistance arises within her. The *mestiza* woman! His son! What had been his explanation? They are 'in his present only because of the past' while she, Kate, was the present? It had sounded satisfactory at the time, more than satisfactory—a commitment, a declaration of love. But now, upon reflection, what does it mean? Was he saying anything more than that seventeenth-century rake, the Earl of Rochester:

> Then talk not of inconstancy,
> False hearts, and broken vows;
> If I by miracle can be
> This live-long minute true to thee,
> 'Tis all that Heaven allows.

To how many other women had he said, 'You are the present'? And should she really put her professional life on hold because he has left a note saying, 'Please wait'? Did she have to stay supine just because he had made love to her? And her missing cell phone? Was it possible that Juan had taken it to prevent her from making a call?

Kate finishes her biscotti and swallows the last of the coffee. She is damned if she will wait. She will go down into the street, find a call box or even push through the crowds to the Vatican press centre. She goes back to her bedroom, puts on her beige jacket and returns to the living room. She turns over the piece of paper on which Uriarte had written his note to write one of her own. What should she write? If she leaves the flat, how can she make contact with him? She has no keys to the flat and the telephone is dead. If Juan has her cell, she could try dialling her number from a call box, but if that did not reach him . . . He would have to find her at the Vatican press centre, but without ID would they let him in? 'I had to go out . . .' she begins but then stops, hearing behind her the sound of keys in the door.

Uriarte looks strange. First of all, he is out of breath, and Kate can see damp patches of perspiration on his shirt. He looks at her and smiles but says nothing, crossing the room to place a bag he is carrying on the floor behind the sofa. His smile, the silence, halts Kate in her tracks. 'I was just going out', she says, but in a fading voice so that the last word 'out' is more or less inaudible.

'Have you had breakfast?' he asks, his eyes looking towards the kitchen then darting around the flat as if to make sure that no one else is there.

'I had some, yes, thank you ...'

'*Necesito un café.*' [19]

'I'll make some.' Kate goes to the kitchen to clean out the espresso machine and make more coffee.

'*Gracias.*' He sits down at the dining table and covers his face with his hands.

Kate waits in the kitchen, watching the milk heat in the pan. Has she been hard on Juan, seeing him as another Earl of Rochester? How does she know that he has had other women? Why should she doubt that for him she is the future as well as the present?

She brings the coffee into the living room from the kitchen. Uriate remains sitting at the table. 'I have had a bad time', he says.

'What happened?' Kate asks. She sits down next to him and pours out the black coffee, then the milk, skimming off the foam from the pan into the cup.

'I was almost taken ... by the *Carabinieri* and the Englishman who was in court.'

'He is here?'

'As soon as he saw me, he came for me.'

'But what does he want?'

Uriarte shrugs. 'Me. If they think I am a terrorist, they will take me, like Abu Omar, and fly me to Cairo or Romania or even Guantanamo Bay.' He speaks calmly, stirring his coffee, waiting for it to cool down.

'Leave Rome', says Kate.

'I will, but first there is something that must be done.'

'Just leave. Come back when the conclave's over. Things will quiet down.'

Uriarte nods towards the bag behind the sofa. 'That has to be taken to the Vatican, today, *antes de mediodía*—before the cardinals return to the Domus Sanctae Marthae for their lunch.'

'What is it?'

Uriarte hesitates before saying: 'A tape-recorder.'

'Why must a tape-recorder be delivered to the Domus Sanctae Marthae before lunch?'

---

[19] I need a coffee.

'Cardinal Doornik is being blackmailed. There is a scandal in his past. The story will be suppressed if he makes a recording of the proceedings.'

'But that is forbidden.'

'Of course it is forbidden. But it is worth breaking a rule to ensure that Doornik is the next pope.'

'But Cardinal Doornik is a liberal ...'

'A liberal, yes. Our best hope.'

'You told me in Africa', Kate says—her voice slow, her tone heavy—'that there was *no chance whatsoever* that the cardinals would choose a liberal pope. You said that John Paul II had carefully packed the College with conservatives and that change would only come if the ceiling of the Sistine Chapel collapsed and killed them all.'

Uriarte looks straight into her eyes and says: 'It was not I who said that, Kate. It was you.'

All at once, she understands. 'This tape-recorder', she says slowly. 'Is it the one modified by your son?'

'He is a clever boy—ingenious, good with his hands.'

Kate looks away from Uriarte, but she can tell from his tone that he knows she knows.

'But does *he* know? Ignacio?'

'What?'

'That it was made to kill ...' Her voice trails off.

'Cardinals? No. He thinks it is to kill camels.'

'Who else knows?'

'About the cardinals? Only you.'

'Your friends in Cairo?'

'No. They think that it is ... for something else.'

'The thermos?'

Uriarte nods. 'Yes.'

'You let me take that through customs knowing that if it were opened ...'

'You volunteered.'

'But if I had known ...'

'You asked to help', says Uriarte. 'You said you would like to risk your life for a cause. And if you had known, fear would have shown in your face.'

Had she said that? Kate cannot remember. 'But this is not a cause, Juan, it is ...'

'What?'

'An atrocity!'

'One man's atrocity is another's—*Comó se dice?*—pre-emptive strike.'

Kate feels faint as images of what Juan envisages enter her mind. 'You mean to kill *all the cardinals?*'

'Kate, it is the only way.' He leans forward, takes hold of her hand, and looks directly into her eyes. 'Remember what you saw in Africa—the terrible suffering of the people with AIDS. Remember what we decided: that it was the stubborn dogmatism of those old men in Rome—Wojtyła, Ratzinger, Sodano, Arinze and a hundred more—which causes the suffering and death of thousands, tens of thousands, of innocent people. Can you really say that it would be wrong to end the lives of one hundred and twenty *sacerdotes geriatricos*[20] who by their own lights will go straight to Heaven if it means saving the lives of *millions*, now and in generations to come?'

Kate's mind does not work: her thought processes are paralysed by the images of bodies piled upon bodies. 'But to gas them like Jews in Auschwitz.'

Uriarte tosses his head. 'Most of them will die soon anyway—more slowly, more painfully and in less glorious surroundings than the Sistine Chapel.'

'How can you know that what would follow would be any better?'

'Of course, it would be better *because it could not be worse.* The whole People of God—a billion Catholics—is yearning for a Church that will prevent the spread of AIDS in Africa. They long to throw off the absurd and intolerable burden of sexual guilt—to welcome homosexuals and divorced Catholics into full communion, to allow women to be priests; above all they long to abandon those meaningless dogmas like Heaven and Hell or the "real presence" of Christ in the Eucharist—*qué absurdo!*'

'But to kill innocent people.'

'Kate,' says Uriarte reproachfully, 'that is a cliché. It is banal. We have ideas. We have convictions. They have consequences. We must take responsibility for the effect on others of what we believe. Calvin's *Institutes* would have made France a Protestant country had not the Catholics slaughtered the Protestants on Saint Bartholomew's Day.

[20] geriatric priests

Cruel? Ugly? Of course, but from a Catholic perspective it worked. History is filled with examples of how small groups of people or even individuals have changed its course. Joan of Arc was told by God to kill Englishmen. Saint Louis of France to slaughter Saracens. Some interventions in the course of history succeed; some fail. Guy Fawkes failed with his Gunpowder Plot, but Bonaparte's whiff of grapeshot succeeded. What if von Stauffenberg had killed Hitler? Or if one of the CIA's cigars had blown up in Fidel's face? Perhaps nothing. But the crew of the one ship, the *Aurora*, and the soldiers of a Latvian rifle-brigade in Saint Petersburg brought about the Russian Revolution. History *is* changed by the actions of individuals—sometimes for the better, sometimes for the worse—and now God has given us the chance to do something *that will save millions of lives.'*

God. History. *Us?* Is she now in it with Juan? Complicit. An accessory? Sarin. Nerve gas. Kate feels like Alice in Wonderland, not in a looking-glass but suddenly behind the headlines of a story in the *Daily Mail*. She thinks back to the trial in Court No. 4. 'When you became aware, Miss Ramsey, of what the accused had in mind, did you alert the authorities?' 'Alert the authorities.' The stock expressions of spooks and policemen reflecting a stock mind-set. David Kotovski: straightforward, normal, happy to live within the box. A steady salary with pension and health plan. A mortgage. A car. Paid to preserve the status quo: a global society of unprecedented prosperity for some, utter and intractable poverty for others. The poor getting poorer, the rich getting richer. Mud huts, air-conditioned malls. Sleek international bureaucrats on tax-free salaries flying hither and thither and accomplishing nothing. Who is there ready to do something effective? Something audacious? Only Juan. And what is she? A journalist? A voyeur of the world's misery? Or someone ready to take the same risks as Juan for the sake of a better world?

'You want *me* to take it to the Vatican?' she asks.

'They are not looking for you.'

'Kotovski knows who I am.'

'But not the *Carabinieri*.'

Kate looks across the room towards the bag behind the sofa. 'Will it blow up in my face?'

'Only if you press one of two buttons—"play" or "record".'

'The plan is—have I got this right?—that I take it to the press centre?'

'Where you ask for Monsignor Perez.'

'I give it to him. He takes it to the Domus Sanctae Marthae and hands it to Cardinal Doornik when he returns for his lunch.'

'Yes. Doornik has contrived *un arreos*[21]—the white tape a priest ties round his waist—so that the recorder will be suspended beneath his robes and strapped to his leg.'

'Uncomfortable', says Kate.

'They walk slowly on these solemn occasions.'

'He returns to the Sistine Chapel for the afternoon session . . .'

'Leans down to scratch his leg and presses the button to start recording.'

'He thinks . . . what?'

'That he is recording the proceedings.'

'Why?'

'To prevent the revelation of something that would prejudice his chances of becoming pope.'

'But he has no chance of being elected?'

'He flatters himself otherwise.'

'Hasn't all this . . . well . . . been left to the last moment?'

'If the cause is just, God provides the means.'

'Did God provide me?'

'*Ciertamente.*' He looks straight into her eyes with a strange expression—determined, desperate, threatening, pleading.

Kate stands, crosses to the sofa and picks up the bag. 'This is the bomb?'

'You have in your hands the means to save tens of thousands of lives.'

Kate thinks of little Miremba, who died in her arms. She looks at Juan. 'You are sure . . . ?'

'I am sure. It is God's will.'

Kate nods. 'Very well.'

'*Vaya con Dios.*'

'I'll be back.'

Kate steps out into the street and walks towards the Tiber. The bag is heavy, but no heavier than her laptop. She sees a taxi and flags it

---

[21] a harness

down. She asks the driver to take her to Saint Peter's Square. He shrugs and says something in Italian that she does not understand. She waits, the door still open. '*Sí, sí.*' He beckons her to get in. They drive only three or four blocks before reaching the Tiber. '*Non posso spingermi oltre in macchina. Dovrai continuare a piedi.*'[22]

Kate gets out, holding the bag with great care. Would the police search it? What if they did? For a journalist a tape-recorder was a tool of his trade. Or should she give herself up? 'Excuse me, officer. I have a bomb in my bag.' Betray Juan. Scupper his attempt to change the course of history. Leave African children like little Miremba to die of AIDs.

Kate makes her way through the crowds, walking slowly towards Saint Peter's Square. Poles. The Poles are everywhere—plumbers in London, pilgrims in Rome. They came for the funeral of their Polish Pope and have stayed on to welcome the new pope. Italians in uniform—Red Cross, perhaps—are handing out bottles of mineral water. How efficient the Romans have been in coping with this influx of three million people. But they are used to it. In 1300, two hundred thousand pilgrims had come to Rome to celebrate the jubilee. And gain indulgences. Big business for Pope Boniface VIII.

But this crowd? These people are not here for time off purgatory. What draws them like swarming bees to Saint Peter's? Curiosity? Superstition? Credulousness? No. An odd other-worldliness. Faith. Devotion. Love. What if Juan had asked her to set off his bomb among these innocent people? She would have refused. Only the guilty old men should die. Guilty of what? Were they not of one mind with the pilgrims? Faith, devotion, love.

'Oh God.' She says it without meaning it because she does not believe in God. He does. Juan. He is the hand of God, smiting the unrighteous. And she is his instrument. Why? If she does not believe ... Compassion. The horror of the suffering of others. If she could alleviate it. Killing a few to save the many. The lesser of two evils. She remembers her Uncle Lolo. Never do evil that good may come of it. The end never justifies the means. But what about the just war? Self-defence? The defence of women whose husbands are infected with AIDS against the dogmatists who deny them condoms? To do

---

[22] I can't go any further with the car. You'll have to continue on foot.

away with superstition. To make the Church relevant to the modern world. Sex no longer a sin. Lovers relieved of the burden of guilt. Men and women free to meet one another's needs. *Compadres* in Salvador. Slappers and players in London. 'If I by miracle can be / This live-long minute true to thee / 'Tis all that Heaven allows.' Religious language to justify debauchery. Debauchery? Depravity? Redundant words. 'This live-long minute true to thee . . .' She hurries her steps, edging the pilgrims aside. The effect is waning. The Uriate effect. The time and distance separating her from Juan . . . Poison gas. She remembers the words of the prosecuting counsel at Juan's trial. 'Sarin is five hundred times as toxic as cyanide. It will paralyse the muscles around the lungs. One hundred milligrams will lead, within a few minutes, to death by suffocation.' Gasping, writhing cardinals. Then twisted bodies in red robes lying in a heap. She is the cause. That the effect. She hears the voice of the judge: 'If you are satisfied, members of the jury, that the accused knew she was delivering a device that would cause mass murder, then you will find her guilty.' But the judge will be Italian, and she will spend the rest of her life in an Italian jail.

For the first time, Kate begins to calculate the consequences of what she is doing. She may have said in Cairo that she was ready to take a risk to help others, but she was thinking of smuggling, not murder. Clearly there were women who had been prepared to kill for a cause—Joan of Arc, Rosa Luxembourg, Ulrika Meinhof—but they were visionaries or fanatics. Who is she to change the course of history? She is a journalist, an observer. Then why is she walking step by step towards the press centre behind Bernini's colonnade carrying a bomb? For fear of what will happen if she turns back? Would Juan's God tell him to kill her? There had been a menacing look in his eyes. And if she goes to the police? At the very least, a charge of complicity and ten years in an Italian prison for bringing the Sarin from Cairo to Rome.

Kate reaches the entrance to the press centre. She shows her journalist's ID and is waved through. Out of the edge of her eye, she sees the man next to the *Carabinieri* talk into the lapel of his jacket. She goes into the press centre. It will soon be done. The bag delivered. The responsibility passed on to another—a Catholic priest. Her hands clean. No, they will never be clean. There will be pictures in the papers of the dead cardinals and a furor. Who had done it? Who would be blamed? Al-Qaida. An excuse for another war. Iran, perhaps, or Sudan. More killing. More refugees. More suffering. Has Juan thought it through? Or is he blinkered by the issue of sex and guilt? Is this the consequence of a young priest sleeping with a slender *mestiza* under the stars in El Salvador? 'If I by miracle can be . . .' Her legs grow weak. If God is with him, who could be against him? Kate, she of little faith. 'If I by miracle can be this live-long minute true to thee . . .' Only seconds remain. She goes to the desk and hears her voice saying: '*Monsignor Perez, per favore.*'

A telephone is picked up; a number dialled. She steps away from the desk and sees, at the entrance, David Kotovski scanning the room. She turns back. There is the priest walking towards her. Perez? No. It is her Uncle Lolo. 'Oh, Uncle Lolo.' Tears break the dyke of her lower lids. She throws herself into his arms. 'Uncle Lolo, I don't know what to do.'

His two arms hold her but only for a moment. 'Is this the tape-recorder?' he asks.

'Yes. Monsignor Perez . . .'

'I know all about it. Don't worry. Leave it to me.' He slips the strap of the bag off her shoulder. 'Say nothing', he whispers. He takes hold of the bag and is gone.

Kotovski in Love

Seeing Kate Ramsey in tears has a strange effect on David Kotovski, and, even as he is asking her to accompany him to the Questura, he feels a strong urge to cherish and protect her—an urge that becomes overpowering when, without remonstrating, she dumbly allows herself to be led from the Vatican press centre. Foremost in his mind is the need to prevent a terrorist atrocity, but, after taking the first few steps in the direction of a waiting police car, Kotovski realises that once Kate Ramsey is in the hands of the Italians he will be unable to protect her. The Italians will take over. He stops and says to Penalta: 'There is no time. We must talk to her now.'

Without waiting for Penalta to reply, Kotovski turns and leads Kate back into the press centre. Penalta comes in behind them.

'We need a room', he says to Penalta.

They are shown into an unused office on the first floor.

'Would you like some water?' Kotovski asks Kate.

She looks up with a puzzled look. 'Water?'

Kotovski turns to Penalta. 'Could you get some water for Miss Ramsey, or a *caffé*.'

Penalta looks uncertain but complies.

Kotovski sits on a chair facing the desk and points to another with its back to the wall. 'Please sit down.'

Kate does as she is told.

'We haven't much time', says Kotovski. 'You must tell me everything you know about Uriarte.'

She looks away.

'Tell me, at the very least, whether he has Sarin and, if he has, whether he plans to use it.'

Still she says nothing.

'There are thousands of innocent people out there who could die.'

She turns back to look at him. '*They* were never at risk.'

'Then who?'

She turns away again.

'Is *anyone* now at risk?'

'No. Not now.'

'Can you be certain?'

She hesitates then says: 'Yes. Quite certain.'

Kotovski glances towards the door, anticipating Penalta's return. 'Kate,' he says, 'I don't know and I don't need to know at this point just what happened or might have happened or how you are involved. If you say there is no risk, I accept your judgement, but we now must think about your position ...'

'My position?'

'If the Italians think you are involved with Uriarte, then you will be held as a material witness and perhaps prosecuted as an accomplice.'

She lowers her head as if presenting her neck for an executioner's axe.

'I would rather avoid that', says Kotovski.

'You? Why?' For a moment she looks puzzled, but then, seeing the look in his eyes, she understands.

'There is a plane that could take us both back to Britain', says Kotovski. 'I think we should take it. But first I must know if there is anything here in Rome that can connect you to Uriarte.'

'My things are in his flat.'

'Things?'

'Clothes. My cell phone.'

'The flat on the via Manzoni?'

'No. Another one.'

'Where?'

She hesitates. 'Not far from here.'

'We must fetch them.'

'Very well.' In the same way as she has allowed herself to be led away for interrogation without protest, Kate now seems happy to agree to anything Kotovski suggests.

'They can't hold you until they have something concrete to link you to Uriarte. Go back down to the press centre. Behave as if you are covering the conclave. Write a story. File it. I'll deal with the Italians and be back at six.'

Habemus Papam

The joy of normality. Kotovski departs with a puzzled Penalta. Kate goes down to the press centre and, recognising a male colleague from the *Daily Mail*, asks if she can borrow his laptop to write a story. He has already filed his copy and so agrees. Kate sits down and starts to write about the atmosphere in Saint Peter's Square, the fervour of the pilgrims, the expectations of different Catholics. Running out of anything to say after writing two paragraphs, she collars a young American Jesuit who has been talking to the man from the *Mail* and asks him who he hopes will be the next pope. She finds it difficult to concentrate on his replies: she behaves as if she were back to normal, but her mind is working on different things at the same time. She tries not to think about Juan and concentrates instead on the work at hand. And the people at hand. The man from the *Mail*, the young Jesuit and Kotovski who will soon return. How extraordinary that he had popped up just when he did—like her Uncle Lolo—to wake her from the nightmare. And what a relief that he, like her uncle, is willing to take things in hand. She knows why: she has seen the look in his eyes. He is in love with her. She doesn't mind.

Or was it not normality that was so wonderful but the serenity of a clear conscience? Not clear, perhaps, but unburdened—the horrible dilemma passed to her Uncle Lolo, the one man who in her childhood had taught her the difference between right and wrong. '*I know all about it.*' How had he known? And why had he been there by the desk at the press centre at that precise moment? 'If I by miracle can be ...' Lolo loves her for more than a lifelong moment. She cannot remember a time when he has not loved her, nor envisage a time when his love will cease.

There was a commotion and a rush to the door. Kate glances at one of the screens: white smoke is coming from the chimney on the roof of the Sistine Chapel. She, too, leaves the press centre and, climbing up under Bernini's colonnade, looks across the immensity of Saint Peter's Square to see the real thing for herself. Is that the chimney? Is that the white smoke? It is too far away to say. Then comes the tolling of the great bells. There is a new pope. She waits and watches. All eyes are on the balcony of Saint Peter's Basilica. The doors are opened. A huge cloth bearing the papal coat-of-arms is thrown over the balustrades. First an acolyte carrying a crucifix, then Cardinal Medina Estevez comes out onto the balcony. '*Annuntio vobis gaudium magnum: Habemus Papam! Eminentissimum ac reverendissimum Dominum, Dominum Joesphum Sanctae Romanae Ecclesiae Cardinalem Ratzinger, qui sibi nomen imposuit Benedictum XVI.*'

The young Jesuit translates what he says: 'I announce to you a great joy: We have a Pope! The most eminent and most reverend Cardinal of the Holy Roman Church, Lord Joseph Ratzinger, who takes to himself the name of Benedict XVI.'

'Poor Juan', says Kate.

'Who's Juan?' asks the Jesuit.

'Oh, a friend who will be disappointed.'

'Well, he's not alone.'

Two for a Penny

Father Luke Scott sits on a bench in the Parco Gianicolense. Beside him on the bench is the bag he had taken from Kate. As soon as he had it in his hands, he had slipped out through a back entrance to the press centre. He had not wanted to run into Perez now, either in the Vatican or the Palazzo Freschi, and so, after walking purposefully in no particular direction other than away from Saint Peter's Square, he had gone into the Parco Gianicolense. He had felt exhausted and yet elated, thanking God for answering his prayers. He had reached Kate before Perez and saved her from complicity in a most dreadful sin. He had also witnessed her change of heart. Like the Prodigal Son she had thrown herself into his arms, weeping and saying that she did not know what to do. She had given him the bag without protest—in her eyes, wet with tears, a look of gratitude and relief.

The park is empty; everyone, Luke supposes, is in Saint Peter's Square awaiting the announcement of a new pope. Now that the drama is over, the adrenalin has drained from his veins and his exhaustion overwhelms him. From a tree a few yards from where he is sitting comes the busy chirruping of sparrows. How beautiful is God's creation. How baffling its complexity and incongruity, ranging from the infinite universe to the smallest creatures like those sparrows, sold at two for a penny in the time of Christ, or five for tuppence. 'And yet not one falls to the ground without your Father knowing', Jesus had told his disciples, adding: 'You have no need to be afraid. You are worth more than a hundred sparrows and every hair on your head is counted.'

Luke remains seated on the bench, his hand on the bag containing the tape-recorder. His thoughts have become disjointed as they do when a fatigued mind slips into unconsciousness. He closes his eyes and dozes. Every now and then he almost wakes but only to decide that he should remain on the bench and rest. Then, half in a dream, he hears the sound of church bells—first a single, deep reverberating sound, then a second and finally the tolling of different bells, one after another. He opens his eyes. The booming sound comes from the direction of Saint Peter's. There is a new pope. Luke feels no curiosity. The Holy Spirit has surely guided the cardinals to make the right choice. 'I will be with you,' Jesus had promised his disciples, 'yes, to the end of time.'

The tape-recorder. Luke had intended to put it in a rubbish bin or hide it behind a bush. But why throw it away? The machine has done no wrong. Why not make use of it, instead, to record the sounds of the bells? He unzips the bag, takes out the tape-recorder and places it on his knees. He is no expert with gadgets, and he has never used an Uher before, but it has the same keys as any other tape-recorder—fast-forward, rewind, stop, play and record. There is a microphone embedded in the machine. All he need do, surely, is press 'play' and 'record' simultaneously, and he will be able to listen at leisure to the magnificent sound of the bells proclaiming 'Habemus Papam' to the city and the world.

Covering Tracks

Kate and Kotovski drive over the Tiber. 'What is the number of the apartment?' Kotovski asks.

'I can't remember, but I'll show you. It's just up here.'

Kotovski stops the car a short distance from the flat.

'You must ring him', he says, holding out his Nokia.

'There isn't a landline.'

'Call your cell. Tell him to meet you in Trastevere.'

Kate starts to dial. 'What will they do to him?'

'It's out of our hands.'

Uriarte answers. 'What went wrong?' He sounds blank.

'I'll tell you.'

'Where are you?'

'In Trastevere.'

He hesitates, then: 'Go to the church of Santa Maria. I'll meet you there.'

She rings off. 'I'm to meet him in the church of Santa Maria.'

Kotovski takes back his cell phone, dials a number and says: 'The church of Santa Maria in about a quarter of an hour.' He looks at Kate. 'Jeans. A white shirt. No. No. He's all yours.'

They wait. A few minutes later, they see Uriarte leave the building. To Kate, he seems like a person she hardly knows. He gets into his Fiat and drives off.

They cross the street, go into the courtyard and up the stairs to the flat. Kotovski fumbles at the lock with a pass-key; after a few false starts, he opens the door and Kate enters. She goes into the bedroom, throws her few clothes into her holdall, then comes back into the living room.

'A nice flat', says Kotovski.

'Yes.'

'Is this yours?' He holds up her cell phone.

'Yes.'

Kotovski looks around the flat. 'Are you sure you have got everything?'

'My toothbrush.' Kate goes to the bathroom to retrieve it.

Kotovski takes a last look around, returning from the bedroom with a frown on his face. 'How long were you here?'

She blushes. ' "A live-long moment ..." '

Kotovski looks puzzled.

'Not long.'

Rendition

'If God is for you, who can be against you?' After Kate has left the flat, Uriarte repeats these words of Saint Paul over and over again, sitting hunched on the edge of the sofa and watching the coverage of the conclave on CNN. Who could doubt that God was for him? His impossible project is about to come to fruition. 'I come to bring fire and the sword', Jesus had said, using the images pertinent to his times. Here was not fire but nerve gas and detonators rather than the sword. But the cause was the same: truth, love, liberation—the end of the perversion of Christianity by a cabal of stubborn old men.

Uriarte does not feel that he is arrogant. His role in changing the course of world history will never be known. The responsibility for the atrocity will fall on Al-Qaida. Who else would want to strike at the heart of the Roman Catholic Church? What else could the extermination of the entire College of Cardinals be but an audacious blow in the cause of *jihad*? If evidence of Al-Qaida's responsibility is needed, evidence will be found: his Coptic friends in Egypt have seen to that. That was surely providential—his encounter with a group of Copts who planned something audacious—an atrocity on the scale of 9/11 that would oblige the Western powers to declare war, not on terrorism but on Islam!

And the girl—the earnest young journalist from London looking for an adventure and a cause. Was her appearance in Rome not providential? And the ease with which he had captured her heart? She had come to him—the inquisitive journalist. He had found her attractive. He had assumed that he would not appeal to her because he was older. Then Lucia had acted up. A jealous tantrum. Women can smell a rival. She knew what he had in mind. But his conscience was clear. It had been Lucia, not he, who had insisted from the start that fidelity was bourgeois, that each should remain free. She had not anticipated, perhaps, that nature is less kind to middle-aged women than middle-aged men. But in her time, she had had lovers, and he had had transitory affairs with young volunteers, though none quite like Kate— none with her class, her style—not aristocratic, perhaps, but *haute bourgeois*: the correspondent of a London newspaper with an Oxford University degree. In what? Theology! Because it was a subject that made it easier to get a place!

Thinking of Kate as he sits on the sofa, Uriarte smiles. How pleasing it had been to discover that the proud young woman—so earnest, so professional, so reserved—should so wholly abandon herself, heart and soul. Had he misled her? Uriarte thought not. He could not now remember whether or not he had said that he loved her, but, even if he had, it was hardly a falsehood: what man would not love a beautiful woman in the prime of life who craved his embraces? Certainly, there had not been a psychological affinity—what one might call 'a marriage of true minds'—but that was hardly likely in a man of his temperament, his experience, his age. It was, after all, the English poet Lord Byron who had written that love is a woman's whole existence, while to a man it is a thing apart. To Uriarte, very much a thing apart. With so vivid a picture of human suffering constantly before him and so clear an idea of what he could do to alleviate it, a passing affair with a British journalist could never be of any consequence—or could be of consequence only if it formed part of his plan.

Why is she taking so long? Why is there no news? Uriarte looks at his watch. It is now past four in the afternoon. The cardinals must have returned from their lunch at the Domus Sanctae Marthae by three at the latest. Perhaps Doornik is waiting for the opening of a debate before starting the recorder? Or could the detonator have failed? Or the Sarin decomposed? No. He had done what Ignacio had told him, and he has faith in his son's expertise. Perhaps Kate has decided that, having delivered the bomb, it would be prudent to remain at the press centre, ready to file her story—and what a story! Not the election of a new pope but the liquidation of the College of Cardinals! The death of one hundred and twenty reactionary old men! That would give those pundits on CNN and BBC World something to talk about. Who would rule the Church? How would a council be convened?

Uriarte looks at his watch again. Ten to five. Then, suddenly, on the television screen there appears a close shot of the chimney on the roof of the Sistine Chapel. Smoke? White smoke! Impossible. Uriarte crosses to the set as if a closer look will rectify his misperception, but the commentators are confirming that the smoke is white. Clearly, unless—perhaps this is a signal that ... No. *There is a new pope!*

Uriarte remains standing, his muscles tense. What has happened? Is it possible that now, at the eleventh hour, providence has betrayed him? Where is Kate? Where is the bomb? Which of the links has broken? Kate? Has she been arrested? Or Perez? Did he lose his nerve? Or is it Doornik? Did he drop the recorder? Did the harness fail? Or perhaps—Uriarte had not considered this eventuality—had Martini or Daniels or even Doornik picked up so many votes in an early round of voting that Doornik had felt confident that one of them would win?

Uriarte goes to open the window that looks out on the street. Over the noise of the traffic, he hears the booming bells of Saint Peter's proclaiming to the city that Rome has a new bishop and to the world that the Church has a new pope. The same sound comes from the television set behind him. He goes back into the room and sees that the television cameras are now focused on the balcony of Saint Peter's. Uriarte watches, transfixed, as Cardinal Medina Estevez comes onto the balcony to announce to the city and the world the name of the new pope!

Ratzinger! Uriarte slumps back on the sofa, his muscles now flaccid, his mind blank. Forty minutes pass before his stunned mind begins to function again. His project has failed. The cardinals are alive. They have elected Ratzinger.

How has it happened? Did he leave too much to God? But had not events encouraged him to trust in God? The acquittal in London, the encounter with the Copts, the girl, her uncle, his story about Doornik, Doornik's vanity, Perez' ambition, the girl again—her turning up in Rome with accreditation, her willingness to serve—all had surely come together in a miraculous manner. Not miraculous—Uriarte did not believe in miracles—but he does believe that God has a purpose, which he works through men.

Uriarte's thoughts are interrupted by another sound coming from behind him: the buzzing of Kate's cell phone, which lay on the marble-topped table. He stands and watches as it vibrates like a dying May bug on the polished surface. He picks it up.

'What went wrong?'

'I'll tell you.'

'Where are you?'

'In Trastevere.'

'Go to the church of Santa Maria. I'll meet you there.'

Uriarte leaves the flat. Why has she gone to Trastevere? Is she afraid that she is being followed? If so, is it wise for him to meet her? Would it not make more sense to disappear—a train to Brindisi, the ferry to Patras, then a plane from Athens to Africa? Uriarte has made no contingency plan for what he would do if things went wrong. 'If God is with you, who can be against you?' Nothing *could* go wrong. But what about Joan of Arc? Or Savonarola? God was with them, but they were burned at the stake. Even Christ on the Cross. 'My God, my God, why have you forsaken me?' Has he, Uriarte, been forsaken? By Doornik? By Perez? By Kate? By God?

Curiosity gets the better of prudence. Uriarte has to know. He reaches Trastevere, leaves his car on the via Garibaldi and walks down the pedestrianised via della Scala. He approaches the Piazza Santa Maria obliquely by the via della Pelliccia and the via de Moro. A part of the

crowd that had gathered in front of Saint Peter's waiting for the proc-
lamation of the new pope has moved on to Trastevere—pilgrims looking for somewhere to have supper. There are no *Carabinieri* in sight, nor
can Uriarte see anyone scrutinizing the faces of those entering the Piazza
from the via della Scala. He crosses to the church, pushes back the squeak-
ing door and for a moment stands in the gloom, waiting for his eyes to
adjust to the dimmer light. The church smells of guttering candles, and
from a side chapel on the right comes the yellow glow of their light. A
number of people kneel at prayer—an old man at the back of the church,
two nuns before the statue of the Virgin. Are they thanking God for
the new pope, perhaps, or complaining about his choice?

Where is Kate? At first Uriarte thinks she cannot be there, but
then he sees her sitting in a pew two or three rows from the altar—he
recognises her white shirt. He walks up the side aisle and slips into
the pew behind her, kneeling to bring his mouth close to her ear.

'What happened?' he asks.

The girl turns. It is not Kate. 'Mister Uriarte?' She has an American accent.

He stands and turns back towards the entrance of the church, but
as he does so two men step out of the shadows. He tries to dodge
them but they grab his arms. As he turns and twists, he sees the
woman come up behind him. Something wet is pressed to his face.
He smells chloroform and, after a last frantic effort to free himself,
Uriarte loses consciousness.

The Gift of Tears

Shortly after seven on the evening of Tuesday, 19 April 2005, two
aircraft take off from the Ciampino military airport south of Rome.
One is a BAC 1-11 of the Royal Air Force, the second a Gulfstream
jet chartered by an American corporation. The first flies north towards
Northolt. The second flies south.

At around the same time, the body of a man found dead on a bench
in the Parco Gianicolense is brought into the Ospedale Nuovo Regina

Margherita in Trastevere. There are marks of scorching on his face and hands, and his clothes are so badly burned that it is only when they are cut away from his body that it becomes clear that the man had been wearing a clerical collar and must have been a priest. The singed passport found in an inside pocket reveals the priest's name and that he is a British subject. These facts are entered on the central computer to be relayed to the British Embassy and the Vatican. It does not seem at first sight that the burns could have been the cause of death: perhaps the shock caused by the conflagration led to a cardiac arrest. The body is sent to the morgue for an autopsy.

Early the next morning, before the autopsy takes place, the director of the hospital is telephoned by a senior official in the Health Ministry and told that, because of evidence found by *Vigili Urbani* by the bench in the Parco Gianicolense, the death of the priest is now a matter of a criminal enquiry and the post-mortem will be conducted by the police. An ambulance comes to collect the body; the staff at the Ospedale Nuovo are puzzled to see that the paramedics are wearing masks.

That same morning, a group of women wait outside the gates to the Parco Gianicolense. They are on their way to shout messages from the park to their imprisoned husbands and lovers in the Regina Coeli prison but find that the gates are closed and guarded by *Carabinieri*. Inside the park, around a dozen men wearing what look like space suits are seen picking up dead sparrows and pigeons and placing them in plastic bags. Someone suggests that there has been an outbreak of avian flu.

Copies of the post-mortem performed on the dead priest are sent to the British Embassy, the Vatican and the priest's family in England. It states that Father Luke Scott died as the result of a cardiac arrest. No mention is made of any burns and no explanation is given for cremating the body without the family's consent. The priest's sister and brother-in-law come to Rome for his funeral. All the arrangements are made by an official from the British Embassy, Tim Eagar. Monsignor Perez from the Vatican says the Requiem Mass at the small church of San Antonio in the via del Orso, and after the funeral a reception is held at the Palazzo Freschi for Father Luke's relatives and his many Roman friends. 'It was the election of Pope Benedict', says the Contessa. 'His heart simply burst with joy! And now he is in the house of the Father with our dear Pope John Paul II.'

Father Luke's niece Kate does not go to Rome for his funeral but attends a memorial Mass for the repose of his soul at Saint James's, Spanish Place. She is accompanied by her brother, Charlie, and David Kotovski, who, when Charlie goes to the lectern by the altar and speaks fondly about his uncle, produces an old-fashioned white linen handkerchief for Kate to wipe away her tears.

[END]